T0245056

THE AURORA REVELATIONS

A PARANORMAL MYSTERY NOVEL

MICHAEL F. WALKER

The Aurora Revelations
A Paranormal Mystery Novel
by Michael F. Walker

Copyright © 2024 by Michael F. Walker.

All rights reserved. No part of this story may be used or reproduced
in any form whatsoever without written permission except in the case
of brief quotations in critical articles or reviews.

This is a work of fiction. Names, characters, businesses, organizations,
places, events and incidents either are the product of the author's
imagination or are used fictitiously. Any resemblance to actual persons, living or dead, events, or locales is entirely coincidental.

First printing July 2024 in the United States of America.

For more information and to receive the author's free newsletter,
check the website :

http://www.michaelwalkerbooks.com

Aurora cemetery gate photo © Tui Snider TuiSnider.com

Smallpox hospital photo © Kevin Walsh forgotten-ny.com

Author photo courtesy of Gerri Hernandez

ISBN - Paperback: 979-8-35095-927-7
ISBN - eBook : 979-8-35095-928-4

For Brenda and Katie, my beautiful wife and my daughter,

The women who captured my heart and whose love makes sense of my life.

Belief is the enemy.

—*John Keel, The Mothman Prophesies*

THURSDAY, SEPTEMBER 10, 2015

Katy Olmos had only two weeks under her belt as a tour guide at Chaco Canyon National Park, but even she knew there was something terribly wrong with the strange man staggering around the bottom of the great kiva at Pueblo Bonito.

"Sir? Sir? This area is off-limits to visitors. You have to stay on the marked trails."

Where the hell did he come from? Katy swore there was no one in sight when she took her last group of the day through Pueblo Bonito not more than forty-five minutes ago. Not many tourists flocked to the canyon in September, and there were hardly any visitors this Thursday. He seemed to materialize out of the thin dry desert air.

"Sir?" Still no answer. Unsteady, one foot dragging on the ground, he was no more than a black shape moving in the shadows cast by the setting sun. Katy initially thought he might be ill. Then she remembered the stories of all the psychedelic pilgrims, some high on peyote, who came from all over the country to worship at this sacred New Mexican site, burning sage and offering ersatz medicine pouches and healing crystals to give thanks to the ancient spirits at Chaco Canyon. They especially gravitated to the forty kivas around Pueblo Bonito—those circular underground spaces where unknowable ceremonies were performed by the Anasazi people over a thousand years ago. Some believed the *sipapu*, symbolic entrances to the lower world found at the bottom of the larger kivas, were real portals to another realm.

Katy steadied herself as she climbed down ten feet into the kiva. She glanced over her shoulder as she wandered around the tumbled stone ruins of the old great house at dusk. As Katy got closer, the figure turned to face her, and she gasped. The stranger was covered in blood. A rich thick crimson spattered across his pale face and down his plaid flannel shirt and corduroy pants, just like the gruesome arterial sprays Katy remembered from those first-person shooter games her boyfriend, Pablo, loved so much.

He seemed as genuinely puzzled by his presence here in the middle of the desert twilight as Katy was. He looked straight at her and asked, "Where?" before he collapsed to the ground as though struck from behind.

"Shit!" Katy was looking forward to ending her shift quickly and heading home, maybe stopping by to visit her *abuelita*, but now she needed to call this in and take precious time to file an incident report.

While she waited for the other park rangers and police to arrive, Katy sat down next to the stranger, slipped on her latex gloves, and examined him gingerly for any wounds. Stopping the bleeding was job one, she recalled from her first-aid training. But she did not notice any obvious cuts, certainly nothing to account for all this splatter. He looked otherwise unremarkable, just another young white dude, close to her own age, maybe twenty-six or twenty-seven. He smelled funny. Not like the desert, Katy thought, but more like something dank and deep, like a root cellar.

Where did all this damn blood come from if not from his own veins? Katy shivered as the shadows of the deep kiva grew longer. Maybe he killed some animal… or maybe some person. Initially wary that this shape shambling about the kiva pit was one of the ghosts of the Ancient Ones she heard about from local legends, Katy now worried she was sitting next to a murderer.

"You didn't come to worship, did you, gringo?" said Katy. "You came to hunt."

A bloodied hand reached out and grabbed Katy's wrist before she could pull away. The man's sudden movement startled her, but she did not dare move. His face was now just inches from her own.

"Did it work?" he yelled. "Did it work? Just tell me if it worked!"

Terrified, Katy barely had a chance to open her mouth before the stranger passed out again.

Katy noticed his backpack just minutes before the police arrived. It was dark blue with a New York Comic Con logo. Inside she found a thermos, a granola bar, and a manila folder filled with typewritten pages, newspaper clippings, and photos, all held together with dozens of paper clips and rubber bands. As the police siren echoed closer along the paved road leading to Pueblo Bonito, Katy pulled off the last rubber band, opened the folder, and stared at the first page.

The first line read: *If you are reading this, you can assume something terrible has happened to me.*

Whether a manuscript, a manifesto, or a confession, she had no idea, but Katy was certain of one thing: if she gave this to the police, she would never discover what happened to the man lying unconscious next to her. She slipped the folder into her own backpack just as the police appeared at the top of the pit.

A dutiful granddaughter, Katy had called her *abuelita* and told her she had to study that night but would happily reschedule her dinner visit, maybe on Monday. Much later that night, she sat down in her kitchen to read the manuscript over a glass of *rosè* and a bowl of leftover *arroz con pollo.*

Much of it seemed organized in vaguely chronological order. Some items stood out as Katy flipped through the pages.

From a podcast transcript: *This summer, we're traveling across this great land of ours to track down every lurid secret buried in the ground, every lurking Damned Thing that science wants you to ignore, every haunted place that's given you goosebumps, and even some you've never heard about.*

From a blog post titled "BREAKING: Kevin Starkly Disappears in Pine Barrens": *That was a pretty irresponsible stunt you pulled on us back in Harrisville, NJ.*

An entry in a dream journal: *The next time I saw Nikola Tesla we were standing in the Rocky Mountains.*

Another blog post: *Meteor Girl had a major breakthrough last night in our experiments with lucid dreaming.*

And a reproduction of an old newspaper clipping from 1897: *The tranquil morning air of Aurora was rudely disturbed today at 6 o'clock, as eyewitnesses reported the appearance of the remarkable airship which has been sailing across the country, flying at an unusually low altitude.*

"Well, I guess I better start at the beginning," said Katy as she poured another glass of wine. "This is going to take a few hours."

This is what she read.

From the note attached to the "Aurora Manuscript"

September 9, 2015

If you are reading this, you can assume something terrible has happened to me.

I wished to compile this information, not so much to rationalize this decision for myself, because I have never felt so clear-minded about any mission I have ever undertaken, but rather that I might leave behind some coherent account. I've attempted to collect the facts—all the things I know to be true—before proceeding. The document you're now holding is the fruit of my single-minded research.

I am astonished by the number of lost souls I've encountered during my travels in the last few weeks, wandering aimlessly across the back roads and small towns, much like that group that ambushed us along that dirt road in Ohio. Some have forgotten their own names. Others feel compelled to tell their stories to every stranger they meet like some cursed modern-day mariner. Most feel safer traveling together so they form large communes for protection, much like the hobo encampments during the Great Depression, I imagine. It's like the blind leading the blind through a landscape of fear.

There are even some who obsessively scrawl "The Pilot Awakens" over every surface because they sense this is some monumental turning point in the course of human history. I've documented many here from my own personal observations. They are too embarrassed or ashamed to tell their families or friends where they are. And all of them, every last man and woman, are devastated by the secret knowledge they've gained.

They don't know what to believe anymore, do they?

I can't help but feel somehow responsible for everything—all the lost, broken people, all the deaths. But I think I finally have a plan to put things right. Does that sound insane?

I've spent my time traveling across several states seeking out every Damned Place on the map. I've explored reports of rifts in the space–time continuum at Camp Hero State Park in Montauk and pursued sightings there of reptile–humanoid hybrids that walk upright on two legs. I've come face-to-face with a monstrous phantom dog that appears regularly near the Ore Mine Bridge in Warfieldsburg, Maryland. The thing is the size of a horse with a single, glowing red eye in the middle of its forehead. I was on my way to West Feliciana parish in Louisiana to stay overnight at the most haunted hotel in the South, but I've since received reports from a small town near the Everglades where the dead are supposedly rising from their graves. So I've been keeping busy.

You need to know one thing before I go any further: This is all real— except for the stories, of course, but even they carry more than a kernel of truth. These are real places, real people, and real events. I've tried to gather together all the necessary documents, all the important evidence, but most of it is also available online for anyone who wishes to verify the specifics.

It's crazy how many people already know part of the story, isn't it? We all have part of the story even if everyone doesn't understand the whole. I've tried to lay out each of the puzzle pieces so the overview makes sense. The easiest step was determining where to begin, because we all know it really started long before that unfortunate incident this past July in the Jersey Pine Barrens. It began before the earthquake, even before Nikola Tesla began his misbegotten experiments in the Colorado Rockies back in 1899. But I'm getting ahead of myself.

As I said, anyone can put together the beginning pieces. The newspaper articles, the websites, all the documents cited are waiting to be uncovered by the ambitious and the patient seekers of truth. But I fear I'm the only one still alive today who can tell the last part of the story, because only I know how it must end.

* * *

From the *Dallas Morning Call*, April 17, 1897

A Windmill Demolishes It

By S. E. Haydon

The tranquil morning air of Aurora was rudely disturbed today at 6 o'clock, as eyewitnesses reported the appearance of the remarkable airship which has been sailing across the country, flying at an unusually low altitude.

However, wonderment soon turned to dismay as the craft, beset by apparent malfunction, collided with Judge Proctor's windmill in the town's northern precinct. The resultant explosion rent the craft asunder, casting debris across the landscape. Judge Proctor's windmill, a landmark of the community, lay shattered and ruined, as well as his prize-winning flower garden.

Amidst the chaos, authorities grapple with the grim reality that the pilot of the ill-fated craft was likely its sole occupant. Though his remains are marred beyond recognition, preliminary investigations suggest he was not an inhabitant of this world. Mr. T.J. Weems, an esteemed officer of the U.S. Army Signal Service, posits that the unfortunate pilot hailed from the distant red planet of Mars.

Also recovered from the wreckage were papers adorned with inscriptions in a hieroglyphic script, whose meaning remains a mystery. These cryptic documents are believed to recount the pilot's celestial odyssey. The very construction of the craft itself remains a riddle. Fashioned from a peculiar alloy, bearing semblance to a fusion of aluminum and silver, the vessel defies conventional explanation. Crowds flock to the crash site, eager to behold the remnants of this alien craft and to glean insights into the mysteries that lie beyond our ken.

The pilot's funeral will take place tomorrow.

From the Dream Journal of Anthony Fermia

July 9, 2015

There I am, sitting in the main reading room of the New York Public Library on Forty-Second Street, where I work, and Richard Harrigan is right next to me, stuffing a load of books into his backpack. It's the same type of dream I've had many times before. Everything is illuminated by a bright, saturated light, almost blinding in its intensity, and everything, every scrap of paper, every piece of furniture, even the scratches on the table, seems to have a life of its own. So I knew right away this is one of those dreams where the dead want to talk to me. That's why I can remember every detail, every word spoken in these dreams, because the dead never want me to forget. That's cool because they haven't spoken to me in a while.

I tell Richard that he has to get out because I'm closing up for the night.

"We'll need all these books for our trip with Starkly," he says.

I turn around and we're standing outside in the dark, except it's not Forty-Second Street or Bryant Park behind the library, but some bizarre, prehistoric landscape that I've never seen before in my life. We're in the middle of some swamp or bog. Gingko trees and towering pines surround us. But the pine trees are all dead, their bare branches tangled together blocking the face of the moon.

We're all walking together through this strange place, Richard and me, Kevin Starkly, and Johnny Walters. We're trudging through this swamp, heading toward this stone wall seemingly misplaced in the middle of nowhere. Veins of ivy crisscross its length. I notice openings in the structure, like windows—or maybe some of the bricks just fell out long ago. Did someone once live here?

Johnny says, "It looks like a medieval castle."

As we're moving along, Richard throws all those books from the library on the ground and walks on them as though they're stepping-stones.

I'm following close behind, stepping on top of these scattered volumes, afraid I'll lose my way if I don't. They feel odd beneath my feet, bobbling and uncertain as if the books are floating on the surface of a pond.

And right ahead of us I see the little ghost girl named Abigail, crying in the dead forest. I've seen her before in my dreams and she always scares the hell out of me. She looks about six years old, and her faded dress is in tatters. Gray-white ash from God knows what incinerated home is plastered to her face like a death mask. Her dark hair is filthy with dirt and soot. The poor thing always looks as though she's walked through a blazing holocaust. And whenever I see her, she always has ugly, horrible things to tell me.

As I get closer, I hear her crying, actually sobbing uncontrollably. Tears from her right eye have worn rivulets through the caked ash on her face. The left eye is an empty socket.

"Why are you crying, Abigail?" I ask.

She stops sobbing just long enough to say, "Please, Mr. Fermia, don't go here. This is a bad place."

The other guys kept walking right past me. I try to comfort her, but it's no use. She keeps wailing. "Please, Mr. Fermia, just go away. Nothing good ever happens here. This is where the bad monster will get all of you."

So I run after the guys, wobbling on the floating books. I'm yelling for them to stop before it's too late. But I see Kevin stepping off the path, and he's crossing past the stone wall heading away in another direction.

I scream, "Kevin, don't go there!"

But I'm too late. Kevin is already sinking fast into the ground. He's flailing around desperately, reaching out his arms, trying to hang on to something. We all ran over and grabbed his hands and started pulling him up. But the force sucking Kevin into the swampy earth is too powerful. It starts dragging all four of us into the ground despite how hard we're struggling. Finally, reluctantly, we released Kevin.

I see him disappear under the ground like a drowning man. He takes one last gulp of air before his head is sucked under with a sickening, plopping sound.

And then I woke up.

* * *

Handwritten note on top of page: *This is who we were.*

From "Journey Into the Abyss: My Escapade Under Atlantic Avenue"

New York Press, June 1, 2015

By Randy Carter

I felt safe assuming that climbing down a manhole in the middle of Atlantic Avenue at midnight would be the strangest situation I'd find myself in last week—but I was dead wrong. I never imagined that I'd be screaming for my life, struggling to hold onto my sanity like a whimpering, neurasthenic milquetoast from a Lovecraft horror pulp.

I just wanted an on-the-job interview with the elusive Kevin Starkly, paranormal investigator and blogger of the weird, and I thought following him underground as he explored the Atlantic Avenue Tunnel, the oldest and most haunted subway tunnel in the world, left shuttered and abandoned for over 120 years, would be no big deal. Well, it seemed like a good idea at the time.

After all, people loved exploring the Atlantic Avenue Tunnel. Thousands have shimmied down that manhole and dropped 20 feet underground since amateur historian Bob Diamond re-discovered the lost tunnel in 1980 and transformed it into one of the most bizarre tourist attractions in Brooklyn, maybe the most bizarre in all of New York City.

Once a month, more than 100 intrepid explorers, equipped with nothing more exotic than sturdy shoes and tiny flashlights, descend from the noonday sun of Atlantic Avenue into the perpetual midnight of the tunnel in search of secrets. Maybe they're looking for hidden pirate booty or the missing diary of John Wilkes Booth, or maybe they're just looking for a good scare listening to ghost stories of old New York. The reason Kevin Starkly is here with some of his self-described

Nerd Legion in tow is because apparently some of the spooks down here have gone bat-shit crazy.

Visits to the tunnel started getting scary a month ago right after that freaky 5.8 earthquake hit New York. People start seeing floating orbs of glowing green mist and then report unexplained cold spots near the back wall. Lights would go out for no reason; even flashlights with new batteries would go stone-cold dead. And then visitors heard the unexplained sounds of footsteps and the eerie cries for help coming from somewhere in the dark. Tourists went elsewhere for safer scares, and eventually Diamond called a halt to the proceedings and invited in an old friend to help him out—ghostbuster-next-door Kevin Starkly.

After climbing down the manhole in the middle of the street, I squeezed through a narrow passageway that opened up into an extraordinary barrel-vaulted brick tunnel. The air temperature dropped about 15 degrees; I could see my breath huffing out in tiny clouds. My mind raced through any number of horror story clichés, which perversely became more overwhelming as I tried to push them aside. I was dropping into the abyss, into the depths of a fungus-covered catacomb, into a cistern more ancient than humanity itself. *"Carter! For the love of God, put back the slab and get out of this if you can!"*

I was dropping into a trap, never to see the light of day again. *"For the love of God, Montresor!"*

And in the back of my head, I kept repeating *I will not scream like a little girl. I will not scream like a little girl.*

I thought I spied Starkly and two pals setting up an infrared video camera on a tripod. He seemed shorter than I'd imagined and with a noticeable beer belly and a prematurely receding hairline.

Was this the same guy involved in that sketchy arson case in Rhode Island? Rumor has it he and his Nerd Legion comrades would be behind bars if it wasn't for the fact that no one was left alive to press charges.

Was this the same guy who was *persona non grata* at Bell House after he bitch-slapped that scientist dude during a Secret Science Club contretemps a few months ago? The guy described as equal parts bullshit and bunkum—and that's from his friends?

Then he turned, looked up at me and said, "Who the hell invited this hack to join the party?" Yeah, that's my guy.

Then, as if to disabuse me of any lingering doubt, he said, "Listen, if you're looking for the hero of this story, I'm your guy, so spell my name correctly. It's Kevin—traditional spelling—and there's no 'e' in Starkly. That punk from *The Times* deliberately kept misspelling it just to piss me off."

Luckily, neither Starkly nor I were interested in making new friends that night. I just held back and watched the team in action. One guy, tall and lanky, Tony Fermia, looked almost normal. Well, passably normal anyway. After all, he does talk to the dead in his dreams.

"I saw this headless man walking toward me in the tunnel," Tony said. "I guess he was talking, but since he didn't have a head it was hard to tell. He said, 'Don't open the wall. Whatever you do, for Christ's sake, don't open the wall.' Then I woke up."

Starkly looked particularly grim in the glow of the fluorescent lamps that lit up the entire half-mile length of the tunnel. "I was afraid of that. The headless spook is probably the English foreman ordered to keep the unruly Irishmen building this tunnel in line.

"According to legend, he ordered that all these upstanding laborers should work every Sunday until the job was done. So those guys responded as any other God-fearing, church-going gentlemen would respond—they shot the foreman between the eyes, chopped off his head, and buried him somewhere in the tunnel walls."

The other member of the team was Richard Harrigan, a portly little professorial type who was really rocking the scholarly look with a neatly trimmed goatee and black-framed glasses. The guy is the only real scientist in the bunch, with a degree in physics or something, which already puts this team a cut above most other self-styled paranormal investigators. Richard is about half the height of Fermia and looked even smaller hunched up over a pile of electronic equipment. A tug-of-war was going on between Starkly and Richard over one of the instruments.

"I told you to adjust the EMF so it was totally unidirectional," said Richard. "With all the underground cables here, the electromagnetic spike could be spillover from another source."

"Excuse me, Mr. Wizard, but unless Con Ed opened a secret generating plant behind that wall, I'm betting our hotspot is located right there," said Starkly as he brushed past me.

Electromagnetic field (EMF) detectors can find even the smallest electrical sources, and this one was going off the charts.

The four of us, alone in the tunnel, headed for the wall at the other end. The ground in front of the wall was littered with a pile of rubble, bricks and stones tossed everywhere. Nobody knew what lay behind that wall. Bob Diamond thought that an old steam train—an American made copy of a British design, the "Planet" type 2-2-0 engine—was entombed there, bricked into place once the tunnel and the rail line went out of business in 1861.

Legends said treasure might have been hidden there by gangs of pirates and bootleggers who commandeered this tunnel as a hideout in the 1880s and 1890s.

"And then there's the story that the railroad company taught a lesson to those workers who killed their foreman. They hired some Pinkerton agents to terminate the ringleaders," said Starkly. "Nobody could prove anything, but it's a fact that many of the men working down here disappeared mysteriously and were never seen again."

I asked about the fourth member of the Nerd Legion, John Walters, and why he wasn't here tonight. "Johnny doesn't like working underground," answered Tony.

In addition to the EMF detectors, the Nerd Legion had a wicked assortment of digital video cameras, fiber optic cables, and monitors set up near that dreaded back wall.

Starkly had worked out a deal with Diamond: In return for checking for spooks, he would get first dibs at posting videos from the tunnel on his Myth-America blog. Starkly garnered quick accolades for his blog and podcasts, especially after that quake turned the world upside down. Within weeks this sketchy dude was one of the paranormal cognoscenti. Hell, Myth-America won a spot on the "25 Best Blogs You're Probably Not Reading" from this very publication.

"Damn, now I remember why I invited you tonight," Starkly paused while lugging a monitor to the far wall. "I needed a reporter to pitch my big summer adventure. Make sure you mention the Myth-America Geek Freaks Across

America podcast starting next month. I'm taking our weird investigations to the next level and the road trip begins with a monster hunt in one of the forgotten towns of the Jersey Pine Barrens. That's the real story here."

I ignored the PR pitch and instead asked how Starkly had met up with Diamond. Starkly smiled and said, "We're both stubborn sonsabitches. Bob knew in his gut this tunnel really existed, even though everyone else in the world had forgotten about it. The more the experts told Bob to drop his pursuit and stop his searching—the more they said all the stories were fake—the more he kept pushing on, bulldozing every naysayer in his path. We're both alike in that way, so I guess we formed a mutual admiration society."

Just as we settled near the foot of the back wall, and I wondered how much colder it could possibly get down here, the lights in the tunnel went out and we were surrounded by tar-pitch darkness.

I will not scream like a little girl. I will not scream like a little girl.

"Ghosts hardly ever come out in the light," explained Starkly. "We need to operate in the dark if we hope to record any paranormal phenomenon."

The Nerd Legion had prepared for an endoscopic examination to try to see behind the wall. Richard had attached an infrared camera to a long fiber-optic cable, and now Tony was threading the cable through a small crack in the wall. We all watched the camera's progress on the monitor as it snaked between the bricks laid down over a century before. The recent earthquake had widened some of the cracks in the wall. The green glow of the monitor made me queasy, but I couldn't look away, no matter how hard I tried. It was a worm's eye view of a vault hidden from the world for ages.

The worms crawl in, the worms crawl out. The worms play pinochle on your snout.

"It's weird how the extreme cold over here corresponds exactly to that freaky electromagnetic field," said Tony.

We were all placing bets, guessing the thickness of the wall. Starkly estimated it at four feet, and damn if he wasn't right on the money. The little camera nosed its way past rocks and rubble and finally came to an opening like a bottomless pit that reflected back no light at all. Tony twisted the cable back and forth to ensure that it wasn't stuck against anything, but the camera moved freely.

"Can we pump up the light levels?" asked Starkly.

Richard was adjusting the camera and shaking his head when I thought I saw something move on the monitor screen.

"Tony, twist the camera back to the right, I thought I saw something," said Richard.

The four of us sat dead silent, gazing at the green glow of the monitor like doctors studying a bizarre brain scan. Something behind the wall, separated from us by four feet of solid stone, was moving toward the camera.

"Are those rats?" somebody asked.

Little pinpricks of light blinked across the screen. First one pair here, then another pair in the opposite corner, until a dozen sets of eyes were staring back at us on the monitor.

"I'm adjusting the resolution to see if I can make out any shapes," said Richard. And that was the last sane thing I recall.

I remember screaming like a little girl as I desperately tried to put as much distance between myself and that wall as possible. You can hear it for yourself on that podcast Starkly posted. I stumbled in the dark tripping on God knows what, as I raced away in a panic. I thought I felt Tony lifting me up from the ground on one side and Richard on the other, but I'm not certain. I don't even remember climbing up out of the manhole. But there I was, leaning on a lamppost on Atlantic Avenue staring at Trader Joe's, thinking, "Christ, is this the real world?"

I know what they say happened. Diamond has shut down the tunnel tours indefinitely. Says the place isn't safe. That it's overrun with rats the size of panthers. But I know I didn't see any rats that night, even though nobody believes me. The Nerd Legion has closed ranks, insisting I saw the rats moving and I panicked. But you notice how they never released all the video recordings or all of the infrared photos? Because if they did, you would see what I saw down there in that stygian gloom, and nobody would ever again say that I'm crazy.

Richard adjusted the resolution on the monitor, and in a brief flash we all saw clearly what was moving behind the wall. The effect was like the lightning storm of paparazzi flashes at a celebrity sideshow. The vision lasted only for a few seconds, but I know I'll be cursed to see those things for the rest of my life. The horrifying image is burned on my retina like a bleeding tattoo.

They looked as if they had once been human—fat, slug-like bodies slick with moisture—ten of them, maybe 12. Eyes glowing green, they seemed to look directly at us through the wall. And those remnants of arms—now spider limbs ending in claws—grabbing at the ground and heaving their bloated maggot bodies through the rubble.

But then I heard them singing. Not a song, but God help me, a sickly sing-song-y taunt. More like a schoolyard threat.

And I swear you would hear it yourself with your own ears if only that damn Starkly would release all the recordings instead of a few self-serving fragments. You would hear them too. Just before I ran screaming down the tunnel, just before I recovered the shreds of my sanity in the night air of Atlantic Avenue, I heard them singing:

We're coming out to play. We're coming out to play. We're coming out to-day!

From Kevin Starkly's Twitter feed

@MythAmerican

Let all the poisons that lurk in the mud hatch out #nycquake #unknown

From "Police Reveal Details in Grisly Murder of Tulsa Antiques Collector"

Daily Oklahoman, May 19, 2015

Police are still seeking suspects in the grisly murder of renowned antiquities collector Todd Sussman who was found dead with his heart cut out in his Tulsa home late last night. Sussman, 58, recognized as one of the foremost collectors of primitive fetishes and ancient weapons, was discovered in a pool of blood in his living room by police responding to neighbors' reports of an altercation at the house. The house was also a gallery and showroom for one of the largest collections of African and Asian religious artifacts in private hands and was featured on several episodes of TLC's "Weird Collectors" and Syfy's "Oddities."

"Strange characters be always coming and going at all hours, other dealers looking to trade or sell to add to their own collections," said housekeeper Dani Mawbry who was not working the night of the murder. "I didn't like the looks of none of them."

Police are concentrating their efforts interviewing any dealers or acquaintances who were in Oklahoma last week. Police confirm there was no sign of forced entry indicating that Sussman probably knew his killer. They also confirm that several artifacts were apparently stolen.

"We don't believe any talk this was some kind of ritual sacrifice or anything else but a bad business transaction with a horrendously violent end," said Sgt. Matt Heckel of the Tulsa Homicide Unit. He described the missing objects as Watusi poisoned arrows, triple-bladed phur-pa knives from Tibet, and kiri daggers used in Kali cults in India. Police are still searching for the murder weapon, but Sgt. Heckel suspects the killer used one of the missing artifacts to remove Sussman's heart. He wouldn't comment on rumors that other internal organs were also removed.

* * *

From the archives of Myth-America.com (posted June 25, 2015)

Curses! New Jersey!

By Kevin Starkly

You have to wonder what the hell the Pine Barrens of New Jersey ever did to offend God. Not that the rest of the "Garden State" isn't ripe for divine retribution, what with its filthy oil factories, waste-strewn waters, and did I mention its corrupt politicians? But you would think that the pine-scented bogs of southern Jersey would be a paradise, a promised land overflowing with healing waters and cranberry and blueberry goodness.

Except, of course, the people who lived and died there didn't see it that way. Over the last two hundred years, town after town trying to carve out a hardscrabble existence from the Pine Barrens has not just failed but been crushed into the ground. The names of these are scattered throughout the history of the state like the memorials of some forgotten disaster, those "lost towns" of the Pine Barrens: Ongs Hat, Harrisville, Calico, and Mount Misery.

Some died a slow death of economic strangulation. Others suddenly disappeared overnight, victims of mysterious fires or senseless panics. You can waste a good chunk of your life searching for the remains of these towns today—and I speak from personal experience. In some places you'll find only scorched earth or the ghostly outlines of a forgotten foundation. If you're lucky, though, you'll come across some still-standing factory walls rising several stories high like the ruins of a medieval castle. A few places have sections of sidewalk leading to nowhere.

And some say that in one of these cursed towns back in 1735, the Jersey Devil was born.

This crazy-quilt chimera sounds like a bad Thomas Nast cartoon nightmare. Check out this terrifying eyewitness account from 1909: Mrs. Mary Sorbinski in South Camden heard a commotion in her backyard during a freezing January night. When she went out to investigate, what she saw made her blood run cold. She observed a dark creature standing about seven feet tall attacking her German shepherd. The dog was barking frantically at this horrendous apparition, which whipped around a snake-like tail, stood on two thin legs, and had a large pair of leathery wings. Mary snapped out of her temporary paralysis and started whacking the beast (the Devil, not the dog) with a broom. The creature bit at her dog, removing a large chunk of flesh, before it finally leaped over her fence and disappeared into the winter night.

Countless tales been told connecting the Jersey Devil with attacks on livestock and on pets. Poor Mary was just unlucky enough to be the first person to witness the Jersey Devil in action. By the way, her pet eventually recovered, but Mary herself was never the same. Legend said the Devil would carry off animals and even small children. Finding the mangled carcasses of goats and chickens miles away from their owners was not unusual, and the missing children were never seen again.

A cab driver in 1927 reported a sighting of a huge dark figure, with two red glowing eyes and covered with hair, start pounding on the roof of his car. (Please see my other entries on red-eyed apparitions in listings for Moth Man and the Flatwoods Monster.)

At least a dozen origin stories are associated with the Jersey Devil. Some legends say the monster was the illegitimate child of a witch who lived on the outskirts of Harrisville. Another says sorcery transformed a normal boy into a demon. The most popular one says that Mrs. Jane Leeds of Estelville was pregnant with her thirteenth, unwanted child. "Let the devil take this one," she was reported to have said countless times to friends and relatives.

Don't people know better than to be careful what you wish for?

They say the creature born that stormy night in 1735 certainly did belong to the Devil. Whatever it was, it didn't belong to this world. It had cloven hooves, a long snakelike body with an elongated head like a horse, and leathery batlike wings. The midwife and all the relatives panicked and bolted out of the house when the unholy apparition slithered up the chimney and flew off into the night. And the legends say that the Jersey Devil has haunted the Pine Barrens for the last 250 years.

An exorcism in 1740 supposedly slowed it down for about a century. But I guess even God's grace wears off eventually, because according to reports, Commodore Stephen Decatur fired a cannon at it in 1800. Police Officer James Sackville shot it with his revolver on January 16, 1909. Later that same week, William Wasso, a railroad worker on the Clayton–Newfield line, swore he saw it electrocuted on the third rail. But despite the best efforts of God and man, the Jersey Devil always returned to stalk the bogs and pine forests of its birthplace.

Before I forget, eyewitnesses have agreed on one other common feature of the Jersey Devil over the last hundred years (aside from its disturbing appearance)—a weird bloodcurdling cry.

Here's how E. W. Minster of Bristol described it (according to James F. McCloy and Ray Miller Jr. in their book *The Jersey Devil*): "Again, it uttered its mournful and awful call—a combination of a squawk and a whistle, the beginning very high and piercing and ending very low and hoarse."

Maybe the poor, cursed child is still pissed off wondering why it has suffered so long for the sins of its parents.

Posted by strangekevin

From Kevin Starkly's Twitter feed

@MythAmerican

If a spacecraft crashes 50 miles outside of Dallas, and the world doesn't hear it, has a new epoch really dawned in human history? #auroracrash

From Forgotten Towns of Southern New Jersey

E.P. Dutton, First Edition 1936

By Henry Charlton Beck

There are many acres of scattered walls, the remains of two-story buildings, skeletons of a dead community…The stone, brick, and lime are in a remarkable state of preservation, considering that it was back in 1893 that the town was swept by fire.

From New Jersey State Police Interrogation Transcript, July 11, 2015

Posted on TheSmokingGun.com

SGT. Z:	State your name please.
JW:	John Walters
SGT. Z:	Were you present at the Harrisville site on the night of July 10?
JW:	Yes, I was there.
SGT. Z:	Please tell me the names of all those present with you at the Harrisville site.
JW:	I've already told this to the park rangers and…
SGT. Z:	Who else was present?
JW:	All right, I was there with Kevin Starkly, Richard Harrigan and Tony Fermia. But as I said already, Kevin was the leader of the expedition.
SGT. Z:	Did you ever hear Mr. Starkly mention anyone named Holly Evers?
JW:	Holly Evers? Who is she?
SGT. Z:	And what exactly was the nature of this expedition that brought you out to the middle of the Pine Barrens at midnight?

JW: I know it was a stupid idea, but it was Kevin's stupid idea. Kevin is what they call an "urban explorer" or an "urban spelunker." It's sort of like a hobby. He's always going on about how he gets this great adrenalin rush when he's risking life and limb climbing over urban ruins. You know, like abandoned subway stations, condemned buildings, ancient cemeteries. That's how he started out anyway. Before you know it, he's doing ghost hunting, paranormal investigations, really creepy, dangerous stuff. Mostly he does his work in the city—New York City—but he recently got it into his head to poke around these "forgotten towns" scattered around the Jersey Pine Barrens, especially…

SGT. Z: Do you know that the ruins in Harrisville are off limits because those structures are falling apart?

JW: Listen, Kevin and even Richard have explored places that are ten times more dangerous. This one time, Kevin snuck over to the south end of Roosevelt Island and climbed to the top of that old smallpox hospital. You know, the one that… I guess I shouldn't be telling you about all this.

SGT. Z: Were you personally involved in any other acts of trespassing?

JW: No. I mean that… (unintelligible)… You think I'm responsible somehow for what happened, don't you?

SGT. Z: Are you feeling guilty, Mr. Walters?

JW: I know exactly what you're thinking. You're thinking, 'He seems like the sensible one. Why didn't he talk them out of it?' I'm supposed to be the practical one, the unadventurous guy who never pulled a dangerous stunt in his whole life. Let me tell you, Kevin assured me that he checked everything out thoroughly the day before our little nighttime excursion. He was taking photos, mapping the area…

SGT. Z: Mr. Starkly investigated the area the previous day?

JW: That's what I'm trying to tell you. Kevin may be stubborn, impulsive, and foolishly opinionated, but he's not totally irresponsible. Do you think I would let Kevin do this if I knew…if I knew what was going to happen? Kevin told me this expedition would just be for laughs. We would scare each other telling ghost stories by the light of the full moon. God, if I knew…

SGT. Z: Is that all you were doing that night? Just telling ghost stories?

JW: It started out that way. We were exploring around, talking crap about the real origin of the Jersey Devil. I told you it was all recorded so Kevin could post it as part of a new podcast for his Myth-America blog.

SGT. Z: Miss America blog? Like the beauty pageant?

JW: No, not miss, it's myth…m, y, t, h…as in… Never mind.

SGT: Z: Were you all working on this podcast with Mr. Starkly?

JW: Sort of, I guess. But it's not like we were getting paid for anything. Doing this was just an excuse to take time off from our jobs this summer and hang out together. It was going to be a road trip to hunt down the weirdest, strangest places in the U.S. Tony described it as the 'Geek Freaks Across America Tour.'

SGT. Z: So you were all getting ready to travel?

JW: Yes, but not that night. That night we didn't go anywhere except camping out in the ruins of that old ghost town. It was almost a dare, like sleeping in a haunted house.

SGT. Z: Did Mr. Starkly ever mention meeting up with Patrick Wayne?

JW: No, I've never heard that name before. Why are you asking about…Wait a minute!

SGT. Z: What is it, Mr. Walters?

JW: Those people…Holly and Patrick what's-his-name? Did something happen to them just like it happened to Kevin? Something happened to them in Harrisville, didn't it?

SGT. Z: Did any of you know Beatrice Longley or Ashani Washington?

JW: Oh my God!

Graffiti on the corner of Bedford Avenue and North 6th Street, Brooklyn, NY:

THE PILOT AWAKENS

Sketch of Harrisville ruins, July 10

From Myth-America.com podcast transcript, July 10, 2015

Kevin: Here she is! As advertised, as promised…
Ladies and gentlemen, I present to you,
the Myth-America Summer Road Trip! Or as
Tony likes to call it: Geek Freaks Across
America Tour!

We're doing something a little different
this summer. I'm dropping all my pressing engagements, all my lucrative writing
assignments…(Laughter)

Please, no snickering from the cheap
seats, gentlemen. You are my guests after
all. Where was I? Oh right. This summer, we're traveling across this great
land of ours to track down every lurid
secret buried in the ground, every lurking Damned Thing that science wants you to
ignore, every haunted place that's given
you goosebumps, and even some you've never
heard about. That's our mission: To travel
across as many states as we can until our
money runs out or the damn rental car col-
lapses…and hunt down and record all the
macabre, weird stuff.

And tonight's first stop is a place close
to my home, if not my heart. A place so
alien, it could just as well be on another
planet. I'm talking about the blasted and
cursed Pine Barrens of New Jersey. And,
yes, ladies and gentlemen, that means
we're hot on the trail of the most infamous monster this state has ever produced…
the Jersey Devil!

Let me just adjust this flashlight so I can
see what I'm doing here… (Fumbling)...
That's better. Ladies and gentlemen, I'm
looking at the most motley crew of paranormal explorers ever assembled. They're
my Nerd Legion, my peeps-in-strange-
ness, my…

Rich: Will you be talking continuously for the
next half hour, or will you give someone
else a chance to speak?

Kevin: And that's the voice of our resident skeptic and scientific know-it-all, Richard
Harrigan. I would never think of traveling across state lines without the company of some of my oldest friends. And
believe me, Rich is pretty damn old. I
think carbon dating indicates around the
late Cretaceous?

Rich: No, I'm definitely after the Age of
Dinosaurs. More like the Age of Aquarius.

Kevin: I've known Rich an embarrassingly long time, since high school, in fact. And Rich is a science teacher. I think chemistry?

Rich: Physics.

Kevin: Whatever. He is a physics teacher at Fordham. Anyway, over here is John Walters. Johnny is the most level-headed artist I know.

John: That's probably because I'm not really an artist. I just play with a lot of them at work.

Kevin: Johnny runs an art gallery in Brooklyn. Mind you, he's got a respectable art history degree from Pratt, but he's curated some of the strangest, weird-ass shows I've ever seen. I mean that in a good way, of course.

John: Did you see our new show? We turned the whole gallery space into a modern interpretation of the old Collyer Brothers mansion from the 1940s.

Kevin: I like the Collyer Brothers.

John: Yeah. Homer and Langley Collyer were the
            original pack rats who surrounded them-
            selves over the years with every newspa-
            per, magazine, and scrap of garbage that
            they ever collected. But I believe the
            Collyers were pioneers in conceptual art.
            The whole of the Collyer House was a "cab-
            inet of curiosities" writ large, or if you
            prefer, a Joseph Cornell box on steroids.

Rich: Please tell me that no taxpayer dollars
            were wasted on this pretentious piece
            of crap.

Kevin: Did I mention that Rich is also a modern
            art critic? Any other complaints while
            we're at it?

Rich: Well, as a matter of fact (Laughter)…Where
            in the world did you get these tinker-toy
            flashlights? Toys "R" Us?

Kevin: Are you implying I'm not prepared with
            adequate equipment and provender for
            this expedition?

John: You're awfully quiet tonight, Tony. You
            feel OK?

Kevin: I was just about to ask that myself.
            Staying up late with your wargaming bud-
            dies? Ladies and gentlemen, allow me
            to introduce the last member of our
            crack Nerd Legion investigation team,
            Tony Fermi.

Tony: Thanks, Kevin. No, I'm feeling fine. It's
           just that back there…back by the dead pine
           trees in the marsh…it reminded me of the
           nightmare I had last night. It shook me up
           a bit.

Kevin: Oh yes, and did I mention that Tony is
           also our very own bona fide psychic? You
           can't have a crack paranormal inves-
           tigative team without a psychic. At
           least that's what they tell me on the
           Travel Channel.

Rich: Starkly, please spare us.

John: What nightmare was this? Were we all in
           this one?

Tony: Yes, we were walking through this creepy
           landscape at night. Just like I'm doing
           right now. Then we started sinking into
           the ground as if it was…like it was
           quicksand. There's no quicksand around
           here, right?

Kevin: Listen, I've told you guys a thousand
           times, we're all safe as long as we stay
           on the hard ground and keep out of the
           bogs. The bogs can suck you under.

Rich: I wish it wasn't so cloudy tonight. At
           least with a full moon we could make out
           most of our surroundings, and we wouldn't
           have to depend on these toy flashlights.
           How long since that park ranger passed
           us by?

Tony: I remember hiding from him in the marsh
           waters about a half-hour ago. My pants are
           still wet.

Kevin: Tony, we don't want to hear about how you
           wet your pants. How about if someone tells
           our audience a little about this lost town
           we're visiting tonight…or do I have to do
           everything myself?

John: The place was called Harrisville, and I
           believe it's up ahead past the pond. It
           was once a booming little town, a real
           success story here in the Pine Barrens.
           The Harrisville paper factory was famous
           throughout the region over a century ago.
           But like so much else in this godforsaken
           part of Jersey, the town was cursed. The
           site is now a collection of vanishing
           ruins and piles of rubble. They say it's a
           haunted place now.

Tony: Then some legends connect it to the
           Jersey Devil.

John: Oh yeah. Many people believe that Mrs.
            Mowas Leeds gave birth to the cursed child
            who would become the Jersey Devil at the
            Shrouds House in Leeds Point, New Jersey.

Kevin: That's why it's also sometimes referred to
            as the "Leeds Devil."

John: Exactly. And, sometimes, poor Mrs. Leeds
            is said to have given birth to the beast
            in Estelville, or Burlington, or right
            here in Harrisville.

Kevin: That's right, folks. We are very likely on
            the hometown stomping grounds of the baby
            momma of the Jersey Devil. So, Mr. Wizard,
            do you have any smartass scientific analy-
            sis of what kind of creature we could be
            dealing with here?

Rich: You mean other than the wild figment of
            some Piney's imagination?

Kevin: Yeah, I mean a piece of imagination that's
            been seen by more than 2,000 eyewitnesses
            over the last 260 years. I was looking
            for something with a little more flesh and
            blood…or at least more shadow and ecto-
            plasm if you prefer.

Rich: Let's try to be refreshingly unpredict-
            able for once and avoid the supernatural
            explanations, shall we? I think you'll be
            surprised to learn that one of the few
            things I believe the Jersey Devil *is not*,
            is a hoax.

John: I'm shocked, shocked!

Rich: No group or community, no matter how well
            organized or isolated from the outside
            world is going to continue a fabrication
            for more than 250 years as you pointed
            out. Good hoaxes get tiresome after a
            decade or two. Even the Piltdown Man was
            exposed after about 40 years.

Kevin: Are you coming to a point here any
            time soon?

Rich: As I was saying, all the eyewitness
            descriptions of the Devil, the leathery
            wings, the long horse-like head, the ser-
            pentine tail, at face value, seem simi-
            lar to a pterodactyl or some other flying
            reptile thought to be extinct since the
            late Jurassic.

John: This whole region seems pretty prehistoric
            to me. The last time I saw mosquitoes
            this big they were in a chunk of amber in
            a museum.

Rich: The comparison to a prehistoric milieu is
          dead on the mark, Walters. These conifers
          and other evergreens you see around us
          are actually reminiscent of the time 300
          million years ago, just before the flower-
          ing of the…well, of the age of flowering
          plants. And that was right at the time
          when dinosaurs walked the Earth.

Kevin: Wait a minute! So you're saying that if
          the Jersey Devil is some freaky flying rep-
          tile left over from the late Jurassic,
          it would feel right at home here in the
          Pine Barrens?

Rich: You see, Starkly, you can sound scientifi-
          cally literate with very little effort.

Tony: What the hell is that thing in the tree?
          Something's glowing in the upper branches
          of that tree!

Kevin: What are you talking about?

Tony: Right up there above your head. It's prac-
          tically on top of you.

John: Oh my God! It's some huge glowing thing!
          It looks metallic.

Tony: Is it some kind of craft?

          (Excited overtalking)

Rich: Calm down everybody! What you're looking
         at is a piece of sheet metal. I'd guess
         it's the door to an Airstream trailer. Or
         maybe an exterior panel. Tony noticed it
         now because the full moon just came out
         from behind those clouds and the light is
         reflecting off of it.

John: What the hell is the door to a trailer
         home doing up in a tree?

Rich: Don't you remember that hurricane that
         came through here a couple of years
         ago? I think it was Hurricane Irene, or
         maybe Sandy? Park rangers are still find-
         ing pieces of mobile homes throughout
         the woods.

Kevin: Ladies and gentlemen, I believe we have
         reached our destination this evening. Here
         before us is spread the scattered remains
         of one of the forgotten towns of the Pine
         Barrens…and perhaps the hometown of the
         Jersey Devil.

John: Look, it's the remains of the paper fac-
         tory! The heart of this community was its
         paper factory, a big structure with walls
         three feet thick.

Kevin: The last time anybody worked or lived here
         was back in 1910.

John: Look at the ivy vines crisscrossing the side of that wall. My God, we could be looking at the remains of a medieval fortress.

Tony: The ruins remind me of something Lovecraft wrote about forgotten old homes left to decay hidden in the deep woods. I think he said something like, "They are almost hidden now in lawless luxuriances of green and guardian shrouds of shadow."

Rich: Leave it to good old Howard Phillips to set the mood.

John: Excuse me, but is "luxuriances" even a word?

Kevin: There's one other point in the legends of the Jersey Devil that I neglected to mention earlier. In addition to scaring the hell out of whoever is unlucky enough to see this monster in the flesh, the Jersey Devil is also rumored to be a harbinger of catastrophe, a bringer of bad tidings, an evil omen.

Tony: Yes, like the legends of the Black Hound.

John: We're now crawling through the fence that surrounds this part of Harrisville, the only part that still has anything left standing that can still fall over and hurt anyone. (Shouting) Kevin, stay away from that wall!

Tony: That's the only part of the paper fac-
            tory which survived the big fire that swept
            through in 1893. Soon after that fire, the
            town started to fall apart. Of course,
            most people began leaving earlier.

            (Excited overtalking)

Kevin: The Italian-Ethiopian war started just
            a few months after Bill Bozarth saw the
            Devil near Batsto in 1935. They say that
            the beast's unholy scream was heard right
            here in Harrisville just before the
            great fire.

Tony: Did they ever find out how it started? Was
            it an accident? Arson?

John: Guys, we're getting too close to those
            walls. They do look eerie in the moon-
            light, don't they?

Kevin: The Jersey Devil scared the hell out of
            the townsfolk in South Camden on the morn-
            ing of December 7, 1941. Oh, and let's not
            forget about the much contested and con-
            troversial sighting that allegedly hap-
            pened on September 10, 2001. Some poor
            tourist in the Pine Barrens…Now, what's
            his name?

Tony: Did you hear that? (Silence) I thought
            I heard something. Like the cry of a
            small child.

Rich: Believe me, Fermia, nobody's around here for miles, especially children.

Tony: No, I heard it distinctly. It was a little girl crying for help. Wait. (Silence)

There she goes again. Can't you hear her?

John: Tony, you're starting to creep me out.

Rich: You're only supposed to hear and see things in your dreams, not…

John: The only other time Tony heard and saw things while wide awake was back…

Kevin: It was the time we were all in the Shunned House in Providence.

(Silence)

John: Oh God! We have to get out of here now. (Shouting) Everybody clear out of here!

Rich: Calm down, Walters, before you slip into complete super-nanny overload. Nothing is happening.

John: You mean…

(An ear-splitting roar is heard. It sounds like the growl of a large animal, or perhaps the screeching of air brakes on a Mack truck. The roar trails off into a chilling scream, the beginning very high and piercing and the ending very low and hoarse. It sounds almost human.)

Tony: Please, dear God, tell me you all
          heard that!

John: We heard it. But what the hell was it?

Tony: It didn't sound…human. Maybe it was some
          wild animal attacking something?

Kevin: How about it, Mr. Skeptical Inquirer? Was
          it the strangled cry of a rare pheasant?
          Or perhaps the sound of swamp gas expand-
          ing under pressure?

Rich: Don't get all cocky, Starkly. It may just
          be the inspired theatrics of some locals
          trying to scare off us city folk.

Tony: And doing a damn fine job of it.

Rich: I suggest we take this digital recording
          of this growl, or cry, or whatever you
          wish to call it, and have it profession-
          ally analyzed.

          (Rapid Overtalking)

John: That's the first sensible suggestion I've
          heard all evening. Let's all get back…

Kevin: The only way anyone is going to identify
          this is if he happens to pull a recording
          of the Jersey Devil out of his ass.

Rich: And the only way you're going to believe
          anything except your stupid superstitions
          is if…

Tony: What's that light up ahead? I didn't see
          that light before.

Rich: It's probably more wreckage caught up in
          the branches.

Tony: No. No, this light is moving. Look, you
          can see it for yourselves over there.

John: It looks like several lights. Fireflies?

Tony: No, the lights aren't blinking. Whatever
          it is, it's a steady light source. Several
          points of light. It looks like they're
          moving closer to us.

          (Silence)

Kevin: This is breathtaking. I'll try to describe
          this as it's happening. I see maybe a
          dozen balls of blue light. No. Make that
          two dozen. And they're just swarming…danc-
          ing…in front of us.

John: (Barely audible, nearly whispering) It's
          like the Ghost Lights of Marfa, Texas. Or
          like the glowing foo fighters flying around
          Allied planes during World War II.

Kevin: The world of paranormal phenomena is chock
          full of strange, unexplained lights. I'm
          going closer to get a better look.

John: Kevin, get back here. We don't know what
          they are.

Kevin: It's like nothing I've ever seen before…
and that's saying something.

(Slight humming)

Rich: Everyone should be careful. The air
seems suddenly charged. Can you feel it?
Ball lightning is still a poorly understood phenomenon.

Kevin: Maybe these lights are the spirits of my
ancestors, just as the Iroquois believed.

Rich: They say ball lightning is mostly harmless, and they simply dissipate.
Other times they explode, or rather
implode, violently.

(Humming increases. Sounds like a swarm
of bees)

Kevin: They're beautiful. Like little flying neon
balls. (Laughs) Maybe they're the van-
guard of an alien armada coming to conquer Earth.

Tony: Look, the lights are…They're completely
surrounding him. Holy…

John: Kevin, step back. Step away from
the lights.

Rich: Starkly, don't touch them. They may have a
dangerous electrical charge.

(Buzzing is deafening)

Kevin: They're all around me…like some glittering cloud (unintelligible)…casting shadows. Can't see (unintelligible).

Rich: What is that idiot doing? Starkly, get out of there.

Tony: I don't think he can hear us.

John: That light is blinding me.

Tony: I can't see Kevin.

Rich: Neither can I.

John: (Screaming above the buzzing) Kevin, run away! Run away!

(Microphone drops to the ground. Buzzing ceases abruptly. After 13 seconds of silence, someone turns off the recording.)

* * *

From the Dream Journal of Anthony Fermi

July 11, 2015

Last night was the first time the man feeding pigeons in Bryant Park spoke to me. I've dreamed about him before. Long after I've forgotten real-life encounters while awake, I'll remember an incident I dreamed about years ago. These are usually the dreams I know something important needs to be communicated.

This time the man looks up at me as he's tossing some breadcrumbs on the ground. It's funny now that I think about it. Here's this dignified older gentleman wearing a dark coat, gray-striped pants, and a derby hat. He has deep-set piercing blue eyes. He looks as though he's about to start a business meeting, yet he's surrounded, engulfed, by a flock of bobbling pigeons.

"Oggi fa bel tempo, non ci sembra?" he said.

I answered that it was indeed a beautiful day. I asked—in English—if I had met him before.

"No, we haven't been formally introduced. But I believe we have much in common. I thought you might wish to speak in Italian today. Still English is fine with me. I am still not as comfortable with it as my native Serbian. Did I tell you I am fluent in six languages?"

When he stood up, I was struck not so much by his height as by his thin build. He seemed so fragile.

"I apologize, sir," he told me. "My name is Nikola Tesla, and it is my pleasure to make your acquaintance."

I offered my hand, but he backed away. He seemed genuinely alarmed. Some spirits don't wish to be touched, even in dreams.

"Do you ever feel that you can barely keep from screaming if someone touches you, even the slightest bit?"

"No, Mr. Tesla, I can't say that I do."

"No? Well, no matter. I'm very sorry to hear of your friend's disappearance, Antonio. Can I call you Antonio? Good. I know you've been troubled lately, considering different options on how best to proceed. But first, let me say that I have the utmost confidence that you shall succeed in my mission...I mean your mission."

"Do you know where Kevin has gone?" Usually my dream guides have been much more direct.

"I believe it is imperative for you to follow the course of action that makes sense to you. You still have something you need to accomplish here in New York." He paused as if considering whether he had something else on his mind. "That is all I wanted to say to you today."

I stood there dumbfounded, watching as he scattered more crumbs to the birds. I couldn't think of anything else to say myself, so I asked, "Are these all your birds?"

I thought I heard him sigh in resignation.

"No, Antonio, they are just pigeons in the park. They are the only friends I have now. Everyone else openly mocks me or simply avoids me altogether. *The New York Times* called me a "dinosaur." Can you imagine that? They all think I'm crazy you know."

As he started to walk away, he stopped abruptly and turned to face me, eye to eye.

"People think you're crazy as well, Antonio. Don't worry, my boy, we'll prove them all wrong."

"Thank you, sir. Thank you, Mr. Tesla."

"Please, I would prefer you call me Niko. I think we still need to talk several more times, and I would prefer just Niko. Did I tell you that's what Sam Clemens called me?"

"Samuel Clemens? You knew Mark Twain?"

"I've known many people and even more secrets. But I will tell you now that Tom Edison once called me a 'crazy rat bastard.'"

He smiled, tipped his derby, and continued walking away.

Then I woke up.

* * *

From eBay auction site

Seven-headed Hydra preserved in glass jar

Authentic piece from Albertus Seba collection

Current bid: US $599.00

End time: 8 hours 52 minutes (July -11-16:42:10)

Shipping Costs: US $10.00

Item location: Tennessee, United States

Description (revised)

Type: Preserved specimen Animal: Unknown (Hydra?)

This critter is the real deal, another Kunstkammer Kids exclusive, not some stitched-together jackalope gaff like those other guys are hawking. This baby is 18-inches-long, and it's the most ferocious looking son-of-a-bitch you'll ever want to see. The gaping mouths on those seven heads are filled with rows of needle-sharp teeth and the heads are attached to snake-like necks, but it's like no snake you've ever seen in your life. *Brother Hank here, I figure to add some details that Frank neglected the first time around because he thinks it sounds like putting on airs. The creature seems to be an extinct or unknown squamate species. The body, clawed feet, and tapering tail seems vaguely like a marine iguana but the seven necks branching off from a single spine and the lack of any back legs seems like nothing else on Earth.* Thanks Hank, I guess Momma didn't waste her money paying for your education. Anyway, if you're the highest bidder you can claim this baby and own all the bragging rights. And it comes with the unmatched Kunstkammer Kids guarantee: if you're not satisfied that this is the strangest, most unnatural, supernatural oddity you've ever encountered on God's green Earth, you just send it back in 30 days and we'll even pay for the shipping. *Hank again here. Just wanted to say that although we don't usually go into the details surrounding the origins of any of our one-of-a-kind collectibles, I did want to add that we have it on good authority that this specimen most likely belonged to the legendary Amsterdam apothecary and naturalist Albertus Seba and was probably last seen in the Zoological Museum of Amsterdam in 1736.* That's enough history Brother Hank, if folks don't know enough to trust the Kunstkammer Kids then who can you trust? We'll even show you the x-ray so you know for certain that no human hand jiggered this thing together. But wait, there's more! If you win this baby, we'll throw in a full-color copy of Seba's Thesaurus book that was reprinted by those fine folks at Taschen as "A Cabinet of Natural Curiosities." Then just turn to page 162, right after those pretty pictures of crocodiles and snakes, and you tell me if that ain't the spitting image of this Hydra in a glass jar!

If you happen to be traveling down I-40 W outside of Nashville, Tennessee, don't forget to drop by our store and dime museum Arcanium and set a spell. Just call ahead first and say Hank and Frank Weir invited you personally. Or check out our latest oddities online at kunstkammerkids.com.

* * *

From Myth-America.com

July 11

BREAKING: Kevin Starkly Disappears in Pine Barrens

By John Walters

Dear Kevin,

That was a pretty irresponsible stunt you pulled on us back in Harrisville, NJ. You should know Tony wanted me to begin this post with the salutation "Dear Jackass," but I thought that too rude. Both Rich and Tony think you staged this whole thing like "fucking Penn & Teller" (Tony again) so we'd witness you disappearing in a swirl of twinkling blue lights.

Anyway, we nearly got ourselves arrested after the three of us went racing out of the Pine Barrens and nearly crashed headlong into a Park Ranger's Jeep on 679. I don't know why, but I feel guilty about this whole episode. I should have talked you out of trespassing on off-limits property. However, if Tony and Rich are correct, and you wanted to generate publicity for our podcast tour across the country, you certainly succeeded. Did you see all the hits that podcast got? I think we started out with something around 10,000 hits after we posted it. Then I thought something was wrong when we were tracking like 50,000 individual downloads the next day. That is until I discovered that several other blogs had linked to it, including Weird NJ and Forgotten New York.

But I'm afraid that something terrible happened to you—something you didn't plan at all. Sorry if I let you down Kevin. You promised we would all be safe. You assured me the road trip was all just "shits and giggles."

Rich and I are packing up to hit the road again. And, of course, we'll continue podcasting and posting along the way, just as we first agreed. So feel free to jump right in and post a comment, or call, or you know…just tell us you're alive and reading this and you'll meet up with us on the road. I'm still not sure where you wanted to go next, but I know we'll come up with something. By the way, Tony says he's not coming. He's always been the overly emotional one of the Nerd Legion. Says he has some unfinished business to take care of in NYC. Not sure what he means by that, but if you're talking to the dead in your dreams you expect to be a little cryptic.

I'm leaving the comments open on this thread for a while. Maybe someone out there knows something or can figure out where Kevin is right now. Hell, I'll entertain any theories you got, half-baked or half-witted, I'll take them all. Kevin always loved a good paranoid conspiracy theory as much as a good bottle of whiskey. And of course if Mr. Myth-America himself wants to reappear from the mists…you have the floor.

Posted by jwalters

Post Comments

Firefly writes:

Did anyone notice any missing time during the encounter? I'm only mentioning it because many researchers (as you know) from Budd Hopkins to John Mack have noted missing time as hallmarks of classic alien abduction cases.

Rich Harrigan writes:

Just wanted to update you. I'm checking with several of my sources to pull any drone images of the Pine Barrens especially around the time of Kevin's disappearance. The resolution may leave much to be desired, but nonetheless, it could offer some interesting leads.

Dw writes:

Have you guys done a Google search on the pine barrens recently? There's been a lot of strange shit going down there! Aside from all the jersey devil stuff there's also bizarre sightings of lights in the sky and ghostly fires that disappear without a trace. Some other disappearances too.

Oddball2001 writes:

> After I heard about Kevin Starkly's disappearance I couldn't stay silent any longer. It's no secret that Starkly knew something or had some hard evidence concerning the Aurora saucer crash. Just check out the links on his own Myth-America site. In fact, it was widely speculated that Starkly would reveal this evidence during his "Geek Freaks Across America Tour." And now he disappears in a flash just as he starts his grand tour. Coincidence? I think not! Obviously, someone or something, didn't want Kevin revealing any secrets. Listen, the life of a ufologist is getting as dangerous as a mine worker or secret black ops grunt. I'm not making this up. Just Goggle "ufologist deaths" and see how many hits you get!
>
> I've also got some links on my blog, www.oddworld.tumblr.com, along with some theories about what's really happening and who is really running this country.

Killjoy writes:

> I don't want to be the first one to start sounding morbid—and believe me, I'm playing the devil's advocate here—but maybe we should admit that the evidence at hand is more consistent with Kevin's "disintegration" and not his "abduction."

Jessie writes:

> Anybody else think there's some connection with these "Collector Killings" taking place across the country? It's no secret lots of folks think Kevin had some Aurora artifact in his possession. Just saying some folks might kill to get their hands on it.

Kevin writes:

> Hi guys, it's me, Kevin! Just wanted to pass on what the aliens told me. They said to send more Chuck Berry!

Cutie writes:

Shout out to the Myth Americans! I got to tell you: Best. Hoax. Ever. How did you get those spooky sounds on the podcast? I'm giving you props dudes…and a little something in the tip jar.

Anonymous writes:

No, I'm Kevin!

Anonymous writes:

No, I'm Spartacus! I mean…er…I'm Kevin!

Anonymous writes:

Thought I saw Kevin sharing a Big Gulp with Elvis at the 7-11 off Exit 10 on the Jersey Turnpike.

Angels writes:

I was looking through the blogs and places where Kevin usually posts, and I found something really strange at the fanfiction.net site. Somebody (maybe Kevin?) posted an old story called "Night Terror" that Kevin wrote years ago. I remember because he showed it to me about a week ago. He posted it under this old pseudonym…mwalker…I think it's like the name of some old childhood chum back in Greenpoint. But here's the strange part…there are several odd changes that were incorporated into the story. Not to go all Nancy Drew here, but I think the changes may mean something. I think they may be clues.

Tony Fermia writes:

I'd like to discuss this with you angels offline IRL if you don't mind. I didn't know Kevin wrote anything on fanfiction.net and I've known him for years. Do I know you?

Angels writes:

Kevin never liked talking about his literary experiments. Too self-conscious I think after that little Night Tours zine of his went under after college. Of course, I know you guys! And, oh yeah, you know me like totally! Kevin even wrote about me on his blog. Maybe you remember? He called me his Meteor Girl—Taa-dah!

* * *

NIGHT TERROR

I swear the horror at Hollis House came alive that first night my son screamed in his sleep. Something old and hungry awoke from a deep slumber and it had no intention of resting. Sometimes I think the shadows of Hollis House have been patiently waiting for me, waiting across the years for the return of the foolhardy son to suffer for the sins of the father.

Just last week we had moved into my old family home hidden away in the Pine Barrens of southern New Jersey outside Crandall Lake.

We got through the evening by making a game of our house cleaning. We pretended that every musty sheet removed from a piece of furniture was an evil ghost biting the dust. Steven quickly picked out his own room on the second floor near the back of the house. I fixed my sights on a spot for my office right off the grand ballroom on the second floor. At last I would have my own private practice, with no more crowded hospital work. And my wife Judy took an inventory of all the family possessions that somehow escaped decades of vandalism: an old stereo turntable and stacks of vinyl LPs, a library crammed with dusty tomes, and an ancient gardener named Silas Powell who claims to be the caretaker of the estate.

Steven was overtired that first night, staying up long past his bedtime listening to Silas spin his "funny ghost stories." But I finally coaxed him into bed with our usual nighttime ritual. I would start singing "Calling Occupants of Interplanetary Craft."

It was our private, eccentric lullaby, and we never tired of cracking ourselves up singing it time and again. Steven would make up some of his own lyrics:

"Hello, friendly Spaceman Mister

Come down and join your spacey brother and sister!"

But within one short hour of falling asleep, my son bolted upright and screamed loud enough to wake the dead. He wailed inconsolably, not even recognizing Mommy or Daddy. Every parent of a child afflicted by night terrors knows the routine. After three heart-wrenching minutes that seemed like an eternity, Steven finally quieted down and went back to sleep as though nothing had happened.

But since that first night I've heard it skittering around the edges of the house, probing for a secret entrance. Every night it grows larger, mutating into a hulking invisible shape knocking over garbage cans in the backyard. I've heard it clambering up the dying silver maple out back, breaking off the lower branches. Some nights I'm convinced the thing is just out of sight in the darkness peering in at us through the broken stained-glass windows. Then Judy will remind me that the most likely explanation for my malevolent monster is a foraging raccoon or a barn owl. But Judy doesn't understand this house like I do.

> *Night terror: n.* A state of intense fear and agitation some-
> times experienced, especially by children, on awakening from
> a stage of sleep not associated with dreaming but character-
> ized by extremely vivid hallucinations. Also sleep terror or
> *pavor nocturnes.*

It is a condition of little interest even to psychiatrists. It's of even less interest to GPs like me. There's no money to be made from a parasomnia disorder with no cure except the passage of time. But since my son is afflicted, I have become quite the expert on this particular health issue.

I've tried to convince Judy that Hollis House is proving unhealthy for Steven. Like most five-year-olds, he's usually bubbling with curiosity and excited fidgeting. Now his typical exuberance seems intimidated by the surroundings. Every tree branch that brushes against the windows causes him to cry out in fear. I remember Steven asking me, "Is grandpa's house haunted?"

"No Stevie, it's just been closed up for a long time. It's a big old rambling house that was too expensive to take care of, but I always thought I'd come back here one day."

It was Judy who eventually convinced me to return to the old family home, arguing that the quiet countryside might even improve Steven's condition. But now she's away on business, called back to the Paris bureau for a week, and I seem unmoored in this familiar, yet strange place. I warned her that it would not be wise for me to stay here on my own so close to the anniversary of my father's death, but she refused to listen.

I miss Judy. She would reassure me that all the noises were just my imagination and not monsters shambling in the dark. I fear that I've been infected by the madness that surrounds Hollis House—a madness that has settled over Crandall Lake.

Tonight, I had a disconcerting conversation with Silas that seemed to reinforce my worst fears. I asked him if he ever noticed anything vaguely peculiar about Crandall Lake. Silas guffawed, obviously delighted with my understatement.

"Peculiar ye say, eh Doctor Hollis! By Gawd, there's enough peculiarities in these parts to fill volumes!"

Silas leaned back in his seat and stroked his ancient snowy beard, as was his custom when he was about to spin his tales.

"What I'm about to tell ye Doc is pure Gawd-honest truth. This here land use to be Iroquois holy land. T'was right here they'd get all their visions and spirit messages. Even to this day, those Indian fellas still swear the great Aireskoi came soaring out the sky to teach 'em the ways of war and hunting. Why, even before most Indians can remember, there was always a wrong feeling around this land. Like something decided to stay here that didn't quite belong. Even nowadays we still hear about spooks and monsters lurking round. Now ye can understand why the folks round here look so queer. Ye'd be quiet and frightful too if ye knew ye might run into some Hell-spawned critter round the next corner. If ye only knew half the things that…"

My son's screaming from upstairs interrupted Silas.

It was the same terrified and familiar cry that has haunted me almost every other night since it first began. Changes in diet and bedtime didn't seem to work, and apparently neither did the change in location from the Upper West Side of Manhattan to the Pine Barrens of New Jersey. Without even an "excuse me" to Silas I bolted up the stairs.

"Everything's alright now Stevie. You're safe." I held him closely to me, offering myself as sanctuary from his fears one more time. But as always, my efforts to comfort him were useless. After a few minutes, with no more rhyme or reason than when he began, he abruptly stopped screaming and fell back asleep.

"Shhh...it's over now Stevie. The nightmare is over."

But that's not accurate. His sleep terror is not so much a nightmare as it is a horrifying hallucination. Medical science has labeled it, but there's no adequate theory to explain it. Everyone is just relieved that it often simply disappears once the child reaches a certain age. I did read one particularly compelling explanation from a Jungian analyst: that these terrors were a remnant of mankind's antediluvian fears that had nestled in the darkest corners of our primitive brain—a recessive memory from a time when our species was the hunted, not the hunter.

It was after I tucked Steven into bed for the second time tonight that I heard it. Outside the house, I heard a rustling, like the movement of something impossibly large in the woods. It seemed more massive and more aggressive than it was only a week ago. I was startled when I looked up to see a hideous face peering through the bedroom window, but it was only my own reflection in the shattered glass. I ignored the sounds, blaming it on the hyperactive imagination that I inherited from my father.

An inexplicable nervousness prevented me from going to sleep. Steven was now peacefully dreaming, and I heard Silas moving gardening tools into the old backyard shed before going into town. A chilling wind was howling through the nearby woods and whipping around the house. The October gales had stripped the trees of most of their foliage and now the wind swayed the branches about in their grotesque nakedness. Several twisted tree limbs scratched at the windowpanes. I tried to forget about the impending anniversary of my father's death, but perversely, I found it impossible to think of anything else.

In his last years my father—an accomplished physician himself—became the victim of a type of early-onset dementia that robbed him of much of his cognitive function. His convulsive delusions and paranoid fantasies grew progressively worse over the course of only a few years. Most commonly, he imagined himself pursued by a large reptilian demon in a trench coat named Mr. Darkly. The occasional trips to the mental hospital in the next town over became just expensive exercises in futility. They couldn't do any more for my father than all of our family prayers and imprecations over that last year.

I can't recall exactly why I started paging through the old family Bible. Perhaps Silas had awakened my curiosity about my ancestors with his tales from the past. I looked through the leather-bound work with its illuminated script and gilt-edged pages. One entry in particular in the family records near the front of the book hit a nerve:

Jeremy Hollis

Born: March 11, 1930

Died: October 30, 1993

I could still remember every detail of that horrible October night even after more than twenty years. I came home late with my mother from some Halloween party in town. My father had left the masquerade earlier in the evening complaining of a headache. My memory is forever haunted by the sight of my father dead on the floor, his face twisted into a madman death mask. The cause of death was officially listed as "heart failure." But I was certain even then that the truth was deliberately hidden from me. I knew that the expression on his face was not one of pain, but fear.

Some well-intentioned relatives said it was a blessing that my father was finally relieved of his suffering. I remember being furious with him and convinced that somehow he was at fault. I cried over the unfairness of it all and felt utterly abandoned.

We closed up Hollis House shortly after my father's funeral. My mother died a few years after that. I think she was physically and emotionally exhausted after the man she loved left her so tragically. Her emptiness was over too. I'm sorry. I thought I had erased that disturbing episode completely from my life, but there it was again after only a week back at Hollis House. If I was testing my fortitude, as my wife had suggested, then I failed miserably.

I fell asleep in the study and had the most disturbing dream. At least I think it was a dream. I thought I heard an odd shuffling sound from the main dining room. I swung open the large wooden double doors and nearly screamed when I saw a tall man with the head of a raven staring directly at me.

"Good evening son. Welcome back home."

Yes, I'm sure now. I was dreaming. What would Judy say? She would patiently explain that this was one of those rare lucid dreams where you could swear you're still awake. Or perhaps I had just gone stark raving mad.

"Dad...Daddy? Is that you?"

"Of course son, don't you recognize your old man?" He reached up and felt a large beak. "Oh, I'm terribly sorry! I forgot that I was wearing this Halloween mask the night I died. Do you remember it? It was an Edgar Allan Poe Party. I was thinking at first of going as The Masque of the Red Death, but that's rather been played out as a bit of a cliché now, don't you think?"

He took off the mask and I nearly gagged as I saw the rotting, maggot-filled flesh of his face. The left eye was hanging by only a few tendrils to its socket, and both cheeks had caved in almost completely to putrefaction. It was truly a skull with only a few traces of my father's face left, including, incongruously, a bit of his moustache.

"Daddy, would you mind putting your mask back on?"

"Hmmm? Oh yes, I'm still not any good at this regeneration thing. I've only made a few appearances over the years, and never as a full-fledged apparition. And nobody has really seen me at all, except for poor Silas."

"Daddy, is this a dream?"

The raven mask looked down at the floor.

"I have so much I need to tell you. I want to say how very, very sorry I am for all the suffering I put you through during my last years. I've finally come to understand the madness that possessed me while I was still alive. I'm sorry you had to witness all the things I did and listen to all my insane mutterings. I don't blame you if those last years have tainted the way you remember me."

I didn't know what to say. What does one say if given the chance to speak with your father for one last time? Should I tell him how angry I was? Do I mention how much I fear I will inherit his dementia as I grow older? Still, I surprised myself with my next words.

"I miss you, Daddy. We all missed you, especially Mom. And I'm sorry that you never had a chance to know your grandson."

At that, he raised his beak and came towards me with a sense of renewed urgency.

"I have to tell you things I've never told a living soul. I have to tell you how I really died, because if I don't tell you now, then you'll be dead before morning. You and your...You and my grandson."

I could feel my knees growing weak. This dream certainly seemed damnably real.

"Silas is right. There's something horribly wrong in Crandall Lake. This thing...it's some freak, an accident of nature. I still don't quite understand it all even now, but I know that this...this cosmic mistake that taints the air around us is a bridge of sorts. It's a missing link between substance and power, a transitional state possessing qualities of both but existing as neither. It acts as an insane midwife, delivering our dreams and nightmares into reality. It gives a solid sentient shape to our madness."

"But that doesn't make any sense at all."

"Listen to me! The Iroquois prayed themselves into a delirium trance looking for a sign from the skies, and it gave them Aireskoi. I imagined that a hideous demon was plotting to kill me behind my back. Remember Mr. Darkly? This beast was at the root of all my paranoid delusions. Well, damn it if it didn't deliver that demon right to my front door on that October night!"

I fell back against the wall and slid slowly down to the ground.

"Is this thing…this demon still here?"

"No. I tried to fight Mr. Darkly with my bare hands, but I know now that no man is strong enough to slay his own nightmare. As soon as I died, as soon as my conscious mind faded into oblivion, the creature born from my paranoid delusions disappeared as well. I believed that it would never more rule over Hollis House, but I was wrong."

"Why are you telling me this?"

My father adjusted his mask as it had started to slip off his decomposing face.

"I'm telling this to you son so that you'll be better prepared to face the creature that was born from Steven's night terrors over the last week."

"No, Stevie would never do anything…"

"I guess I'm not making myself clear. We don't really have any control over it at all. It only responds to intensity. It feeds off the sheer magnitude of the passion or madness that goads it into action and it gets fatter and bolder and more corporeal until…"

"Don't worry Daddy, I won't let anything happen to Stevie."

"Remember everything I told you son, or else you'll both meet me face to face before the sun rises."

I seriously thought that if I just closed my eyes and screamed as loudly as possible, I would force myself awake from this nightmare. I remember awakening with a scream that tore through the night. It was a cry desperately clutching at sanity.

As I tried to snap myself into full consciousness, I wasn't sure if the scream was real or just another part of my dream. I went upstairs and found Stevie sleeping soundly, then I went into the garden. What I saw out back shocked and sickened me. There laid Silas on the grass, his wrinkled face transformed into a wide-eyed witness to terror. The chilling wind tugged playfully with his white hair. Silas's heart had just stopped. Was it *his* scream that awakened me? In my confusion over this tragic coincidence between my dream and Silas's death, I didn't even think of calling the police. Was my father's warning really coming true?

Then I heard rustling in the trees that was not caused by the howling autumn wind. I stopped breathing as I heard the sound of immense wings flapping directly above my head. It was still here! Somehow, I knew I mustn't look up or turn around. Terrified I heard the splintering of dozens of tree branches, and I knew that something impossibly large was diving straight for me. It was only a few yards above me when my legs regained life. Fear-triggered adrenaline pushed me forward in a spasm of movement towards the still opened back door. Even as I ran I could feel it close behind me with its hellish wings beating the night air. Finally, I flew through the doorway, spun around with my eyes closed and slammed the door shut. The deadbolt fell into place. I stood up and glanced quickly about me making sure all the first-floor entrances were secure. After an intolerable breathless silence, I heard at the back door a distinct…knock. This nightmare outside was knocking at the door as casually as a salesman.

For one insane moment I entertained the notion that maybe this was all a hallucination. Maybe that was Silas at the door wondering why I had raced back into the house like a madman. Almost against my will, I moved closer to the door. Just as I reached for the knob, a massive weight crashed into the closed door. It shook violently in its frame throwing me backwards in shock, but the old oaken panels miraculously held firm.

At that instant I remembered what my father had said. This was the night terror from Steven's mind. That must be the answer. This freakish cloud over Crandall Lake had latched on to my son's ultimate terror and brought it to life. I was equally certain that it had somehow killed Silas.

I rushed upstairs to my son's bedroom feeling my heart pounding in my ears. Steven was already sitting up in bed, rubbing his eyes, oblivious to the thing below.

"Daddy, is it morning already?"

How could I possibly explain to him what was really downstairs? I didn't understand it myself. But I knew that one look at this living night terror and the intense shock will lead first to madness, then death.

My father had given me a clue on how to stop it. I knew I had to move quickly, so I picked up Steven in his flannel pajamas and carried him down the hall, past the ballroom, to my makeshift doctor's office. What would my father do? I decided this is where we would make our last stand.

"You're scaring me, Daddy."

As I closed the door to my office, I heard something that froze my heart in sheer terror. The thing was moving in Steven's room! I could hear the hideous sound of its feelers or tentacles...or whatever monstrous extremities it possessed...moving noisily about in the room. Chairs and lamps were being overturned inside. Just listening to that abomination could bring a man to the edge of madness. How did it get inside? My mind was screaming, "You don't belong here. Leave us alone!"

Now the thing, or at least a part of it, was crawling in the corridor, moving towards the office. My trembling fingers managed to remove the hypodermic needle from its sterile wrapper. My plan of attack was actually a retreat, a retreat from reality.

"As soon as my conscious mind faded into oblivion, the creature born from my paranoid delusions disappeared as well." My father had guessed the key weakness of the phenomena: these creations from the ether require active thought to perpetuate themselves. Once the thought ended, so did the creation. I was hoping that death wasn't absolutely necessary to accomplish the desired goal.

I reasoned that a heavily drugged state would also effectively end any conscious thought as well. And therefore end this rampaging horror.

I administered a large, but harmless, dose of phenobarbital to Steven, who was only half awake.

"Daddy, sing me the song again."

I began in a low voice, like praying, and Stevie joined in immediately as he always did every night.

"Hello, friendly Spaceman Mister

Come down and join your spacey brother and sister!"

Immediately, Steven was unconscious.

But something was wrong. I could still hear the night terror writhing its way towards us, pulling forward with hideous spasms. I could feel its dark presence just outside the door. I failed! Maybe I misunderstood the warning. Was it only a meaningless dream? I wiped the sweat from my forehead and felt a fever chill shake my body.

Then I realized that it was feeding off my thoughts as well. Yes, that had to be the answer. It was using my mind to continue itself!

I sensed its dark hideous mass waiting outside, probing the door's surface. Quickly, I injected the phenobarbital into my own veins.

At that moment, the door of my office slowly swung open. I remember seeing, or rather sensing, an ultimate blackness, like charred flesh peeling off muscles and bones. I gave a soul-wrenching scream and welcomed the loving void.

As I write this, the dawn is smothered by storm clouds. Steven is resting in my arms. I'm afraid to look beyond my office door. Maybe it was all a horrible nightmare. Maybe Silas will come back to the house and wonder why we've locked all the doors.

Or maybe not.

Maybe my greatest fear has come to pass, and I am afflicted with the same crippling dementia that cursed my father.

Maybe I have barely survived a monster born from my son's night terrors, a monster waiting to be reborn.

Either way, I am damned.

I know that whatever I see in the morning's darkness, we will be leaving Crandall Lake as soon as Stevie awakens.

I know this experience has marked me forever. I suspect that this terror crawled to life from my own mind and not Stevie's. Like my father, I fear I have found my own Mr. Darkly, and it will follow me beyond Hollis House until the end of my days.

Published July 11, 2015 on Fanfiction.net

* * *

From the archives of Myth-America.com (posted April 14, 2015)

The Girl Who Fell to Earth

By Kevin Starkly

Meteor Girl had a major breakthrough last night in our experiments with lucid dreaming. She imagined that she was back in school. But it was one of those crazy-quilt environments that everyone experiences in their dreams—here are the desks you scribbled on in first grade, but the hallways have the lockers you remember from high school. Anyway, she was told she had to report to the principal's office with her best friend, Susan. Then she hears the music, softly at first as though it's drifting down the hallway from someone's radio, reminding her of her dream state.

So she remembers the mantra we've worked out, the saying that I've coached her to use every single day since we've been investigating the mystery of her alien abduction.

"If this isn't nice, I must be dreaming."

And in a flash, she recognizes the reality of the dream, as she's dreaming!

She tells me she was soaking in every detail of the moment. She looked at the blackboards, the institutional slate grey color of the walls, even noted the greenish terrazzo flooring. Here's the thing, though: As she's walking down the hallway with Susan, she remembers that Susan died in a fiery car crash on the LI Expressway back in college.

Finally, she looked at Susan and asked,

"You're dead, aren't you?"

I wish I was walking next to her to catch this double take! Susan first shoots back a real quizzical look, but then she starts to smile with this wide grin, as though she has finally gotten the punch line of some inside joke.

The next thing she knows, she's back in bed, and I can barely keep her from bouncing around as she's yelling, "It worked! It worked!"

We had some success earlier with using music as a triggering mechanism to signal REM sleep and clue the sleeper into the fact that they're dreaming. I have to tell you that when I first began my probing into the world of alien abductions, I never imagined that it would lead me into the Elysian fields of lucid dream research. I've told you the details of her case before (you can check the details here). I'm sticking with our agreement to keep her totally anonymous. No names, no revealing details about how we met. You probably wouldn't look twice at her if you passed her on the L train. Just another Neo-Goth chick who's probably meeting up with friends at the Korean horror film festival at BAM. But you would never guess that she was snatched out of her bed one night last February and came face to face with an alien creature.

She claims she felt a tingling sensation throughout her entire body, and in that same moment she realized to her horror that she couldn't move a muscle. While she was still trying to make sense of her paralysis, she swore she could feel herself lifting off from her cozy bed and levitating towards the ceiling. Then *through* the ceiling, and then…

She doesn't remember much after that. Maybe she simply doesn't want to remember. She told me she sensed a shadowy presence, a short creature with a large head. She vaguely recalls hearing it speak to her, but the words came right into her brain.

I think we've made significant breakthroughs in our research. She's open to exploring other theories beyond the clichéd alien abduction scenarios of every single sci-fi potboiler since 1956. We've adopted John Keel's cautionary motto: "Belief is the enemy." Always question your own paradigms before you find yourself enslaved by them. Maybe what we're really exploring is an invasion of dreamtime.

Listen, if you're some higher race of alien intelligence looking for a quick and easy way to communicate with the primitives here on Earth, what would you do? Maybe you sneak in through the back door of dreamtime and start manipulating our shared consensus of reality one beautiful dreamer at a time? Impossible? Ladies and gentlemen, I believe it's not only possible, but it has been going on for decades. And the only way we may be able to understand the entire phenomena is if we confront them head on through lucid dreaming.

Before she came to me, Meteor Girl came up with her own solution to the problem. Before she went to sleep each night, she would faithfully handcuff herself to the bedpost. She sleeps in a big brass bed, damn heavy too. She often told me she felt light as a feather before she drifted off to sleep, almost weightless, as though a stray breeze would send her helplessly drifting into the sky. The handcuffs kept her anchored. They were a crude but effective insurance that she would never be taken away against her will. Not ever again.

Last night she put on Mendelssohn—from the oratorio *St. Paul*—to help her get back to sleep. Every so often she'll ask me to stay the night. You know, just watch over her, make sure nothing happens. Not many people would trust me like that. In fact, most would tell her to run in the opposite direction.

How lovely are the messengers

That preach us the gospel of peace!

Maybe the soaring music caused my flight of fancy, but I was reminded about that famous meteorite fragment preserved in a cathedral in Ensisheim, France. The object crashed to Earth in 1492 while Columbus sailed the ocean blue. Of course, the good townspeople of Ensisheim had no idea what had boldly disrupted their daily routine. Nobody knew about meteorites in 1492. The heavens were perfect, completely unchanging. Many thought the thing was some rare gift from heaven. So the people of Ensisheim hung the meteorite in chains because (and this is the part I love) they were afraid it would escape back into the sky. So that's my Meteor Girl. She's a woman who's so afraid of flying into space that she's tethered herself to her own bed. Damn, but don't we just find security in the strangest acts?

Posted by strangekevin

From Kevin Starkly's Twitter feed:

@MythAmerican

You start messing with precious preconceptions, you're going to wind up with a bad case of cognitive dissonance—and upending reality on its sorry ass! #alternate reality

From Craigslist.org

Lost daughter (Jersey City)

Reply to: xxxxxxx@craigslist.org

Date: July 1, 2015, 11:27AM EDT

Holly Evers left our house on the evening of June 10 in a stretch Hummer packed with her friends heading to her Senior Prom. That was the last time we saw her.

Her friends tell us that after the Prom they all drove to the Pine Barrens to a spot just past Harrisville Pond on the Old North Main Street. Somehow, she disappeared from the rest of the group and nobody could find her. We searched all night long and into the next day but there was no sign of our little baby. The police say they're doing all they can to find her but I don't believe them. I can't say I blame them too much. After all, there are so many, many missing people nowadays.

Holly is only 18 years old. She stands about 5'1 and has long, straight black hair. She thinks she looks like Beyonce, but she always looked like my sister Kay. She was last seen wearing a lime green cocktail dress with matching high heels, pearl necklace, and an adorable little beaded handbag that belonged to her grandmother.

Please if you have any idea where she is please tell her to call her Mommy. Tell her that her Mommy is worried sick over her and misses her very much and just wants to know that her lovely daughter is safe and healthy. Please tell her to call right away. God bless you.

- it's NOT ok to contact this poster with services or other commercial interests.

PostingID: 555849724

From After the Quake Twitter feed:

@Afterthequake

>**One night I dreamed I was abducted by an Evil Alien.**

>**Now I'm not so sure it was only a dream.**

From Angel McQueen's personal email

July 12

Hi Doc,

Hope you're getting a good night's sleep. Lol!

So I can't believe that Tony remembered me. When he called and heard my voice, I swear he said, "Wait a minute. Are you Angela…Angel McQueen from the Prep?" Damn! I said something witty and sophisticated like, "So who do you think I was, Sherlock?" But what I really, really wanted to say was "It's good to finally stop hiding."

He has this deep reassuring voice. It was good to hear his voice again.

Omg! I am so getting off the track here. I want to write you about what I told Tony about the clues in Kevin's story. You know, that "Night Terror" Lovecraftian homage that mysteriously was posted to Fanfiction.net with all those odd changes? So I told Tony that the really strange thing was that I'm probably the only person who would have noticed those changes. It was as if Kevin (I guess it has to be Kevin) was writing directly to me. He wanted to send a message to me.

Yeah, I know I promised Kevin that I would never reveal my identity to anyone, but here's the thing…I figure it's no biggie now. I mean there are like what…five other babes online claiming to be THE Meteor Girl? This was forced on me against my will and I swore up and down that I would never let it define me. Well it's too late to stop it messing with my head because that was job one. So I've decided to follow your advice and claim rightful ownership of the experience. You were like so right about how it was never all of me, or even the best part of me, but to keep denying it ever happened is just too schitzo. So yeah, I'm Meteor Girl. And yeah, I've got no problem with that! Besides most of my Bff figured it all out months ago.

Ha! Tony couldn't believe I was Meteor Girl. In fact, Tony said "We we're taking bets that Kevin just made up the whole story." I assured him that the story was all too true, and that I was real flesh and blood. I hesitate on the line and Tony goes all Lord Byron on me and his voice gets real serious and he says, "I think we should meet right now and talk about those clues."

Did I mention that his voice is really deep?

I keep telling myself that I'm all nervous because maybe this will help bring Kevin back. Maybe this is an important piece of evidence that will help Tony and Rich and Johnny. But I think I'm also a little nervous (excited?) to finally see an old friend I haven't seen in years. I'm thinking of the first time I met Tony in Mr. Judge's World Literature class and Tony is reading this drunken character from Chekhov's Cherry Orchard...Wait, maybe it was The Seagull? Anyway, I'm absolutely mesmerized because he's got this character nailed completely. What's the name of that guy? Omg! I haven't thought about that in what, ten years?

* * *

From an advertisement in *WIRED* Magazine

DISCOVER YOUR INNER WORLDS: UNLOCK THE POWER

OF LUCID DREAMING

Do you ever know when you are dreaming?

If so, you know that lucid dreams are filled with fantastic freedom, joy, and wonder.

Have you ever directed your dreams?

If so, you've tasted the awesome healing power and potential of lucid dreaming.

If you have not unlocked the power of your own dreams, we will show you how at

The Dreamtime Research Institute.

We are dedicated to helping people develop lucid dreaming ability. Our training program employs the latest cutting-edge technology developed and perfected over the last ten years by leading sleep researcher Dr. Jeanette Stryker.

Our classes employ the Dreamscape Induction Engine (DIE). It combines the most effective lucid dream induction methods with our proven state-of-the-art digital technology in a compact, easy-to-use, and affordable device suitable for any sleep environment. The combined LED light display and audio headphones will guarantee success in alerting you to wake up in your dreams. The DIE will even improve your dream recall.

Dr. Stryker explains that great thinkers throughout history have harnessed the power of their dreams:

- The chemist Friedrich Kekule discovered the structure of benzene while dreaming.

- Elias Howe designed the sewing needle after awakening from a vivid nightmare.

- After a fever dream in the jungles of Malaysia, Alfred Russel Wallace uncovered the secrets of natural selection.

- Electrical genius Nikola Tesla drew the intricate workings of the AC motor after seeing it in a vivid waking dream.

- Samuel Coleridge composed his great epic poem "Kubla Khan" while in a dream state.

- What will YOU do when you unlock the power of YOUR DREAMS?

- Will you dream yourself into good health? Dream a great invention into reality? Create the epic adventure of a lifetime?

The Dreamtime Research Institute will show you how!

Online classes are available now for **ONLY $24.95 a month**. For a limited time try our introductory class and receive your **first month FREE!**

Sign up for six months and receive a **FREE** autographed copy of the best-selling *The Key to Lucid Dreaming* by Dr. Jeanette Stryker.

Log on today to dreamtimenow.com

* * *

From the Myth-America.com archives (posted January 12, 2015)

My ETH Rant: Part 2

By Kevin Starkly

As I've mentioned before, I fully believe that what is commonly referred to as the Extraterrestrial Hypothesis (ETH) has done more damage to the study of the UFO phenomena than all the crackpot conspiracy theorists and fucking Adamski-style Space Brother contactees put together. I'm talking about the hard-core nuts and bolts saucer freaks who swear that all those unidentified aerial phenomena (UAP) are nothing less than real alien craft rocketing through outer space. Of course, once you start arguing about flight paths from Alpha Centauri and faster-than-light warp drives, you've left all the serious scientists at the front door. They can't ignore all the logistical and logical obstacles that crop up when you start arguing about alien visitors buzzing the Earth.

And the ETH plays right into the skeptical hands of every UFO debunker from Phil Klass to Carl Sagan to Neil Tyson: Why haven't we seen these craft through our telescopes? How can they travel through space in direct violation of all the known laws of physics? Why are they more interested in contacting housewives and farmers than scientists and government authorities? And this is always the big one: Why the hell would any advanced interstellar civilization bother to visit our half-assed planet anyway?

The skeptics say that since UFOs don't act as we imagine real extraterrestrials would act, then therefore, UFOs can't possibly be real.

Now don't misunderstand me. I continue to believe that UAPs or UFOs or whatever you call them are very real. I just don't happen to believe that they are alien space shuttles.

I mean creatures and strange beings have been flying through our skies since the beginning of recorded history. Ufologist Jacques Vallee quotes Plutarch on the matter of these sky ships from Magonia:

"The famous Cabalist Zedechais,…bethought himself to advise the Sylphs to show themselves in the Air to everybody: They did so sumptuously. These beings were seen in the Air in human form, sometimes in battle array marching in good order, halting under arms, or encamped beneath magnificent tents. Sometimes on wonderfully constructed aerial ships, whose flying squadrons roved at the will of the Zephyrs."

Unless you believe that medieval faeries and sylphs were flying around in spaceships, I think we must seriously reconsider the nature of these unidentified craft in the skies. Why do these creatures need any craft to travel at all? Beats the hell out of me. But the evidence for it is everywhere, from cabalist writings to the flying *vimana* in the *Mahabharata* to the legends of the Iroquois. Maybe they have limitations on how far they can travel in this sphere. Maybe it's more akin to recreation and less like a morning commute. Or maybe it's not traveling as we understand it at all, but something completely unfathomable and alien. All I know is that trying to explain alien modes of transportation to an Earth scientist is like explaining the difference between jet propulsion and bicycling to a baboon.

I think Vallee made the point best in one of his later books. He compared our present efforts studying the UFO phenomena to a scientist setting out to study film projection technology by sitting in a darkened theater watching movies on the big screen. After decades of study we are all still seduced by the play of shadow and light and we are no closer to locating the damn projection booth, let alone figuring out how they get those pretty pictures on the screen.

Posted by strangekevin

From the Dream Journal of Anthony Fermi

July 12, 2015

Last night I dreamed again about that frightening incident that happened when I was ten years old. I was back in my old bedroom on the second floor of my parents' home in Corona, Queens. I was just getting over a bad cold, or maybe it was the flu. My grandma was caring for me while my parents were working. This involved large amounts of Vicks VapoRub applied to my chest and constantly refilling the humidifier next to my bed.

I was trying to go to sleep or maybe I had awakened suddenly from a nightmare. I can't remember which it was now. I only remember wanting to run from my darkened room into the safety of my parents' bed next door, but I was frozen in place. The more panicked I became, the more I was unable to move a muscle. I couldn't even scream out in terror. Then I noticed that I couldn't hear the humming of the humidifier by my bedside. In fact, I couldn't hear anything at all—no passing cars in the street, no television from the living room downstairs, nothing. All of my familiar comforting sounds disappeared. Even the smell of the mentholated rub was gone from my nose. I realized that whatever had paralyzed me was now stealing away all of my senses. As a child I always felt vulnerable, but now I was truly trapped.

During this entire time, which was probably no more than ten seconds, although it seemed an eternity, I was looking at my bedroom door which was always opened a crack to allow some of the reassuring hallway light to filter into my room. I noticed now that someone or something was blocking the light from the hallway. I couldn't make out the figure very clearly because now my sight was disappearing as well. The fear of my fading vision was eclipsed only by the horror of the creature I saw at my bedroom door. As the room grew darker, I saw the shadowy figure turn towards me. The head seemed all wrong, as though it was way out of proportion to the rest of its body. The last thing I saw before the darkness overcame me were two glowing red eyes staring straight at me.

God, I haven't had that dream in years.

From Kevin Starkly's Twitter feed

@MythAmerican

I love studying alien encounters because at least with abduct-ees we have a real interaction with the mystery of the phenomena. #alien abductions

From Snopes.com

Was This Death of an "Occult Book Collector" Really Evidence of a Serial Killer of Paranormal Collectors?

Claim: The apparent suicide of a self-styled expert in occult literature in Hobart, NY was really the latest victim of a serial killer (or killers) targeting collectors of paranormal paraphernalia across the country. The FBI is deliberately covering up these incidents.

Rating: Mostly False

As reported in the June 15 edition of the Oneonta Daily Star, Henrietta "Etta" Swallow, 48, was found dead from an apparent heroin overdose in her home outside Hobart, New York. And that would have been the end of this tragic and all-too-common story, except for the fact that Swallow had made a name for herself as a frequent expert guest on "Coast to Coast AM" and other paranormal-themed radio programs and podcasts propounding her theories on mystical forces and powerful cults secretly existing among us. Also, there were some unusual circumstances surrounding her death that appealed to those enamored of conspiracy theories. Almost immediately, warnings circulated by email and on numerous websites that Etta Swallow "knew too much" and "had to be silenced" by a mysterious murderer who has supposedly already killed and robbed dozens of other paranormal collectors over the last several years. As always, we caution readers to be wary of some form of crime that is claimed to be a widespread phenomenon but actually has taken place only in a few unrelated, isolated incidents. While there are several unsolved homicides over the years that roughly correspond to this vague description, there is no evidence that any of them are connected or even share the same modus operandi whether by stabbing, hanging, blunt force trauma, decapitation, mutilation, or poisoning. In fact, according to police records, the only common denominator was that all these victims were eccentric characters who lived in high crime areas. As for Swallow's death, police found no evidence of foul play, just another one of the 50,000 opioid overdoses every year in the U.S. Some valuable tomes were allegedly stolen, including a rare "rock book" by Richard S. Shaver that Swallow mentioned in several interviews, although there is no evidence that she ever possessed it. Swallow also intentionally blinded herself before her overdose. Although rare, self-enucleation or mutilation of the eye, is not unknown. Police have not determined the implement used by Swallow to remove her eyes, but they believe the blinding was self-inflicted.

* * *

From Angel McQueen's personal email

July 13

Hi Doc,

Good News! Tony gets mucho bonus points for not asking about my alien abduction within the first five minutes of our conversation. Meteor Girl is like this private persona I shared only with Kevin and you and to tell you the truth, I still feel sketchy talking about it with anyone else. That's why I still don't mention any of that alien abduction stuff on my blog. Meteor Girl gets enough unwanted attention in some of the real unsavory corners of the blogosphere. Like I'm doing cartwheels if I clock 100 page views on my latest post, while one of those other babes calling herself Meteor Girl (some bitch pretending to be a "performance artist") is getting couple thousand per posting. She even paid one of those Gowanus comic artist dudes to draw a logo. It's a caricature of her (pretty accurate I'm guessing) and she's straddling a raunchy phallic-shaped meteor through space like a bucking bronco wearing nothing much except a pair of cowboy boots.

More good news! Tony looks taller and hunkier than I remember him from the Prep. I'm glad I went with the Goth Lolita look instead of the black jeans and Hellboy t-shirt. So I'm wearing this little black leather skirt and fishnets combo and I'm bending over fetching some of Kevin's papers and I swear Tony is checking out my ass! Don't get me wrong. I'm not going anywhere with this like it's anything real. I mean Tony's a good guy and everything but he's not the type to inspire passion, or drama, or anger and tears. You know, all the usual stuff that signals true love, right? I'm just messing with Tony's head just like in high school. Except I'm not the same geek gal pal playing Velma with the rest of the Scooby gang.

From Myth-America.com

July 14, 2015

The "Geek Freaks Across America" Road Trip Continues!

By Richard Harrigan

Our original quartet may have diminished to a dynamic duo—Fermi is staying put in NYC and Starkly is still lost in the ether—but we are valiantly motoring on with our original mission. And please note that this is not some misguided notion that "Kevin would want it this way." I happen to believe that Starkly may be carrying on this road trip solo and in secret for reasons known only to himself. Walters, being possessed of enormous paranoia, is of the opinion that Starkly is in danger from the "Collector Killer" allegedly stalking the land.

So, I believe that we may find ourselves intersecting paths with him deep in the heart of West Virginia. I claim no precognitive abilities (indeed I would argue that no such abilities exist at all), but in consulting with Walters I think we've hit on an advantageous course of action. My sleuthing here extends no further than reviewing some recent postings on this blog and uncovering a number of mentions of the Mothman incident in Point Pleasant. This certainly would be an appropriately supernatural follow-up to our hunt for the Jersey Devil. So without further ado we are heading to the heartland of the Mountain State riding something called a Prius Hybrid—which Walters assures me gets excellent mileage—where we may find some much-needed answers.

– posted by drrich

Post Comments

Firefly writes:

Kevin also recently mentioned the Flatwoods Monster case, so please keep that in mind as a possibility as well. Good hunting!

Cicero writes:

I suggest a detour to the famous Mystery Hill here in North Salem, NH. Always some strange rituals taking place around here especially by the Sacrificial Table.

Polly writes:

I think you all should be ashamed of yourselves for abandoning the search for your friend so quickly. I say you stay in Jersey and scour every inch of the Pine Barrens until you find Kevin.

Rich Harrigan writes:

Police are handling things Polly, and may in fact, find Starkly before we do. But I believe he is not "missing" but hiding. God only knows why.

Jerseyjim writes:

If it's bizarre creatures you're after I say go to Little Miami River in Loveland, Ohio to track down those scary half man/half frog creatures that were sighted there years ago. Maybe they've spawned some tadpole babies by now.

Tony Fermia writes:

Change of plan, dudes! I think Angela and I have figured out the clues in that Night Terror story. I think somebody—maybe Kevin—wants us to meet somebody special. Give me a call.

Email from Anthony Fermia to John Walters

July 14, 2015

Hey Johnny:

Here are the details: Angela noticed immediately that the lullaby sung by the father in "Night Terror" (the lullaby by the way was not mentioned anywhere in the original story) is from a real song with special significance to only three people in the world! "Calling Occupants of Interplanetary Craft"—aside from being an obscure song originally recorded in 1976 by the band Klaatu—is also the triggering song Kevin used on Angela to aid in her lucid dreaming experiments. When I researched the song, I knew instantly why Kevin would be attracted to it. It was the "official" song for World Contact Day—a wild scheme hatched back in 1953 trying to tele-pathically summon extraterrestrials to Earth—so it resonated perfectly with Kevin's favorite notion of "interacting with the mystery of the phe-nomena." Anyway, Angel assures me that nobody else knew they were using that song…except for one other person. Kevin shared the details of his dreamtime experiments with Dr. Jeanette Stryker—she's some kind of nationally-recognized expert in lucid dreaming. He consulted with her before on his alien abduction theories and then again with Angela. I didn't know what to make of all this, so I contacted Dr. Stryker at her Dreamtime Research Institute. I've forwarded her reply:

>> How extraordinary! And how very clever of you to make the connection to me in regard to this night terror tale. I'm quite sure I wouldn't know what to make of it if I happened upon that tale on fanfiction.net.

First, I was going to write to tell you that I had not heard any-thing from Kevin since his unfortunate disappearance. I lis-tened to that podcast with utter disbelief and horror, as had a number of other people I'm sure. Perhaps Kevin intended that we should get together and compare notes so to speak. I'm giving a talk at the upcoming Starship Invasions Convention next week outside Adams County, Ohio. Perhaps we can get together there. Anyway, I'm sure we can get this sorted. I know Kevin was paranoid about a number of subjects, but particularly about anyone stealing some evidence he uncovered concerning the Aurora Texas spaceship crash. But then I'm sure you already know all about that!

Original World Contact Day Message from the International Flying Saucer Bureau (IFSB)

March 15, 1953 (Selected excerpts)

We of IFSB…would like you to make an appearance here on EARTH.

We will do all in our power to promote mutual understanding between your people and the people of EARTH. Please…help us in our EARTHLY problems.

Be responsible for creating a miracle here on our planet to wake up the ignorant ones to reality.

Let us hear from you.

* * *

Handwritten note on top of page: *First mention of "Aurora artifact"*

From Myth-America.com podcast transcript May 5, 2015

Kevin: We're back again with Part Two of our
         ongoing discussion on the history of UFO
         investigations. And back with me for
         another round of intellectual abuse is my
         old friend Richard Harrigan. We're record-
         ing secretly from the second floor of the
         Old Town Bar and outside New Yorkers are
         celebrating our favorite holiday, Cinco de
         Mayo. Now back to discussing flying saucers
         and aliens that go bump in the night…and I
         believe this round is on me?

Rich: When have I ever challenged your beliefs?
         Pay on Macduff!

Kevin: Here let me help you conserve that big
         fat teacher's salary of yours. Hello?
         Sally, we'll have two more Sam Adams here.
         Thanks, doll. Now where were we?

Rich: You were sitting there, and I was sit-
         ting here. Oh, and you were making an ass
         of yourself.

Kevin: I object to that characterization. I don't
         deny it, but I certainly object to it.

Rich: I was demanding some physical evidence to support your indefensible proposition that flying saucers are worthy of continued scientific research. I mean, certainly a supposed investigation that has been going on for what? 70 years? Certainly by this time, you would have something to show for all your troubles.

Kevin: And I'm saying that there's significant progress made just over the last twenty years. Just look at the research done by John Mack at Harvard into the alien abduction phenomena.

Rich: Excuse me, but I believe I specified physical evidence. I was not talking about the deluded babbling of some unfortunate hypnotized mental patient. And by that, of course, I'm referring to the late disgraced Dr. Mack himself.

Kevin: Oh, that reminds me of my new drinking game. I take a drink every time you make an ad hominem attack on someone. At this rate I'll be under the table in fifteen minutes. Cheers!

Rich: Listen, if I can't bitch about other academics, especially dead ones, there's no point in being an academic.

Kevin: Really, Mr. Physics, you should be the last person demanding physical evidence for anything. When was the last time an astrophysicist produced physical evidence for dark matter? In fact, when was the last time anyone even agreed on a definition for it?

Rich: Now wait a minute, that's a legitimate branch…

Kevin: And for that matter, where's all that physical evidence produced in support of string theory? Hell, where are the testable hypotheses?

Rich: That's unfair. You know full well that scientists in good faith are still debating this issue. In fact, I personally believe that string theory is as bogus and full of holes as the cheesecloth "ectoplasm" that Madame Blavatsky would pull out of her bloomers during her infamous séances.

Kevin: As much as I would love to dwell on that disturbing image, please allow me to make my point. All I'm saying is that if this was a court of law, UFOs, or Unidentified Aerial Phenomenon as I prefer to call it, would have won their case years ago. You don't need physical evidence, you just need a preponderance of facts, including eyewitness accounts, that prove your case…

Rich: Don't think I haven't noticed how you've just wormed your way out of a scientific discussion to a legal debate since neither one of us is trained as a lawyer. Every single investigative body that has looked at the eyewitness testimony has concluded that practically all UFO cases, let's say 98 percent of them, are simply misidentifications of natural phenomena. And this finding goes back to the Condon Report.

Kevin: Oh my God, I can't believe you have the audacity to mention the Condon Report. Are you getting back at me for bringing up John Mack?

Rich: You can shoot the messenger all you want, but the bad news isn't going away. And the simple fact is that once these flying saucer cases are thoroughly investigated by non-charlatans they are practically all handily identified as lenticular clouds, meteors, mirages, or even Russian satellites burning up in the atmosphere. And the other two percent of unknown cases may never be satisfactorily explained simply because we don't have enough information.

Kevin: Oh please, Richie, that is a bullshit argument and you know it. Every debunker starting with Phil Klass has tried to fool the uninformed into thinking that with just a little more research all those flickering lights in the sky could be identified as Venus or Mars or possibly swamp gas. So there's really nothing significant to worry your pretty little head over so just move along, nothing to see here.

Rich: I've got three words for you: Ockham's Razor, fool. Look for…

Kevin: What the debunkers conveniently forget to mention is that some of those pesky "unknown" cases are actually the strongest, most compelling UFO sightings on record. These are the cases that have stood the test of time not because they're vague lights in the sky, but because they are startlingly clear, shockingly clear reports of alien occupants.

Rich: You're not going to mention…

Kevin: Richie, please shut up and let me make my
point. Let's talk about the famous Socorro
case from 1964. Police Officer Lonnie
Zamora is on patrol outside Socorro, New
Mexico…it's about dusk…when he comes
across something that he has never seen
before in his entire life. There is a
metallic egg-shaped craft resting on four
legs by the side of the road. He clearly
sees two small figures moving around outside this bizarre structure. They're
dressed in white. Clearly humanoid but
quite strange. The figures quickly retreat
into the craft and with a flash of light
and a loud roar the thing rockets up into
the sky (makes a rocket launching sound)…
and then disappears within seconds. But
here's the amazing part: when Zamora
calls in his report and his fellow offi-
cers respond, they find four indentations
in the ground corresponding to the landing
legs and scorched brush in the middle of
it all. Ladies and gentlemen, to this day,
nobody has come up with any explanation
for the sighting except for the frighteningly obvious…something or someone that
doesn't belong on this planet paid a visit
to New Mexico on April 24, 1964.

Rich: That's a lovely fairy tale Starkly, but what justification do you have for invoking ETs when a simpler explanation—that it was a hoax concocted by Officer Zamora to boost tourism in the town—covers the known facts?

Kevin: Woo-hoo! Another ad hominem attack. Keep up the baseless accusations and you'll be paying for the next round in record time. Actually, that reminds me—Hello, Sally—Sally, could you bring me a shot of Glenmorangie with a little water on the side. Thanks doll!

Rich: And I'll have another Sam Adams please.

Kevin: And here's another old sighting that is still unidentified. Remember the Father Gill case in New Guinea? Several eyewitnesses, including the good Father himself, saw an orange, saucer-shaped craft hovering close to the town of Boianai on the night of June 26, 1959. The sighting lasts what…two, three hours? They get a good clear look at this thing for a long while. And here's the clincher—they all report seeing four humanoid occupants standing on the top deck of the saucer. The townspeople start waving to them, because, you know, they're friendly people who don't know that they're supposed to be scared shitless. And the occupants start waving back! It's the first documented case of human/alien contact and it goes back over 50 years ago.

Rich: And in two hours nobody locates a camera to take one picture? Even leaving aside a deliberate hoax…

Kevin: Can't you just admit…

Rich: Look, I hate to belabor the obvious, but we're still talking about a lack of any physical evidence. And I know my harping on this peeves you tremendously because it forces you to acknowledge the lack of unambiguous evidence ufology has collected over the last 70 years.

Kevin: Alright, you want physical traces, you say
you want in-controversial...I mean...incon-
trovertible...evidence of UFOs? Then just
take a shovel and start digging up that
alien pilot that's buried in a cemetery
in Aurora, Texas. It's been laying underground for over a century.

Rich: You can't be serious about bringing up
that old chestnut Starkly. It was dismissed almost immediately after the story
was resurrected back in the 1970s. And
certainly nobody believed it for a minute
back in 1897.

Kevin: As usual, Mr. Skeptical Inquirer, I beg to
differ with you. The town of Aurora today
is about evenly divided on the matter.
Half of them pooh-pooh the whole thing
as a local reporter's joke, and the rest
believe that something alien crashed into
Judge Proctor's windmill that April morning, destroying the craft and killing the
only occupant on board. Many believe the
truth is out there buried in an unmarked
grave in the Aurora Cemetery.

Rich: This is all urban folklore. Now perhaps you can make a good case that this phenomenon should be studied by sociologists or psychiatrists as a modern mental aberration, but I still see no reason why serious scientists, like physicists, chemists, or even biologists, should waste their time and their reputations by investigating this crap.

Kevin: What would you say if I told you that I have some evidence…precarious…no, I mean precious…evidence in my possession that proves that something crashed in Aurora, Texas over a hundred years ago?

Rich: First, I would say that you've definitely had too much to drink. Are you serious?

Kevin: And this something was not of this world, and not a hoax. Would that just blow apart your orderly little mind?

Rich: You've never mentioned anything about this before.

Kevin: This is exactly why…You want to know why nobody trusts scientists any more Richie?

Rich: Not particularly, but I have a feeling you'll tell me anyway.

Kevin: People don't trust scientists not because
of their monumental arrogance, not because
of their annoying habit of telling us all
what to eat, what to drink, how to live,
how to raise our kids, based only on the
slimmest amounts of evidence. No, people
don't trust scientists because they have
succeeded in sucking dry all the mystery
from life. They have drained all the awe
and wonder from the world and replaced it
with what? What? Mathematical formulas
and evolutionary theories used to explain
everything from free will to human emotion? Scientists are the killjoys at the
party, and everyone is anxious to show
them to the door.

Rich: I've told you this before Starkly, science is not a popularity contest. Our job
is to present our evidence to the people,
regardless of the outcome.

Kevin: Well, I've probably said too much already.
I'll get back to this later, but now is
not the time. In fact, I think we've quite
worn out our welcome here at the Old Town
Bar. You can subscribe to our series of
podcasts or just check back at Myth-
America.com for the next one. So ladies
and gentlemen, have a happy Cinco de Mayo,
and remember to watch the skies.

* * *

From Kevin Starkly's Twitter feed

@MythAmerican

Maybe what happened at Aurora is like a badly-kept family secret: the evidence is gathering dust in attics—or it's buried in the ground. #auroracrash

From WNYC Morning Brief

May 1, 2015

Shaken, Rattled and Rolled: A 5.8 magnitude earthquake—one of the largest ever recorded in New York State—seriously shook up a number of jaded New Yorkers last night. The quake was centered in the southwestern part of the state near the town of Lily Dale, but the shaking and aftershocks cracked walls, tumbled construction scaffolding, and jangled nerves from the Bronx to the Rockaways.

Emergency Overload: Police reported record-breaking number of 911 calls last night involving property damage, strange lights in the sky, rumbling and moaning sounds from underground and missing pets. Thankfully, no deaths or injuries reported.

A River Runs Through It: Morning commuters dealing with suspensions of the 7 and F service—the MTA is checking for possible earthquake damage to the elevated platforms—can take a break and enjoy the most unusual, and pastoral, aftereffect of last night's quake: the sudden appearance of a small lake in the southwest corner of Washington Square Park. Experts speculate that the quake unleashed the full strength of the forgotten Minetta Brook, covered over since the 19th century, causing it to bubble up to the surface. City officials caution against skinny-dipping in the seemingly clear waters until environmental regulators give the green light, notwithstanding the inevitable killjoys reporting "strange creatures" swimming in the new lake.

From the archives of Myth-America.com (posted June 15)

All Shook Up

By Kevin Starkly

All hell really did break loose after the quake, didn't it?

I mean, maybe everyone wasn't talking about how the world had changed that night, but MY world certainly changed, and let's face it, that's the only thing that matters.

I remember waking up just before dawn yelling at my parents to stop that damn monster truck rally shaking things up on our brownstone roof. But the shaking didn't stop. It seemed like forever, but only two minutes passed. And it wasn't just our house, but all New York was rumbling out of its sleep.

Just when you thought it was over, that's when the cacophony started. Like some penny-ante Philip Glass score for the apocalypse, it started with car alarms honking up and down the block, followed closely by screams and house alarms blaring one after another. And like a subtle chorus, you could hear church bells ringing in the distance throughout the entire borough of churches.

From that moment, nothing in our lives were certain again, if they were ever certain to begin with. The trains we took to work every day were now potentially unstable. The stores we shopped in were condemned. Our secure little world could collapse around our ears at any minute.

And then people started hearing whispers from the cracks in the basement walls. Ancient graves opened up. They reported great lights in the night sky and floating orbs close to the ground. Something shook loose during that unexplained, unnatural earthquake—and it turned out it was our tenuous hold on reality. Things that should have stayed in the shadows were set free. Of course the skeptics—God bless 'em—came prepared with armloads of explanations about methane-induced hallucinations and piezoelectric effects from fault lines and other paltry offerings. But who are people going to believe: a scientist with his head up his ass or their friendly neighborhood paranormal investigator? Yes, ladies and gentlemen, I had stepped in shit and was enjoying every minute of it! I was a little porker wallowing in more ghost sightings and cryptic creatures than I could shake a stick at. Me and my blog were bona fide sensations, covering haunted houses in Gravesend, alien abductions in Fresh Meadows, and even a plesiosaurus sighting in Minetta Lake. Within a short time, Myth-America. com was bookmarked by every weirdo in the five boroughs.

What caused the quake? We'll probably never know, but I've heard every conspiracy theory possible, from the Coast Guard testing Tesla vibration rays to Deros warring under the Adirondacks to ancient curses coming to pass. But I say anything that makes people doubt their comfortable notions of how the world works is great for business!

Posted by strangekevin

* * *

From Newsday, May 2, 2015

Quake Halts Excavation Work On Tesla Museum

Construction on the much-delayed Tesla Museum and Science Center at Wardenclyffe located in Shoreham hit another major setback yesterday as work was halted after the discovery of a deep well that was supposedly backfilled nearly a century ago. Yesterday's earthquake shook loose ground around newly installed foundation supports revealing the 12-foot-square vault which some estimate to be 120 feet deep.

According to sources connected to the Friends of Science East, the local nonprofit overseeing construction of the museum, the well is a remnant of Nikola Tesla's original Wardenclyffe laboratory which he shuttered back in 1911 after his ambitious project to wirelessly transmit electrical power around the world went bankrupt. Most of the original laboratory, save for the main brick building designed by architect Stanford White, was demolished and salvaged in 1917.

"The vault probably housed the network of iron pipes that connected Tesla's oscillator and transmission tower with the Earth," said Michael Savino, spokesperson for the Friends of Science East. The only other remnants of the 187-foot-high transmission tower topped by a 68-foot-diameter copper-clad dome are the eight concrete foundations of the original tower still clearly visible about 60 feet to the right of the White building.

The Tesla Museum and Science Center, first proposed in 1996, will be a memorial to the inventions and accomplishments of Nikola Tesla, the flamboyant Serbian inventor considered one of the great scientific pioneers of the 20th Century. Tesla is credited with creating alternating current, providing electricity for the 1893 World's Fair in Chicago, and developing the original patents that made the invention of radio possible. Tesla is said to have never recovered his reputation or popular support after the failure of his Wardenclyffe transmitter. Experts believe his notions of a world system of intelligence transmission, self-directed robots or "tele-automats," and particle ray beams were decades ahead of their time. Tesla died penniless in 1943 at the age of 86.

The museum will contain artifacts, documents and photographs collected for the Tesla Remembrance Project and will be equipped with interactive exhibits designed by Ralph Applebaum and Associates.

Construction is expected to resume after a thorough site safety reevaluation within the next two months.

* * *

From the Myth-America.com archives (posted May 2, 2015)

My Hero, Nikola Tesla

By Kevin Starkly

Today's article on Wardenclyffe in *Newsday* got me thinking about the strange, sad story of Nikola Tesla.

For those who don't know, Tesla is like a Nerd God. He was a successful inventor, the smartest guy in any room, but he was an awkward weirdo who never even dated a girl.

By the time he returned to New York in 1901 from his wild experiments in Colorado Springs, he was a world-famous genius. He was only in his mid-40's but his accomplishments were unequaled: he invented alternating electric current, demonstrated radio-controlled craft, and held more patents than probably anybody except maybe Edison. But his biggest experiment was still ahead of him.

He went out to Long Island where he purchased farmland from James Warden, 75 miles from Manhattan in Shoreham.

As far as his investors were concerned, Tesla was out to build a wireless telegraph station at Wardenclyffe, the first of many. But Tesla's vision was much grander. He dreamed of information flowing freely from Wardenclyffe—words, pictures, music—a world system of intelligence transmission to whoever wanted it. And all by harnessing the power of the Earth. It was a 1901 fever dream of an information superhighway that wouldn't exist for about another century.

Where Tesla got his visions remains a mystery to this day.

Like all great geniuses ahead of their time, everyone was just waiting for Tesla to fail, counting on it, in fact. Once Marconi triumphed with the first trans-Atlantic telegraph message (using several Tesla patents, by the way), Tesla was old news. His investors left him in droves, even J.P. Morgan. And without the necessary funding, his grand vision for Wardenclyffe died.

The 187-foot-tall transmission tower was torn down and the lab a distant memory by 1917.

There were all kinds of unsubstantiated stories, of course. Rumor had it that Tesla was really working on a death ray capable of killing at a distance. Maybe an army of his remote-controlled robots were waiting to crawl out of the ground. Locals speculated that miles of underground tunnels branched off from Wardenclyffe filled with God knows what unnatural experiments.

But we'll never know the real story because the U.S. government confiscated all of Tesla's papers as soon as he died. That's right. Uncle Sam has filed away all of his secrets in wooden crates and shipped them to Area 51.

The real story of Wardenclyffe—the last of Tesla's workplaces left standing anywhere in the world—has dropped down the memory hole.

Posted by strangekevin

* * *

From Myth-America.com

The "Geek Freaks Across America" Travel to Ohio

By John Walters

July 16

And that brings us to the question, "Why are you two booking to Seaman, Ohio?"

I figure every other alien freak, conspiracy nut, and officially certified loser is heading that way, so why not join the fun?

After all, it's the home of the largest serpent effigy mound in the world. That impressive quarter mile-long Serpent Mound with its coiled tail and gaping jaws has been attracting crowds of curiosity seekers since it was studied and excavated back in 1883.

So there's that, but did you know it's also the location for the biggest Starship Invasion Fanvention in the last five years? No, I didn't know either until Dr. Stryker told us about it (I'm not much of a fan myself).

So we're packing up the t-shirts and Tostitos and leaving NYC for the Comfort Inn on Route 32 for a weekend of aliens, cheap beer, and maybe… just maybe…a reunion with Kevin Starkly.

Posted by jwalters

From After the Quake Twitter feed

@Afterthequake

My husband went camping in the Badlands last week and came back a different man.

I want my real husband back now please.

From Angel McQueen's personal email

July 17

Hey Doc,

I can't believe all the stories Tony remembers from ten years ago. Omg! But it's not all those fond "those were the good times" recollections. He still remembers the time I dropped those ice cubes down his pants in the middle of some intense Dungeons and Dragons action in my room. God, I was such a little jerk.

So Tony says, "I thought you moved to London with some indie-rocker guy." I swear I don't know where these sketchy rumors get started! I mean, OK, so I joined Brian in England for a little while, but it's not like I intended to live there forever. Then he looks at me in that distracting intense way of his and asks, "Why didn't Kevin tell us that you were the mysterious Meteor Girl?" I give him the expected answer—I had Kevin pinkie-swear not to tell another living soul, not even his best buds, not even the other dudes who remembered Angel from the Prep—blah, blah, blah. But I don't even believe that answer. I've never told you before, but I always suspected that the real reason was that Kevin was a little embarrassed about me. Oh, he was sweet about it. Well, as sweet as Kevin can manage. He told me that if we were seen together too often in public that rumors would start percolating around the blogosphere and eventually my secret would be out. So I never joined Kevin when he played his Nerd Legion games. And I never pushed it. What did I expect? That he was going to proudly introduce me to everybody as this former Elf Warrior from back in high school who now claims that she was sucked up into the sky by little green aliens? Pathetic!

Email from Anthony Fermia to Kevin Starkly

July 17, 2015

Dear Jackass,

I just finished chatting face-to-face with Meteor Girl this evening. Or should I say Angela McQueen? Bet you never imagined that would ever happen!

And don't pretend you've conveniently forgotten how I talked about her back at the Prep. Remember how you kidded me mercilessly about the bad poetry I would write about her?

I actually believed all the bullshit you told me about how I shouldn't pursue her and make a fool of myself. You said that if we were fated to come together, it would just happen. I must have been an idiot to take romantic advice from you of all people!

And I believed all the bullshit about how you wanted to preserve Meteor Girl's anonymity. You said that you had this sacred pledge to protect her identity. Now I suspect the real reason you didn't tell us about Angela was because you knew how I felt about her, and you didn't want the competition. Thanks dude, I owe you for that one. Because I almost had myself convinced that this was all some delusion on my part. Maybe, it was only a stupid teen infatuation that I would look back one day and just shake my head wondering what the hell was I thinking. After all, Angela seemed more attracted to those hipster types she was forever checking out in Williamsburg and Greenpoint. Why would she bother with some geek who was into war gaming and reciting Lovecraft? But then I saw her last night after all those years, and I'm right back in Judge's world literature class, and I can't take my eyes off her. I can barely speak. Even remembered scribbling this line in a notebook somewhere: "Never a day goes by that I don't dream of seeing your face again." Ok, so not great prose, but those old feelings were real, and I wanted to hit myself in the head for wasting all that time without her next to me. Or was my tortured revelation part of your master plan? You don't know how much I wish you could get your sorry ass over here so I can kick it back into the great beyond. Honest. – tonyf

From Myth-America.com

July 17

The "Geek Freaks Across America" Travel to Ohio--UPDATE

By John Walters

A car crash today closed down most of OH 32 West.

News said some lunatic driving the wrong way plowed into oncoming traffic at 80 mph. The head-on collision killed at least four people and I forgot how many injuries, but the main road was a mess. We're already running late and I started to panic. Rich suggested that we pull off and drive through the woods until we hit a local road—which was a pretty impressive feat considering our Prius would never be mistaken for a four-wheel-drive SUV.

After crashing through brambles and shrubs and running over God knows what else, I finally stumbled onto a dirt road that wasn't on Google Maps. I hit the gas hard hoping to make up for lost time. Both Rich and I saw the figure on the road ahead of us about the same time. He seemed to fade into existence out of the heated air like a mirage. The hitchhiker was blurry, just a silhouette with a backpack holding a tattered cardboard sign. I slowed down immediately. I'm not a great believer in picking up strangers, but I figured this was just another Invaded fanboy making a pilgrimage to see his cult film and hear the Gospel according to Goodbody.

Just when we were less than a quarter mile away, the hitchhiker dives into the tall grass along the side of the road and disappears in the blink of an eye. Where the hell did he go?

Now it's getting darker and I'm beginning to think to myself that this is an awfully God-forsaken spot to catch a ride. Our phones hadn't caught a signal for the last few miles. As I got to the spot on the road where I saw the hitchhiker dive out of sight, I came to a complete stop thinking he must be somewhere nearby.

"Close the windows. Quick!" Rich is the first to spot them.

As the power windows shut tight, I noticed some movement in the grass. It takes a full second or two before I finally see all the eyes staring back at us from the field. Not just a single mystery hitchhiker, but an army of them. All of these shadowy figures crouched in the grass, lying in wait for us. As if on cue, they all start moving towards the car and I can see now that some of them are just kids no more than 15 or 16, but others are older men and women. Their clothes are dirty and torn as though they had crawled through brush and deadfall for days.

Then I think, "Shit! We're surrounded."

Of course, I've read about them before—although you can only believe half of what you see online. These are crazy homeless mobs wandering the country. Most just hide out in abandoned buildings and malls eating whatever they can find. But I hear some can get really violent stealing what they want. They say these people dropped out of the mainstream two or three years ago. They just abandoned everything and started traveling together in packs. They didn't leave their jobs and families looking to start a new life. They had no life at all—just a shared emptiness.

Rich grabbed the wheel from me and put his foot on the gas. That snapped me out of my stupor immediately. The car was nearly completely surrounded by this mob. I gunned the engine and flew through the only opening in their ranks. I heard some pounding on the side of the car and a yank or two on the door handles, but what spooked me more than anything else was how the whole event unfolded in such complete silence.

Rich and I just looked at each other and didn't say another word.

I didn't look back and I never slowed down until we reached Seaman.

Posted by jwalters

* * *

Email from Angela McQueen to John Walters, Tony Fermia, and Richard Harrigan:

July 17

Hold the phone dudes! Just found this email on Kevin's backup laptop he kept at my place. I've cut and pasted the important bit here:

Dear Kevin:

Thank you for your submission. I am delighted to inform you that your book proposal, tentatively titled, "Myth-America Road Trip: A Paranormal Adventure Across the Country," has been accepted for publication by the Editorial Board, subject to approval of the final manuscript. I understand that you're unable to submit your first draft until your summer podcast travel series is completed on July 30.

The formal offer to publish is based on the terms outlined below....

Yadda, yadda, yadda!

I swear I didn't hear a peep from Kevin about this!

John Walters writes:

OK, so it's not exactly a smoking gun, but damn, it does look like Richard's suspicions about Kevin are on target. Is a pending book deal enough motivation to fake your own "abduction" hoping to generate advance publicity?

Sorry, but Kevin never told me he was writing anything.

Has Kevin ever told the truth to anyone about anything? –JW

Richard Harrigan writes:

A rhetorical question, certainly.

Anthony Fermia writes:

Still a secret book deal is sketchy, but not incriminating. We were all there when Kevin disappeared in those buzzing blue lights. How the hell was he faking that?

Richard Harrigan writes:

Damn it Fermia, I'm a physics teacher not a magician! Just because I can't do the trick, doesn't mean it's not a fake. Rather ask *cui bono?* Who benefits?

* * *

From the Starship Invasions Fan Convention Program

FIFTH ANNUAL

STARSHIP INVASIONS

FANVENTION

JULY 18-19, 2015

COMFORT INN

Seaman, Ohio

Program of Events

July 18

10:00 AM—5:30 PM

Dealers Room Open (Grand Ballroom)

Starship Invasions Fanvention is proud to offer the largest selection of SF and fantasy/occult merchandise once again in Ohio. Special commemorative items are also on sale.

11:00 AM

Special Guest Appearance: Robert Vaughn (Conf. Room A)

Television and movie star Robert Vaughn (*Man From UNCLE*) will speak about his distinguished film career, and in particular, his starring role as Professor Duncan in *Starship Invasions*. Autograph session scheduled at 12:30 PM in the Grand Ballroom.

12:00 Noon

Screening of *Starship Invasions* (Conf. Room B)

The cult classic that continues to bring us together after almost 40 years will be screened in a special HDTV format. Extraterrestrial bad guys from the Legion of the Winged Serpent headed by Captain Ramses (Christopher Lee) attempt to conquer Earth. They are opposed by good guy aliens Captain Anaxi (Daniel Pilon) and Gazeth (Victoria Johnson) representing the pacifistic League of Races. After their secret underwater base in the Bermuda Triangle is captured by the evil Captain Ramses, the League reaches out to Earth's #1 UFO expert Professor Duncan (Robert Vaughn) for his help and expertise. The two alien forces battle for the future of our planet in spectacular spaceship shootouts. This remastered digital copy is taken from a pristine original print recently discovered by director/screenwriter Ed Hunt.

1:30 PM

Special Guest Appearance: Dr. Jeanette Stryker (Conf. Room A)

Best-selling author and sleep expert Jeanette Stryker (Dreamtime Research Institute) will discuss her latest research into the fascinating connections between lucid dreaming and reports of alien abductions.

3:00 PM

The Invaded Manifesto Explained (Conf. Room B)

Starship Invasions' most provocative fan, Robyn Goodbody, will answer questions about her controversial treatise "The Invaded Manifesto." Does this cult classic from 1977 really contain clues revealing a secret human/alien connection?

7:30 PM

Masquerade Ball (Serpent Mound Park –weather permitting)

Grand prizes for the best SF or fantasy costume. As always, special recognition for Starship Invasions re-enactments. Please remember: 21 and over only!

From Myth-America.com

July 17

The "Geek Freaks Across America" Travel to Ohio--UPDATED

By Richard Harrigan

A quick look at the map and it becomes glaringly obvious that something is horribly wrong: Why is there a 1,300-foot-long serpent slithering atop Adams County?

Indeed, the origins and purpose of the infamous Serpent Mound is just as shrouded in mystery today as when Frederic Ward Putnam of Harvard University's Peabody Museum first mapped its contours back in the early 1880s. Putnam had never seen anything like it. He wrote, "The most singular sensation of awe and admiration overwhelmed me..." It is, from the tip of its coiled tail to its mammoth 75-foot-wide gaping mouth, an impressive sight. Archeologists now believe that Native Americans (not Atlanteans nor Lemurians, or some other fanciful lost race) built it up from the earth over 1,000 years ago. But why? Was it to mark the passing of the summer solstice, to commemorate an auspicious event, or did they celebrate some forgotten rituals we can never even imagine? If anything, the Serpent Mound, along with all the other assorted earthwork shapes and figures scattered across the country (some of which can only be seen to full effect from above), reminds us that the landscape of ancient America was exceedingly different from today. In fact, I remember Starkly once pointing out to me that the area around the mouth of the serpent is most likely the remnant of a meteorite crater. Starkly often speculated that the ancient Indians constructed this serpent to recognize some otherworldly energy that emanated from the spot. Personally, I think Starkly was reading too much vintage von Daniken. Next stop: into the lair of the serpent!

Posted by drrich

Email message to Myth-America.com

ObviousFakeFan writes:

To Nerd Legion: If you want to know what happened to Kevin Starkly contact me immediately for a private meeting. And bring the Aurora artifact from Starkly's collection. Don't contact the police.

John Walters writes:

Who are you? What have you done to Kevin?

ObviousFakeFan writes:

You'll find out tomorrow Walters. Meet me alone at the abandoned Mobil station off Rt. 32. No tricks and no police or you'll never see Starkly again.

John Walters writes:

If you want Kevin's "Aurora artifact" we'll not be meeting alone in any abandoned location. You can meet me here at the Starship Invasion con tomorrow night during the Masquerade Ball or no deal.

ObviousFakeFan writes:

Agreed. Will only make deal directly with you Walters at the Masquerade at 8:30 PM.

Don't waste my time.

* * *

MICHAEL F. WALKER

From *The Invaded Manifesto* (Self-published)

By Robyn Goodbody

Let it be known that we, the Invaded, believe that *Starship Invasions* is more than simply a Grade B *Star Wars* knock-off. We believe that it is self-evident that Writer/Director Ed Hunt used the popular "space opera" format to communicate a greater truth about humanity's secret relationship with the space aliens. Hidden within the 87-minute running time of this classic movie is a message on the next steps we must take to join the Intergalactic League of Races.

We believe that the more you know about the UFO phenomena, the more you'll understand the brilliance of *Starship Invasions*. The opening scenes showing a very close encounter of the erotic kind between an Earth farmer and the naked alien woman Sagnac (Sherri Ross) is a clever recapitulation of the infamous Antonio Villas Boas alien abduction case from 1957. Sadly, this intimate rendezvous is merely suggested in the film rather than graphically portrayed, otherwise *Starship Invasions* would have garnered at least an R rating and perhaps an even greater cult following.

Other familiar images are displayed throughout the film for the secret delectation of true UFO connoisseurs.

We spot an exact duplicate of the much-studied "Marjorie Fish Star Map" of Zeta Reticuli seen by Betty Hill during her famous abduction in 1961.

The robots in the League's undersea base are based on the "creatures" seen by Charles Hickson and Calvin Parker, Jr. during their abduction in Pascagoula, Mississippi on October 11, 1973.

Professor Duncan (played by Robert Vaughn) is loosely based on real-life UFO researcher J. Allen Hynek.

We believe that the most startlingly prophetic part of this overlooked masterpiece is the accurate depiction of the current "suicide epidemic" sweeping the country. Psychologists are still trying to formulate theories to explain the tragic increase in suicides across all age groups, but especially among 16-30-year-olds. In the film, the "suicide ray" is the first line of attack on humanity by the evil aliens headed by Captain Ramses (Christopher Lee). There may be a more chilling scene in cinema than the moment when Professor Duncan's lovely wife (Helen Shaver) slits her wrists in the kitchen sink, but I can't recall it. That this wave of suicides was accurately predicted almost forty years ago demands our attention.

Ed Hunt uses the eerie suicide ray as a narrative gambit to slap us out of our movie-watching stupor. The major clue is the winged serpent emblem worn by Christopher Lee and his minions. Why did Ed Hunt choose this provocative image? It is an obvious reference to the Herb Schirmer abduction case in Ashland, Nebraska in 1967 where he recalled under hypnosis that his abductors wore uniforms with a flying serpent emblem.

Do I need to remind anyone of the preponderance of serpent images found mysteriously entwined around all of human history and culture? From the Ouroboros of the ancient Egyptians and Greeks—a symbol of eternity pictured as a serpent swallowing its own tail—to the celestial dragons of Chinese legends, the serpent has been a powerful image of renewal, life and death, and secret knowledge.

The Egyptians called him Kneph, the great sky serpent. It was from his jaws that the "cosmic egg" came forth. The great beings associated with feathered serpents in Mexico and South America, whether called Quetzalcoatl or Kukulkan guided their cultures instructing them in agriculture and law. It's a shame that the Catholic Church completely misappropriated and twisted the true meaning of the serpent—as they have done over the years to other perfectly good pagan icons—for their own limited moralistic purposes.

We believe that these beings associated with the serpents were actually space aliens guiding the development of humanity through crucial junctures in our evolution. We believe they were preparing us to make the next jump in human consciousness—the final step in our development before joining them as space-faring gods.

* * *

From transcript of Dr. Jeanette Stryker talk

"Dreamtime Invasions"

July 18, 2015

Jeanette Stryker:

I was greatly amused, and I'm sure you were as well, watching the recent coverage commemorating the 50th anniversary—or was it the 55th anniversary? —of the SETI Project. You know what I'm referring to, of course, the search for extraterrestrial intelligence. All those years pointing our Very Large Arrays into the night sky waiting patiently for a whisper in the dark, waiting for some sign of intelligent life somewhere out there. And of course, SETI, the poor darlings, have come back empty-handed. All those years scanning the heavens with their sophisticated radio telescopes and not hearing a single peep or beep…nothing.

So the response from the SETI officials being questioned about all this time and money spent on essentially nothing has modulated back and forth between quite pissy posturing and rather forced bonhomie. Really, how many times can you hear scientists brag about the importance of null results?

I don't know about you, but I've always felt that those SETI darlings could find out more about extraterrestrial intelligence by turning off their radio telescopes and simply start interviewing some of the alien abductees gathered right down here at this convention.

(APPLAUSE)

And think of all the savings in fundraising. Instead of budgeting $50 million or whatever it's up to now, they would only have to pay out $15 or maybe $30 in admission fees. Really, I like to think that those of us involved in researching alien abduction cases are like the popular coed packing her purse with lipstick and condoms as we race off to our next party for the night, while the SETI researchers are like the poor sorority sister stuck at home waiting for her date to call.

I remember one particularly cheeky reporter asking a SETI official why they were not investigating alien abduction cases. You know what that official had the audacity to say? "We're not interested in exploring abductions because it's not real science."

(LAUGHTER)

Clearly our poor SETI darlings are more comfortable waiting for a long-distance phone call from an extraterrestrial, rather than say...I don't know...chatting with that same alien chap parked in his spaceship outside our window.

Yes, that's a sterling distinction in the annals of science, isn't it? That's brilliant, is what that is. I think it's far past time for us to start searching in other directions and in other media for extraterrestrial intelligence. Why should we limit our communication possibilities to only radio transmissions? Because Frank Drake believed so?

I believe this communication...or information exchange if you will... has been taking place for years, if not decades through the medium of dreams. Maybe as far back in our past as the ancient legends of the Dogon tribe in West Africa which describe the star Sirius and the orbit of its invisible companion. But where did they get this knowledge? Astronomers only discovered the existence of Sirius B centuries later. Could alien intelligence transmitted instantly across light years, maybe transmitted on another dimensional plane, come directly into our dreaming brains? Certainly my theory is no more bizarre than that lovely physicist Paul Davies who suggested that we seek out extraterrestrial messages imprinted on the human genome. Why limit the means of expression of an alien intelligence?

Now let me take a moment to make myself clear. I'm quite afraid my own message has gone awry in transmission, for many seem to misunderstand what I'm saying. At least I'm in good company. Both Carl Jung and Jacques Vallee are both misquoted when it comes to the subjects of extraterrestrials and UFOs. My critics would have you believe that I'm claiming that alien abduction stories are all fantasies, just dreams cooked up by overactive imaginations. It's all in your heads. Let me tell you right now that this is a deliberate misinterpretation of my theory and is either disingenuous or an outright lie. It is pure bollocks.

An invasion of our reality is no less real if it is taking place in our dreams than if it is happening along a country road. The alien manipulation of our minds…the minds of abductees or "experiencers" as my dear friend John Mack referred to them…is still an alien intrusion into our lives. I believe this brings a new understanding to the phenomena without diminishing it in the least. Who can say if this alien intelligence…wherever or whatever it is…will ultimately be satisfied by only intruding on our dreams?

* * *

Email from John Walters to Anthony Fermia

July 18

Hi Tony,

I've arranged to meet a mysterious someone tonight at the Masquerade Ball who claims to know what happened to Kevin. Rich—our perpetual cynic—still thinks Kevin is somehow behind this, like this is a big Myth-America PR stunt. Sorry, but I'm afraid whoever I'm meeting is involved with that alleged "Collector Killer," so I'm not taking any chances. Rich thinks it's a waste of time, but he's agreed to cover my back. Our mystery man (woman?) thinks I have some "Aurora artifact" to hand over. Just when he finds out I'm empty-handed, Rich and I grab him and get the truth. That's the general plan anyway. After tonight I'll just be relieved to finally beam the hell out of here. You're lucky not to be stuck here Tony. I know the Starship Invasion Fanvention is devoted to a cult film, but I didn't know it was so...cult-like.

And I'm not just talking about the costumes. I mean practically everyone is dressed in alien-appropriate fashion, and as every Invaded follower knows that means men are covered head-to-toe in a black unitard and the women are modeling shimmering space bikinis.

But it seems people you run into are more likely to talk about alien abductions and the Apocalypse than about, I don't know, say the relative merits of Heinlein versus Niven—which in my experience is pretty unusual for a SF convention crowd.

And outside the hotel, the army of the missing is gathering like some evangelical tent revival. I'm not kidding. The homeless encampment stretches as far as you can see down the road to Serpent Mound Park. They all look dazed and disheveled like the ones we saw on the road who tried to grab our car. Some of them actually staggered into the lobby grabbing croissants and muffins off the complimentary breakfast tray before hotel security showed them the door. I'm embarrassed to admit that I thought they were some cosplayers practicing for a *Walking Dead* skit.

Did I mention I'm not a big fan of *Starship Invasions*? To say it was a justly obscure film would be an understatement. Remember Dante? He refuses to believe the film even exists because he can't stream it on Netflix. It never had the cult following of *Troll 2*, but it soon became insanely popular for obvious reasons. Then that Goodbody babe wrote her "Invaded Manifesto" and that sealed the deal. Wish me luck! --JW

Email from Anthony Fermia to John Walters

July 18

Johnny, keep yourself safe man. We're keeping ourselves busy back home here.

I'm going through Kevin's pig sty first. I can't believe he was really living in his parents' basement all this time. Maybe some new eyes will pick up something that Angela hadn't noticed before. Don't ask me what I'm looking for because I have no idea, but I think I'll know it when I see it. If Kevin had something really valuable, I believe he would hide it Purloined Letter style in plain sight. Maybe Kevin did engineer his "abduction" to escape from this Collector Killer. It would certainly explain why he's still hiding from us.

Angela buys into a bunch of Kevin's more extreme conspiracy theories so she believes that Kevin would never keep his secrets out in the open at his own apartment. If government agents from the CIA or NSA were behind this (and she really thinks they might be after Kevin and the rest of us), they would have searched through his place immediately.

So she had this flash of intuition based on some passing remark from Kevin that he may have sent his "secret" over to the Collyer Brothers art installation at your gallery.

So we're splitting up next week: I'll be picking through the debris here at Kevin's place and Angela's sampling some culture at your art show.

Email from John Walters to Anthony Fermia

July 18

Sorry Tony, but I think you and Angela are wasting your time looking through Kevin's stuff. Rich thinks all this speculation about a UFO "Rosetta Stone," or secret revelation just came out of Kevin's fevered imagination because the Aurora crash simply didn't happen. You might as well start rummaging through his sock drawers looking for a little grey alien in a pickle jar! –JW

Email from Anthony Fermia to John Walters

July 18

Yeah, we may be wasting our time, but after the last few days I've decided to take Kevin's claims seriously. Remember, we didn't believe there was a Meteor Girl either, after all.

* * *

From transcript of the Robyn Goodbody talk

"The Invaded Manifesto Explained"

July 18, 2015

Robyn Goodbody:

Was the prominent serpent image in *Starship Invasions* a simple coincidence? I think not. I think it was intended to lead us to the final secrets of how we can contact our space brothers.

I believe the answer can be found in the teachings of kundalini yoga and the practices of Tantric sex, exotic disciplines whose origins may well go back over a thousand years. Kundalini yoga practitioners say that everyone has prana or life force, lying dormant at the base of her spine that can be awakened to full consciousness with the proper techniques. But here's the part that truly sends a chill down my own spine. Can you guess how this secret life force, this prana, has been pictured for centuries?

Yes, it is pictured as a coiled serpent waiting to strike! With the proper training, this great kundalini serpent will uncoil upwards from its spinal base to give birth to ultimate enlightenment in the conscious mind. I believe this is the next step for all of us.

(APPLAUSE)

We already recognize the reality of alien beings visiting our planet. They have been guiding all of us to save us from ourselves. They want to rescue us from the mess we've made of our lives. They want to save us from the crimes we've committed against our Earth. Save us from the crimes we've committed against each other. And they've supplied us with the techniques to save us from our baser desires.

(APPLAUSE)

The secrets of Tantric sex show us how to tame our selfish desires to deliriously prolong our pleasure until we reach overwhelming orgasm— "la petite mort" or "little death." This is the ultimate sacrifice of self. We believe the recent "suicide epidemic" and the legions of the missing who have abandoned their lives must play a significant role in the grand plan, if only to remind us that great leaps in knowledge often requires self-sacrifice and equally great leaps into the unknown.

The message has been repeated through all time and all cultures until it becomes foolish to ignore it: Follow the Serpent! Follow the Serpent!

(AUDIENCE CHANTING: FOLLOW THE SERPENT!)

Whether it's Quetzalcoatl directing the Aztecs, or the sky dragons guiding Chinese dynasties, the path is clear. Once we awaken the kundalini serpent-power in all of us, humanity will evolve to the next level. At the moment of ultimate orgasm, the perfect release, we leave this life behind and enter a new plane of existence. I believe this evolution—or should I say revolution—will bring us to another location in space and time.

When that time arrives, we will be welcomed by all the other sentient beings of the universe as brothers and sisters. Maybe they already exist, and have existed, in this separate place for a millennium—maybe for all eternity?

But is humanity ready to take that next step? Are you ready? Are we all ready for the next revolution?

(APPLAUSE)

* * *

From text messages on July 18, Serpent Mound Park, OH

8:00 PM EST

Rich: Where r u?

John: By the bonfire

Rich: Which 1?

John: By the mouth of the snake, I think

Rich: Still can't see u 2 crowded

John: I think the hot action is happening by the tail bonfire

Rich: I haven't seen this much fire and freaks since the last Burning Man

John: This is more like The Wicker Man!

Rich: I hear the human sacrifices begin at 9

John: Can u see me now?

Rich: OK. Where r u going to meet?

John: I set it up for 8:30 at the serpent's mouth

Rich: Isn't that near the costume contest?

John: I wanted a crowded spot

Rich: Did I just see a kick-line of pointy-nosed robots pass you?

John: Ha! Those are the good robots from the underwater base.

Rich: OK, I knew you're secretly a fan of this movie

John: I am so NOT a fan

Rich: Then why were you so pissed when Robert
            Vaughn cancelled?

John: I just said it was uncool how he blew off the con. And
            Starship Invasions is no Star Wars

Rich: It's not even Battle Beyond the Stars

John: Vaughn was in that film too. When did u see Battle?

Rich: When u dragged me to that John Sayles film festival
            at MOMA

John: That was cool!

8:30 PM EST

Rich: Who's the young lady undressed as Barbarella?

John: I think she's dressed as Gazeth.

Rich: Who?

John: Wait I think she's my mystery date

Rich: How did she find u? The competing geek vibes
            r overwhelming

John: I'm the only 1 wearing a Myth-America t-shirt

Rich: What is she saying?

John: Hold on

Rich: Can't see u now. Where r u?

John: She's asking me for the Aurora artifact

Rich: Hold her there, I'm coming over

John: She just realized I don't have it

Rich: Who is she?

John: She's Goodbody.

Rich: I lost u again

John: Wants me to follow her

Rich: No, don't move!

John: Something about joining the awakening.

Rich: I can't see 2 many freaks blocking you

John: What?

Rich: I lost u again. Where r u?

Rich: Where r u?

* * *

From *Portsmouth (OH) Daily Times*

July 19, 2015

39 Found Dead at Sci-Fi Film Con

A weekend-long celebration of a popular cult film ended abruptly in tragedy yesterday when local police discovered 39 bodies at a masquerade ball held in the Serpent Mound Park in Adams County, all apparently poisoned as part of a bizarre suicide pact. This is believed to be the largest mass suicide in county history.

Officials say that all the dead were registered attendees of the Starship Invasion Fanvention, an annual event celebrating an obscure science-fiction film released in 1977, held at the nearby Comfort Inn in Seaman. Police Chief William "Bill" Patterson reports that they have no apparent motive for the crime, but several witnesses have come forward who claim to have seen the killings.

"We have it on good authority from at least a dozen eyewitnesses that these poor kids were involved in some ceremony going on at the Serpent Mound," says Patterson. "They all took some kind of pill, and some of the group started dropping to the ground."

The official cause of death for the 39 convention attendees has not been determined, but results of the toxicology tests are expected next Monday.

The deaths took place during a popular masquerade ball. A convention spokesman estimates that over two hundred people gathered at the Serpent Mound for various activities, including a costume contest, but insists that no special ceremonies were officially scheduled that evening.

The names of all the victims are being withheld by the police until all next of kin have been notified. However, Chief Patterson has confirmed a rumor that UFO cult author Robyn Goodbody, a featured speaker at the convention, is missing and is currently being sought for questioning.

Police say there appears to be no connection between last night's deaths and the suicide of five seniors at West Union High School last week.

* * *

From eBay auction site

Mystic Tibetan Dagger

Current bid: US $29.00

End time: 4 hours 32 minutes (July-17-16:42:10 PST)

Shipping Costs: US $10.00

Item location: Tennessee, United States

Description (revised)

Type: 18th Century phur-pa

This gorgeous-looking toad-sticker is as useful as it is beautiful. Another one-of-a-kind item from the collections of the Kunstkammer Kids, this Tibetan phur-pa is said to have slain a real demon back in the day and you can even still see the blood staining the blade after all these centuries. *Brother Hank here just adding that the phur-pa or mystic daggers are mostly known for their ceremonial uses, but there are many times when push came to shove that these artifacts were wielded as deadly weapons. Legend says this dagger was used by the Tibetan deity Hayagriva to slay nasty serpent demons known as nagas.* Boy Howdy! I bet you could have used one of them knives when that hairy werewolf jumped you in the Cascade Mountains near Spokane. And you wouldn't be needing that eye patch either. *You know what Momma always says Frank, "Scars are like tattoos except with better stories." And speaking of stories, I almost forgot that the legend of this phur-pa says that the blood stain on the blade will liquefy and start dripping again but only in the presence of another demon.* We haven't tested that out yet, but whoever wins this beauty please report back to us, hear now. It's not every day that a supernatural weapon comes on the market, especially one this beautiful with gold inlay and an emerald stuck on the hilt about the size of a walnut, so we expect some brisk bidding to commence on this one. And as always, it comes with the unmatched Kunstkammer Kids guarantee: if you're not satisfied that this is the strangest, most unnatural, supernatural oddity you've ever encountered on God's green Earth, you just send it back in 30 days and we'll even pay for the shipping. Just remember the place to go for all your occult oddities, freaks of nature, and supernatural shopping needs in this life and the next is the Kunstkammer Kids store available online at kunstkammerkids.com. Or if you're visiting our neck of the woods just stop by our brick-and-mortar Arcanium and dime museum out on I 40 W outside of Nashville. Just call ahead and tell them Hank and Frank Weir invited you personally.

* * *

From Myth-America.com

July 20, 2015

The Geeks Escape the Serpent's Lair—Barely

By John Walters

This is just to alert everyone that despite the alarming reports circulating across the blogosphere, Rich and I are both alive and continuing the quest.

Like an idiot, I thought this would be a simple transaction.

Believe me, I would never knowingly place myself in harm's way. I'm a good friend and all, but I'm no action hero. Anyway, after we spoke with Dr. Jeanette Stryker, the lucid dreaming expert (she says she first worked with Kevin during his investigation of that alleged alien abduction off the Brooklyn Bridge), we were contacted by a mysterious party who claimed to know about what happened to Kevin. In fact, implying they might be responsible for his disappearance. In exchange they wanted Kevin's Aurora artifact. Of course, the only problem here is that Richard and I had no idea what Kevin was talking about when he claimed some mysterious inside information about the Aurora crash. So that was my mission: meet Mr. X in a very public location, find out what they knew about Kevin and then grab them without handing over the Aurora artifact—whatever the hell that is.

I talked it over with Rich and I was pretty sure I had it all figured out. Rich was convinced this was all some elaborate scheme concocted by Kevin himself to bring us together so he could make his grand re-appearance. And to tell the truth, I was really hoping, right up until the last minute that Kevin would come waddling up to me out of the crowds at the Serpent Mound and say something like, "Hi Johnny, how the hell are you doing? Hey, check out this cool first edition of *Flying Saucers Are Real* I picked up in the Dealers Room."

Then I saw this stunning brunette heading my way wearing a strapless space bikini just like the one Victoria Johnson wore in *Starship Invasions*. I found it extremely unlikely that I was suddenly transformed into a babe magnet by wearing my Myth-America t-shirt and cap. Rich was watching over me from a discreet distance just as we had arranged. As it turns out, Rich was handicapped in his guardian angel role by all the convention attendees crowded into that one spot. As I considered various pick-up lines, she said, "Do you have the Aurora artifact?" I wonder how many other bewildered guys she tried that line on before she found me?

That's when she asked me if I wanted to make a trade—what she knew about Kevin in exchange for the secret evidence I had concerning the Aurora crash.

I told her to spill her information first.

She then said, "The earthquake set certain events in motion. Certain alignments had formed. There were collectors searching for the Aurora pilot—if the story was true. Kevin is probably hiding from them now."

Finally, I recognized her voice. This Gazeth-wannabe was the aptly named Robyn Goodbody. I didn't recognize her at first seeing how she was nearly naked and wearing a wig. Then I fessed up.

"Sorry Robyn, but it looks like I have about as much secret information about the Aurora crash as you have about where Kevin is hiding."

Initially, she seemed really peeved that I pulled a bait-and-switch job on her.

"So you have nothing?"

I said "No, but I was hoping you might know who would want him to disappear."

She started looking around nervously, as though her date for the evening was late. Then she did the oddest thing—not that anything leading up to this moment was otherwise lacking in oddness—she grabbed my arm and started blabbing some gibberish about an important ceremony that I should attend.

"Maybe you could join us for the serpent awakening. The alignment here is perfect."

I admit I panicked a little and pulled away abruptly. "I'll ask one more time. What happened to Kevin Starkly?"

She smiled. Then something hard and heavy hit the right side of my head.

I staggered back but didn't fall. I couldn't quite understand what was happening to me. I'm in the middle of a friendly crowd. Is someone really trying to crack my skull? Even when I reached up to feel the lump on my head and saw my fingers covered with blood, I thought maybe I was getting sick and I should take an aspirin. Then something hit me again with such force that I swear every tooth in my head shifted in its socket. That's when I hit the ground and lost consciousness.

The next thing I remembered Rich was hauling my sorry ass across the parking lot and into the back seat of the rental car. So we were heading back to the hotel as the biggest mass suicide in Adams County, Ohio, was going down. We missed the part of the ceremony where they drank the Kool-Aid or popped the pill or did whatever they thought they had to do to join the benevolent Space Brothers. I wasn't surprised when I discovered later that most of the dead were guys in their twenties who had recently embraced the new religion of The Invaded. The temptation to acquire forbidden knowledge is a powerful force, especially if someone like Ms. Goodbody is doing the tempting.

Rich figured it out first, but then he is the smartest guy in the room. This was all a trap for us from the start. Someone or some group wanted to tempt us to hand over Kevin's mysterious "evidence" for the Aurora crash. Rich admitted—reluctantly—that the guy who set this up might indeed be the serial killer going around the country murdering paranormal collectors. So if we didn't arrange this meeting in a public place—if we had met in private as was first requested—I could very well be dead right now instead of nursing a concussion. Kevin if you're reading this, you sure as hell owe me a drink the next time we get together at the Old Town Bar. And maybe you'll tell me who is after you dude. And what the hell do you know about Aurora that nobody else knows?

Posted by jwalters

* * *

From Angel McQueen's personal email

July 20

Hi Doc,

I just found out that Johnny was way more freaked out by what happened to him at the Serpent Mound than he told everyone on the blog. Of course, I suspected as much. I mean, really, when was the last time that Johnny was even in a fistfight? Maybe sophomore year at Prep? And this wasn't even a really fair fight. It was more like someone jumping him and kicking the crap out of him. And for what reason?

You see the really scary part is that some shadowy guys are going around hunting for Kevin, and now they've figured out that the best way to get to Kevin is through the rest of the Nerd Legion. And it's pretty damn obvious that they'll do anything to get what they want!

So Tony is telling me how freaked Johnny and Rich are (even though they are all full of that macho "I'm a fearless paranormal investigator" bullshit that Kevin patented years ago), and Tony asks me if Kevin ever said anything about this mysterious "evidence" he had about the Aurora airship crash back in 1897.

So I get all indignant on him, like Wtf!? Am I some co-conspirator hiding evidence? But Tony calms me down and says he's not accusing me of hiding anything. In fact, he's pretty sure that if Kevin didn't play show-and-tell with the bros, he probably didn't tell me either. But maybe, just maybe, he let something slip. Hello, News Flash! Kevin was all about hiding EVERYTHING! And he was sooo good at it too. He hid his secrets as well as he hid his feelings. I was just Meteor Girl to him, another piece in the UFO puzzle.

So Tony leans in closer to me at the bar (did I mention that we went out for drinks tonight?), and he says he's worried that the creeps who attacked Johnny might find out about me too.

Whoa! It never occurred to me before that moment that I was sort of unofficially voted into the team. I guess we're all in this together now, whether we like it or not.

So Tony downs another PBR and says, "Don't worry, I won't let…I mean, we won't let anything happen to you." Too late on that one, Sherlock!

The conversation had taken a precarious turn for the personal and I decided to go with it. Now I'm starting to feel all super awkward about not friending Tony on Facebook. You know what I mean?

I mentioned that Kevin had told me all about Tony's strange experiences as a kid. I mean not just the creepy ghost dreams and voices, but also his freaky nightmare encounter with that thing with the glowing red eyes. Normally I don't want to hear about that personal stuff from a third party. I mean, if someone wants to pour out his most intimate thoughts and fears, I'll just wait until he tweets about it. But I told Tony that I felt we shared this connection that most people would never understand in a million, million years. That something inexplicable and terrifying had possessed us against our wills and maybe changed us. Anyway, so I said that's why I specifically contacted him when I thought it was time to "out" myself as Meteor Girl.

So he gives me this big goofy grin (which was great because the high-octane melancholy Tony is kind of cool in a "Johnny Depp plays Hamlet" sort of way, but he's so much more adorable when he's making stupid, self-deprecating jokes and laughing) and says, "And here I thought you called because of my good looks and charming smile."

Wait! Was Tony actually flirting? I mean, I thought he was constitutionally incapable of flirting. Like he's had a major flirt-ectomy or something. This boy might prove to be full of surprises after all!

* * *

Texts recorded from July 23, 2015

Angel: What r u wearing now?

Tony: Just jeans & t shirt…I'm hot here.

Angel: Depends on the jeans!

Tony: Damn Kevin…2 cheap for AC in the basement.

Angel: I'm hot too

Tony: Depends on what ur wearing

Angel: I mean I'm hot on the trail u dirty boy

Tony: Ha! So what r u wearing?

Angel: That little black dress I save for hipster art openings

Tony: Wish I was there with you

Angel: You never told me J has such a cool art installation

Tony: Site specific art is not my thing

Angel: Any luck for u?

Tony: Zip…nothing here but K's accumulated crap

Angel: Lots of Goth types here…cute guys too

Tony: Find anything?

Angel: I just got here

Tony: Did u find Bubble?

Angel: J's assistant?

Tony: Yeah…the 1 who looks like Bubble from Ab Fab?

Angel: Lol! He's helping me now

Tony: Did K ever throw anything out?

Angel: K would luv this…the Collyers were the mac daddies
          of packrats

Tony: What does it look like?

Angel: Like landscaping by Tim Burton…mountains of stuff,
          not just paper but strollers, bikes, old computers, parts of
          an SUV

Tony: I found K's 1st computer stuck in a closet, plus copies
          of the Saucerian Bulletin from 1959…where did he get
          this garbage?

Angel: Bubble's back…This is cool: they have a list &
          map of everyone who donated anything to the
          Collyer installation

Tony: What did K donate?

Angel: Oops!

Tony: What?

Angel: Kevin's name is not on list!

Tony: U sure he said he was sending something?

Angel: Yeah! He def said: I'm sending something special to
          J's project

Tony: Let me think.

Angel: Did I screw up?

Tony: No…read me the list of recent donors and what they sent

Angel: How recent?

Tony: Just before the trip to NJ…just list all the names, K prob used an alias

Angel: Or this could be a waste of time like J predicted

Tony: No, I trust you

Angel: OK…M. Sullivan, old TV;

           package from D. Hresko;

           baby stroller from J. Rodriguez;

           package from S. E. Haydon;

           G. Sankner, old Superman comics

Tony: That's it!

Angel: What?

Tony: S. E. Haydon is the reporter who wrote about the Aurora crash

Angel: We have a winner!

Tony: Stay there…I'll meet you at gallery and we'll both see what K put in that package

Angel: I can meet u back at K's place…I'll take the L

Tony: No…ur safer over there

From Angel McQueen's personal email

July 23, 2015

Hey Doc,

So Tony really freaked when he saw the package from Kevin (or should I say S.E. Haydon?) We snuggled into that Mexican café; you know the one right off North 6th?

Inside this manila envelope was an old-fashioned White Owl cigar box. It was made of real wood too, not some cheap laminated crap from Walmart. And it was stacked full of old letters…yellow, yellower, yellowest…all tied together with some fishing line.

So my excitable boy tore through this stuff scanning every page. I even grabbed a dozen pages myself for a quick read. Talk about pulp fiction! Boyhood recollections from this guy, Lawless Starkly, that sounded like Huck Finn on acid, followed by weird war stories, and weirder tales about working the docks. Tony and I figured out that this Cigar Box of the Damned came from Kevin's grandfather who passed away back in April. I remember Kevin talking about going to the funeral in Astoria and then crawling around his grandpa's attic clearing out tons of trash. I think he was going to sell some of the tchotchkes on eBay and keep some of the cool dime novels and bloody pulps and such for himself. So this Lawless dude was Kevin's grandpa's daddy. He was Kevin's great grandpa. So I figure the weird gene must run in his family, huh?

After about 30 minutes and a second cup of espresso, Tony finds this letter, I mean THE letter. If the other stuff was wild, this was epic. This is sooo totally the "Aurora artifact" that everyone is looking for! Tony is so jamming with adrenaline that he jumps up and plants a big smooch right on my lips. He's such a sweetie that he actually blushes! He grabs me real close so we can read the letter together and I'm practically sitting on his lap in the booth. We're both buzzed by the contents of the letter and what it means. And I think we're equally buzzed by the epic spontaneity of the moment. I've told you already that Tony has a deep-rooted fear of spontaneity. I mean this is the dude back in high school who had to work up his courage to ask me if our two avatars could go on a quest together. And I'm like, dude, my Elf Warrior and your Cleric have been covering each other's backs for the past three months!

Before I say anything, Tony is talking about catching a plane to Dallas maybe and joining up with the Nerd Legion before they head to Aurora. I mean, I understand what he's talking about. Kevin probably thought that this was his destiny. Like a Roots-style family imperative to connect with great-grandpa Lawless. No doubt this is the final destination that Kevin was keeping to himself. But here's the thing—I'm actually surprised by how much I don't want Tony to leave. I'm going to miss hanging with him. He's such a reassuring presence in my life. Is "reassuring" the right word? Don't know. But I do know I'm not going to go all "clingy girl" on him and ask him to stay with me. Arrgh! I'm such a jerk. Did I really think we were going to play Nancy Drew and Joe Hardy all summer long? Time to cut the crap and get real, babe. Sometimes I wonder how much of my life I waste on these pathetic fantasies. I think both of us are feeling a little awkward as Tony gets up to go with THE letter. But at least he promises that we'll get together before he leaves. I guess that's something, right?

From the collected letters of Lawless Starkly

June 30, 1936

Dear Jesse,

Postcard from the Texas Centennial came today from old Jeb Haskell. Knew Jeb from the time we were boys in Plainview. We went to school together. Played hooky together. Signed up together to fight in the Great War too, but that's another story.

Jeb took the family to the celebration in Dallas. He said it was "educational." Now if you ask me, I'd sooner go to the jubilee over in San Antonio, the one with the dancing girls and big top circus shows. I hear they even have a Pavilion of Negro Life. Damn, but those colored folks can put on a fine show.

Anyway, that got me to thinking of the time when I was a boy just about your age now. I was about 8 years old and living outside Dallas, Texas. My Momma, that's your Granny, she would always say that I had "the devil chasing my behind." I guess she meant that I was always racing hell bent into all sorts of scrapes. Although sometimes I wonder if she really meant I was possessed by the devil. Certainly I was obsessed by the supernatural in a way that probably wasn't healthy for a normal little boy. I know my folks were awful worried about me and had me sit down more than once with Reverend Jimmy to discuss the saving grace of Jesus. Of course, I didn't say anything because if I told the good reverend about all the things I had seen and heard in the dark places around town it surely would have turned his hair snow white.

I had quite the hankering for tales of the unknown. I'd save my nickels and pennies and buy every dime novel about werewolves, vampires, and restless spirits. When Momma wasn't looking, I would read the stories in Scribners about people contacting the dead with those "talking boards." My folks would have thought it was those Godless tales that inspired my most foolhardy adventures. There was the time I broke into that séance underway at the Partridge Sisters place with that famous medium from back East. People paid good money expecting to see ectoplasmic spirits trooping out of the wardrobe. Instead what they got was a rambunctious 8-year-old getting his britches caught on the invisible wires holding up the "spirit" instruments. Good lord, they must have heard all that clattering and commotion and screaming all the way to Dallas. Then there was the time I slept overnight in the haunted Haverstraw house off Main Street, but that's another story.

What I wanted to tell you about was the real reason I started chasing after spooks and unnatural things. I haven't told a single person the whole story, but I think it will do my soul a world of good if I set it down here now for you when you're grown. Didn't have anything to do with all the dime novels and werewolf stories I hid from my Momma. What really inspired me and set me on this dark path was a peculiar conversation I had with the strangest dead man I ever did see.

I couldn't have been no older than six or seven at the time. In those days, I traveled with my Daddy when he went on his many sales trips around the dirt-poor towns of Texas. He'd think nothing of pulling me out of school when the mood struck him. Thought I got a better education on the road than in a schoolroom anyway. Daddy never made much money on his sales trips as far as I can remember. Guess there wasn't much call for sheet music or stereopticon shows if you were dirt poor. But Daddy just liked exploring out on the road and getting out of town I guess.

But I remember this particular April day we came into this town where people were running around like it was the Gold Rush. Woman and children combing the ground picking up shiny pieces of God knows what. My Daddy asked around and sure enough found out that some flying contraption had crashed to the ground just the other day and exploded into a million pieces. Thank God, nobody was hurt, but the poor pilot of the airship was killed outright, and they were set to bury him the next day.

There was rumor that the strange little fellow was a "man from Mars," but my Daddy, being a God-fearing man, would have none of that foolish talk. Nothing in the Good Book talked about no life on other planets so all this chattering was too close to blasphemy for my Daddy's liking. We passed the house where the dead pilot was being waked. Judge Proctor's place, I heard someone say. You understand that back in those days people paid their last respects in the living rooms of your relations, not in some orchid-scented funeral home like nowadays. They say homes were overflowing with the dead during a plague that settled on this same town just a few years back. I wanted to go in and see the body, but my Daddy said he's got no time to go to a stranger's wake. He smells a likely sale at the general store off the main road, so he pulls me along and tells me to wait outside. Strangest thing was watching all those good folks picking up shiny slivers no bigger than my thumb up and down the road. Without meaning to do so, I found myself kicking at some of the pieces with my shoe as I wandered around and before I knew it, I found myself back at the Judge's house.

Easy enough to sneak in seeing as how the door was wide open and people were coming and going. I was too young to know about funerals, never having even seen a single dead person. The living room was set nicely, like you would fix it up for company. Except here there was a little child's coffin closed up tight as a tick and set where you would have the drinks and serving trays. Struck me right away that something didn't seem normal. Maybe it was the small coffin, or maybe the scared looks on the faces of some of the mourners. Didn't take too long before most of the grown folks had cleared out of the room and I found myself alone in the Judge's parlor. Maybe they were getting ready to close up shop for the day, I don't rightly remember. But I'll never forget to my dying day what happened next. I swear to God that the coffin lid started creaking slowly open as I stood there just like in that Nosferatu movie. I didn't want to see what was moving around in that coffin, but I couldn't move a muscle, not even to close my eyes.

Sweet Jesus, Mary, and Joseph, but didn't that dead pilot sit straight up in his coffin! Still can't keep from trembling all over as I think about it even now. He turned to look at me, or at least I think he was looking at me because his head was wrapped all around in bandages. Bandages covered everything like he was King Tut's mummy. Even standing there shaking in my britches, I knew this thing didn't look human. The head was too big. It was clear double the size of a normal head bloated up it was like the stinking belly of a dead dog. Rest of the body, or at least what I could see of it, was about my size or maybe a bit bigger, like a ten-year-old. So it looks at me with it's covered-over eyes and bandage-wrapped mouth and asks me clear as day, "What time is it?"

It struck me that this was a most unnatural question, even coming as it was from a dead man. Was he running late for some appointment? Had a pleasant enough voice, I'll give him that. I stuttered some cock-and-bull answer because I didn't have a pocket watch and didn't rightly know how to tell time anyway. Then it said, "Who are you?" And quick as a whip, I answered, "I'm Lawless Scott Starkly, sir." And he said, polite as you please, "A pleasure to meet you, Lawless Scott Starkly. My name is Max As Abraxas."

Didn't sound like much of a proper name to me, so I had to ask several times for a spelling of it before I knew what he was saying. Then he said, "I think I'm going back to sleep now for a long time, but I just had to introduce myself to somebody. I have important work to do later." I gulped hard because it struck me then that maybe nobody else in the whole wide world knew who this fellow was laying here. Was anybody else seeing this? Then I heard my Daddy calling for me outside in the street. He sounded real angry. "I have to go now Mr. Abraxas," I said just like I would be saying goodbye to my Sunday school teacher. "Goodbye, little Lawless, I'm sure you will always remember our meeting today, won't you." He didn't say it like a question. It was more like a command. Then he laid his bloated bandaged head back down and the coffin lid slammed shut.

My Daddy found me soon enough when I ran out of that house like a jackrabbit with its tail on fire and he whupped my bottom till it was sore. Did I tell him what happened inside the Judge's house? What do you think?

Kept the story to myself I did as though it was the deepest, darkest secret in the world. Even a brain-addled six-year-old knows enough not to go around telling folks he had a "how-you-do?" visit with a corpse like it was exchanging small talk on Sunday morning. I recall telling Jeb Haskell and your Momma, God bless her soul, but I never told anyone the whole story, not till now that is.

But after that day, I reckon I changed myself inside out, if you take my meaning. I knew there were more things hidden in the world than they were telling me in the schoolroom or in church. Once you know that you can't rightly get it out of your head. And I wondered how many more secrets were out there that nobody was talking about. First, I started reading as many dime novels about spooks and haunts as I could lay my hands on. Then I started hunting them down myself. Sometimes with Jeb, but mostly just by myself. Never was that fearful about anything, although I don't know why that was so.

Now you're probably thinking right now that your old man just dozed off that April afternoon in that dusty Texas town and dreamed up the whole visit with the dead Martian. I guess it sounds like a dream now that I put it down on paper. Believe me, I tried to convince myself it was just a dream the first night after it happened.

But here's the strangest part, as I get older and older my meeting with Mr. Abraxas seems more real with every passing day and everything else in my life seems more like a dream. Fighting in the trenches in the Ardennes, meeting your Momma when I thought I had no more love left to give, seeing you the day you were born, all that and all the other stories I have left to tell, they all seem like dreams now. And sometimes I have to fight real hard to keep those memories from fading away after I wake up. But that spring afternoon in Judge Proctor's parlor seems more solid and more real, just like it happened the other day. Don't seem natural, does it? Every once in a long while I try to forget it, but it won't fade away. It seems stuck there in my head like it was nailed to my brain. Maybe now that I wrote it down here and passed it down to you, maybe now I can forget it.

Guess that's enough writing for today. I'll set more memories down on paper when the mood next strikes me. I promised that to your Momma and it's a promise I intend to keep.

Sincerely yours,

Your Daddy, Lawless Starkly

* * *

From Angel McQueen's personal email

July 24, 2015

Hi Doc,

Whoa! Did I have the strangest dream last night or what?

OK, so I haven't been keeping up with my lucid dreaming exercises since Kevin disappeared. I figure if Kevin skips town, why should I bother? But I was getting pretty good (if I say so myself) at recognizing when I was dreaming without waking up.

But I never could get down with that whole "controlling the dream scenario" thingie. I'd catch on real fast that I was dreaming, but I could never do anything to change it or even alter my behavior within the dream. So instead of feeling trapped in my dream, I was like, let's tighten the seat belts and go with the flow. No need to get my panties in a twist and go all control freak. I'd just go along for the ride and see where it takes me.

But last night I had an abduction nightmare that really scared the shit out of me.

So I'm dreaming that I'm lying in bed with the covers off because it's sooo hot and I'm wearing that cute Doctor Who collector's t-shirt that Brian bought for me when he was in London. But I can't move a muscle! I'm paralyzed from head to toe just like the time back in February. Then I start to lift off the bed and I'm fucking levitating, and I get this sick feeling in the pit of my stomach like I'm about to throw up. But I keep it together and I'm saying over and over again, "If this isn't nice, I must be dreaming."

I know I'm dreaming but I can't do anything about it. Arrgh! There's this God-awful shimmering light coming from the window. A sickly, green-tinged lurid glow that looks like something coming up from the bottom of the sea. And I know I'm being pulled right out that window. Ouch! I can feel the cuffs cutting into my wrist. The only thing holding me back is the handcuff attached to the headboard, but the brass rails are bending under the pressure twisting out of shape. I mean in another few seconds, maybe ten seconds tops, the cuffs will come loose from the bed and nothing is going to stop me from flying out that window feet first.

So I close my eyes because I'm terrified and I don't want to see what happens next. But while I have my eyes closed, I remember this lucid dreaming exercise that Kevin taught me. About how I can introduce something or someone new into the dream if I feel I can't handle it myself. I close my eyes and I wish that someone was in the room with me who could just grab me and stop the abduction. Just someone to hold me. My eyes are closed so tight and I'm wishing so hard that tears are streaming down my cheeks. I feel the cuffs break free from the bedpost with a POP. My eyes are still closed and I'm in complete freefall mode, unmoored from the world— from everything—and flying deeper into some nightmare.

Omg! But someone catches me before I go sailing into oblivion! These strong arms are wrapped around me holding tight. And nothing is pulling me anymore. There's no paralysis, nothing, nada. It's like some spell is broken.

So I can't wait to open my eyes and see who I conjured up to save my sorry ass, because honestly, I have no idea. I swear to God. I almost don't want to open my eyes. I just want to savor the mystery. So I'm thinking, "Is it Kevin?" Maybe it's Brian from London? Or maybe Josh, the first boy who ever kissed me when I still wore glasses. Maybe I've subconsciously summoned a Frankenstein-like amalgamation of all my old boyfriends. Gross!

So imagine my surprise when I open my peepers and come cheek-to-cheek with Tony Fermia. Damn! I swear I wasn't even thinking about that boy, at least not that particular night anyway. And there he is holding me, and he has this distracting goofy grin and those big moody dark eyes, and…you know. Now what do you suppose that all means?

From After the Quake Twitter feed:

@Afterthequake

I promised that we would both go together.

I watched as you ended it all last night in our kitchen.

But I didn't have the courage to follow.

Now I'm alone and afraid of what happens next.

Every choice fills me with terror.

From the Dream Journal of Anthony Fermi

July 24, 2015

The next time I saw Nikola Tesla we were standing in the Rocky Mountains. We were on a verdant plain surrounded by snow-capped peaks, like some ski resort postcard. Tesla was wearing a white lab coat and an odd pair of goggles when he came over to greet me.

"Welcome to my Wonderland in the Rockies, Antonio."

No sooner did I reach out to shake his hand than the scene shifted to the inside of a high-ceilinged laboratory. Machines with twitching dials and switches were everywhere and the air buzzed with electricity. It was like I dreamed myself into the middle of a James Whale Frankenstein movie, complete with mad scientist. The one thing I remember vividly were these two metal pillars each topped by a large copper sphere. Brilliant veins of lightning arced from one sphere to the other. I swear I could smell the ozone in the air. It was both oddly beautiful, and utterly terrifying.

"It is impressive, isn't it? Back in my laboratory in New York, it was impossible to produce electrical sparks twenty or thirty feet long; but here I produced some more than one hundred feet in length. The conditions in the pure mountain air proved extremely favorable for my experiments, and the results were most gratifying."

"What kind of experiments were you performing out here?" I asked.

Tesla seemed lost in thought as he rapidly flicked several switches while closely monitoring a gauge or two. After a minute he seemed genuinely startled to see me, as if he had quite forgotten that I was standing next to him.

"Didn't I tell you about my experiments? Well, I guess I assumed that every schoolboy has learned about my work in the same classes where they are introduced to the miracles of Edison and Marconi."

I had no idea what he was talking about. Would I be quizzed now about "pioneers in electricity?"

Tesla saw my hesitation and continued. "Don't worry, Antonio. Many people in my own profession have wondered what I am trying to do. Have you ever had that experience of trying to convince someone of your point of view, only to be interrupted abruptly by some vision taking form before your eyes, and the vision has solidity to it as if you could reach out and touch it?"

"No Niko, I don't ever recall that happening."

"No? Well no matter. At any rate, after my success with alternating current, I devised some simple apparatus for the wireless transmission of energy. But I knew I needed to use the Earth itself as the medium for conducting the currents. The difficulties I encountered at first in the transmission of currents through the earth were very great."

Tesla went on to describe some machine that was like a pump drawing electricity from the Earth. I didn't understand a word of it.

"Is that the machine over there?" I finally asked pointing to the sparking metal columns.

"This you see here is but a prologue to my greatest experiment, and alas, my greatest frustration." He looked away from me for a moment before he continued.

"I remember my work here near Pike's Peak with great fondness. When working with these powerful electrical oscillations the most extraordinary phenomena take place at times. Veritable balls of fire are apt to leap out to a great distance, and if anyone were within or near their paths, he would be instantly destroyed."

I stepped back a few feet from Tesla and his machine.

"A machine such as this could easily kill, in an instant, three hundred thousand persons. As you might imagine, the strain upon my assistants was telling, and some of them could not endure the extreme tension."

"Yeah, I could see that happening." I took another step back and started looking for an exit, but I couldn't see any doors or windows.

"But do you know the discovery I made here that truly captured my imagination? Heed me, Antonio, as you will need this information later. I can never forget the sensation I experienced when it dawned on me that I had observed something of incalculable consequence to mankind. I felt as though I were present at the revelation of a great truth."

"What did you discover?" I asked.

"My first observations positively terrified me, as there was present in them something mysterious, not to say supernatural."

"Niko, what are you talking about?" I noticed now that some of the instrument panels were sparking, as though some fuse had blown out. The electrical buzzing from the great metal columns increased in intensity until it sounded as though a thunderstorm was approaching. Even though Tesla was now shouting at me, I could barely hear him over the noise.

"Antonio, I am convinced that I had been the first to hear the greeting of one planet to another."

At that moment the laboratory exploded into a storm of electrical fireballs. Brightly charged plasma spheres whirled around us like meteors. My mind was filled with paralyzing images of death, of being disintegrated in an instant by the touch of one of the fireballs. Tesla stood frozen on the spot.

"You have to help me. How do you stop this?" I screamed.

"You have to do this yourself my boy. I can't help you."

I grabbed a valve and turned it frantically. I flicked switches up and down as fast as I could, all with no effect on the chaos flying around me.

"I don't have the knowledge to do this. I can't do this alone."

Then I clearly saw Angela standing firmly amidst all the flaming cacophony. Oblivious to all the danger swirling around her, she stood there smiling at me and holding out her right hand. There was a broken handcuff dangling from her wrist. When I looked at her face, I couldn't help but feel momentarily calmed. I heard her speaking clearly to me above the tumult, as though she was whispering in my ear.

She said, "Don't worry Tony, you'll know what to do."

I ran as several flaming spheres swooped down on me. I dropped to the floor and curled myself in a ball waiting for the inevitable fiery impact.

This time I awoke shaking and covered in sweat. I hate it when that happens.

* * *

From *The Last Days of Nikola Tesla: Secrets Behind the World's Greatest Mad Scientist* **by E.G. Hardwicke (Penguin Books, 2013)**

September 5, 1917

Dear Luka (*Tesla's nickname for longtime friend, Robert Underwood Johnson—Ed*),

Against your best advice I returned to Wardenclyffe, a day after they had dynamited my transmission tower into rubble. I'm afraid I should have listened to you. I did not exactly cry when I saw my place after so long an interval, but I came very close.

The notion that my tower was used as a spy nest for German saboteurs is too absurd to warrant any serious consideration at all.

However, it reminded me of an important piece of unfinished business that I'm hoping you may attend to at a future date.

I apologize in advance for any burden you may suffer in fulfilling my request. To be honest, I don't know who else I could possibly entrust with the task.

I will give you full details and instructions when we meet at the laboratory next week. I know I don't need to mention that this is all to be held in the strictest confidence—even from Madame Filipov—and not even a hint in *Century*.

It would not be an exaggeration to say that you not only do me a great favor, but you perform a great service for all mankind.

Yours truly,

Nikola

* * *

From Snopes.com

Claim: The U.S. Government is behind the increase in suicides across the country

Status: Inconclusive

Example (collected on the Internet): There is a secret U.S. government mind control program headed up by the spooks in Homeland Security or the NSA that is causing the alarming increase in suicides across all age groups around the country, and maybe the world. One often-repeated theory is that it is a counter-terrorism experiment that went tragically out of control and has affected thousands if not millions of innocent civilians. The next most popular theory is that this "suicide plague" is a deliberately orchestrated action by the U.S. government to cause a nation-wide panic so that draconian measures severely limiting our Constitutional liberties can be enacted by the White House and rubber-stamped by a fearful Congress.

Origins: Certainly the reality of the so-called "suicide plague" is undisputed. The best overall review of the situation is probably this recent Lancet article (www.lancet.com/articles/suicide-watch) or any number of consumer reports in the media. Following a small increase in suicides among boomers starting in 1999, the suicide rate nearly doubled across all age groups within a few short years. Among men and women ages 25-39, suicides increased anywhere from 45-50 percent, with an even greater incidence of attempted suicides. Unfortunately, this unfolding tragedy is the perfect breeding ground for any number of paranoid conspiracy theories to take root. The only fact experts can agree on is that the cause of the suicide outbreaks (and a 23 percent increase in missing person reports, we might add) is undetermined. The medical community is baffled, but a number of hypotheses have been offered, ranging from depression caused as a side effect of allergy and pain medications, to mental illness caused by social media, to a general millennial ennui. Political blogs and pundits are spinning the recently called Congressional hearings into the matter as "evidence" for the most half-baked paranoid fantasies. There is no typical victim profile with recent cases cutting across all age, race, and class boundaries. We'll take a wait-and-see attitude as we follow the Capital Hill investigation, but it seems unlikely that any political mischief is driving this phenomenon.

Graffiti spotted on the corner of NW 17 and Classon, Oklahoma City:

THE PILOT HAS AWAKENED

From *An Examination of the Youth Suicide Epidemic*

Harvard Institute of Epidemiology Research

Between 1950 and 1990, youth suicide rates tripled (particularly among young men), while suicide rates for adults fell by 7 percent and suicide rates for the elderly fell by 30 percent (See Fig. 2). As we approach the middle of the second decade of the 21st century, suicide is the leading cause of death for youth in the US overtaking accidents and homicide, while it is the second leading cause of death for youth in Canada, Australia, New Zealand, and much of Western Europe.

If youth suicide is an epidemic, attempted suicide is a plague of biblical proportions. For every teen that commits suicide, another 1000 teens report attempting suicide, 400 report requiring medical attention for a suicide attempt, and 100 are hospitalized for a suicide attempt.

Why have youth suicide rates increased so much, even as suicide among the elderly has leveled out? Why are there so many suicide attempts?

This paper will examine several of the theories advanced to answer these questions. The following two case studies are representative of the recent rise in youth suicide. They also foreshadow several questions that we address later in this paper: What factor do "missing time" occurrences and other social stressors play in the suicide epidemic? What is the role of peer pressure or social contagion in youth suicide? The first case is reported by Wilcox and Wilson (2015):

"It was on June 1 when the parents of 18-year-old Cliff Peters brought their son to my practice outside of Boston. He had slit his wrists in the shower the day before and passed out. Aside from a mild concussion and two superficial cuts he was relatively unharmed. The parents reported that Cliff had recently gone on a camping trip to Mount Shasta with several friends during spring break. Somehow, he had gotten separated from his friends for several days, although Cliff claimed to have no memory of his lost time. After his return, the parents noticed a marked change in his behavior. He appeared sullen, depressed, and uninterested in school activities. Previously, Cliff was a talented track and field athlete who was looking forward to his senior prom. He professed to have no appetite and often had trouble falling asleep at night. During my initial examination he told me that sleep no longer relaxed or revived him. It offered him no solace. Or as he reported to me, 'My dreams are all wrong now.' I could detect no obvious signs of drug abuse or personal problems. There was nothing beyond the typical stresses of final exams and worries about college. We arranged for another session the following week and I prescribed a selective serotonin re-uptake inhibitor (SSRI) immediately.

The next day during the middle of his World Literature class, Cliff Peters without warning crashed through a closed window and fell to his death. He was impaled on the metal gate under his classroom."

The second case occurs in Miami Beach, Florida and was witnessed by one of the authors (Nilssen, 2015). Within a six-month period, a suicide epidemic swept through one of the white, predominantly high-income gated communities of the city affecting an unusual proportion of young women. The community was perceived by many observers, both insiders and outsiders, as relatively insulated from many of the social stressors common to the surrounding area. Organized crime and substance abuse were not widespread problems. The decline in housing prices and increasing foreclosures, while not unknown in the neighborhood, were nowhere near the levels seen elsewhere in the city. Yet, given an estimated population of about 1300 teenagers and young adults in this community, there was a 48 percent higher suicide rate in the community than the year before; and at least a ten-fold increase in cases requiring medical hospitalization.

The case of 24-year-old Cindy Hutton is representative of many of the suicides in that neighborhood. Recently married with a six-month old daughter, Cindy was a stay-at-home mother who volunteered at her local church. The family had no unusual health problems and Cindy in particular had no history of psychiatric problems. Both Cindy and her daughter were found dead in the front seat of their SUV. She had closed the garage doors and left the engine running soon after the husband left on a weekend business trip. Both succumbed to carbon monoxide poisoning. The police found the following note left in the daughter's crib: "I'm sorry for what I must do. I can't think of any other way around this. Any other good mother would push her child out of the way of an oncoming train. Little Cherie is safe now in heaven. God forgive me."

It may be significant that local news coverage was fixated day and night on many of the successful suicides taking place in the area. In fact, two of Cindy's closest friends, both members of a local book club, had hung themselves in their homes the previous week.

* * *

Email from Anthony Fermia to Kevin Starkly

July 25, 2015

Dear Kevin,

I don't know if you're even checking any of your emails anymore, but I had to tell someone about what happened last night. If you see Rich and John before I do don't blurt it out to them all at once, OK?

I guess you should know that I've decided to come along on this misbegotten adventure after all. I promised you in the beginning that I was part of the team and I pledged to stay in this game all summer long until the bitter end. The library's not expecting me back on the job until August anyway. I might even still attend Gen Con.

I realize now that it was all about Aurora even from the beginning. All that talk about evidence "buried in the ground" is fairly obvious in retrospect. But I couldn't have done it without Angela's help. She's such a gem, a real treasure. But you know that already. She says she's cool with me leaving NY and traveling to Texas, but I don't think she's telling the truth. We got together the other night for a "kickass farewell party" arranged by Angel. She invited me to hear her perform with this group she hangs with called the Bushwick Nipple Magnets at that place in Greenpoint we always joked about. The band is OK—they do mostly covers of classic New Wave and Goth stuff but the drummer says they're working on some original material too. But the real revelation was seeing Angel performing on stage. You never said how great she is!

Oh wait. I forgot; you never told me anything about her at all.

With her long legs and dark bangs, she's more Bettie Page than Elvira. And she kicks into those guitar riffs with a self-assurance I never see offstage. I think she calls herself Angela Starr. One time she took the mike and did the lead vocals on that Flock of Seagulls song "I Ran." She exudes this scary sexy longing like Annie Lennox circa 1984, and I fall in love with her all over again. I think we both had too much to drink and I probably should have declined when Angel invited me back to her place.

That's what I want to tell you. I want to tell you that Angel is such a major part of my life now. She started as just a fond memory shining out from an otherwise forgettable high school experience. And now I can't imagine being apart from her. I remember one of our first conversations after she told me about "Night Terror." I asked her how she's doing after all these years. And she said, "You know how it is, you try to do something with your life before life does something to you. I guess I'm running a little behind on that score." She mentioned making most of her money from freelance music PR and marketing work, but she really loved performing onstage herself.

Then tonight while Angel played a few of her prized vinyl LPs—some 70's rock anthems, The Cure, some R&B, I think—she told me, "You should know Tony that I've done really stupid things with boys over the years." It was such an out-of-left-field comment that I didn't know what to say. So as usual I said something completely lame like, "You mean like the time you slipped those ice cubes down my pants?" Thank God, she started laughing just as I realized what a clueless jerk I am. "All things considered," she said, "I probably should have slipped a lot more ice cubes down a lot more pants."

Then just like that she's off showing me this compilation of science-fiction movie soundtracks she just ordered from Rhino. And just as I start to think we're headed into another trivial conversation comparing and contrasting our favorite B-movies, she reveals that she's always wanted to start her own indie Goth band. "Maybe something like Angela Starr and The Flying Serpents of Death," she says only half-jokingly. You know how Angela has this disarming habit of starting to undress right in the middle of a conversation? Maybe you don't know. Anyway, she starts unzipping her leather boots and sliding them off, and then she gives a little provocative sideways glance just to check that I'm enjoying the view. It's all part of her casual sensuality that leaves me tongue-tied and so aroused I can't think straight. Then she flops on the bed feigning exhaustion. At this point it was around midnight. Without looking at me, almost as if she's addressing the books on her bedside table she says, "Sometimes I wonder if I'll ever be anything except Meteor Girl. I'm afraid this one terrifying incident has trapped me forever." I sit down next to her and for some reason which I still can't fathom I reveal this deep fear that I've never told anybody. In fact, I don't think I've ever admitted it even to myself. "I'm afraid that I'll always be this freak that talks to dead people in his dreams. Sometimes, I wish it would just stop so I could at least pretend I was normal." We sat together silently on her bed for a minute or two listening to the music playing. Then, as if on cue, your song comes on— "Calling Occupants of Interplanetary Craft" by Klaatu.

I look over at Angel and she's smoothing down a part of the bed sheet and I realize that neither one of us wants our time together to end. Trying desperately to think of something to say, I ask, "How does it feel sleeping with handcuffs on every night?" She smiles and grabs the handcuffs from her bedside table. "Do you want to find out?"

Before I could even think of an answer, let alone protest, Angel was already instructing me in the finer points of manacled sleep. "Lie on your back and stretch out your arms behind you…just like that." She nonchalantly starts shimmying out of her skirt as she says, "It doesn't hurt if that's what you're worried about you big baby." I lay back on the bed as Angel straddles me at waist level. She stretches over me so closely her breasts brush against my left arm as she snaps the cuffs shut on my wrist. She clasps the other cuff to a spot on the big brass headboard that looks well-worn from repeated rubbing. As she rises over me her dark hair falls across my face and I'm completely trapped by her presence, locked in by her scent and her body heat. She looks down on me tantalizingly out of reach and I know that I wouldn't want to be anywhere else in the world but here.

"How does that feel?"

I can't think of anything else to say except, "If this isn't nice, I must be dreaming." Yeah, I stole your line. So sue me.

"Sweetie, this is your dream come true." And then she started slowly unbuttoning her blouse, her body swaying to the music. I tried to reach out to touch her with my right hand, almost forgetting that my left hand was shackled to the bedpost. She only smiled and slapped my hand aside saying, "Patience!"

Angel accommodated my desire by caressing herself. Tenderly, she moved her hands across every curve of her body, stroking her breasts, then down to her thighs. And just when I thought I couldn't stand it any longer, she stretched her body on top of mine and our mouths came together with a hunger and longing that was frightening. I kissed her everywhere, desperate to taste every inch of her body. First her lips, then the flying serpent tattoo on the back of her neck, then her shoulders. If this was a dream, it was one we both wanted to share for at least this one night.

Sometime after we made love, Angel removed the other cuff from the headboard and attached it to her right hand, so we were joined together as we slept. There we were face-to-face, two freaks in love. And in chains. We're the only pair known to exist in captivity.

Don't worry Kevin, I'm not pissed with you anymore about jealously hiding Angel away from me. I've figured out that Angel was never anything more to you than just your secret dream experiment. You just used her to prove another half-baked theory. The fact that I had a crush on her since high school was irrelevant—if you even remembered it at all. So no hard feelings, but dude, you've really got to work on honing those social skills. And if you're out there monitoring this in some way, just remember not to tell Rich and John about this Angel stuff. I want to do it myself first. – Cheers, Tony

* * *

From "Headless Body Found in Morbid Maze Gallery"

New York Post, July 25, 2015

Jumbled props and relics—from obsolete computers to plaster death masks to broken mannequins—are everyday fare at Brooklyn's own Last Round Gallery; so co-curator Patti Halyak didn't think twice last night when she saw a decapitated body in a blue suit sitting in the gallery.

But this was no art display.

It was the remains of security guard Dennis Halloran who was butchered last night while making his rounds of a maze-like exhibition of junk and reams of paper based on the infamous Collyer Brothers' home.

"I thought it was like a movie prop or something," said Halyak. "But then I see the bleeding head just looking at me from a smashed vitrine on the other side of the room, and I knew it was real."

The only other person in the gallery who saw the bloody spectacle before police arrived last night was artist Lilith Greaves who was rushed to Methodist Hospital in Park Slope suffering from shock.

"She was just laughing and laughing like she couldn't stop. She couldn't breathe, she was laughing so hard like she was in hysterics," said Halyak.

Police are asking anybody with any knowledge of the murder to step forward. The owner of the Last Round Gallery, John Walters, could not be reached for comment. The exhibition "Collyer Brothers Redux" has been closed until further notice.

* * *

Emails from Anthony Fermia to John Walters and Rich Harrigan

July 25

Tony Fermia writes:

Sorry guys, I missed my flight on Delta, but I reserved another direct flight to Nashville airport arriving at 12:10. I hope you can still pick me up. Angel is terrified after hearing about that murder last night at Johnny's gallery. We were just there the other day and it's pretty obvious what the Collector Killer was searching for. This is getting too close for comfort. Anyway, Angel's staying with her cousin out on Montauk.

Also, if that's not enough, there's a new scare story posted by Kevin on fanfiction.net. It's titled "Peabody's Last Patient", and I don't know what it means, but I'm pretty sure it's some kind of warning.

John Walters writes:

Wish to God we could all just go back home. Sorry now I left Patti all alone with this mess. Maybe Angel's got the right idea. We're all targets now—need to hide.

But Rich reminds me that we're getting closer to the truth. We have to finish this mission and find Kevin even it means traveling to a cemetery in Aurora, Texas.

Still puzzled by a number of things that don't make sense. I'm still trying to figure out why Kevin posted "Night Terror." Clearly it was to hook us up with Angela and Dr. Stryker, but why? Thank God, we were traveling to meet with Stryker at Fanvention when that freak (Collector Killer?) contacted us, otherwise we might have faced him on his own terms, and I would be dead right now. But how could Kevin have known that? Has his abduction given him the power to see the future?—JW

Rich Harrigan writes:

I've just read "Peabody's Last Patient" and I've spotted a disturbing similarity between the two tales from Starkly. Both involve mentally damaged physicians with unsettling secrets. Maybe Starkly unconsciously is revealing more about himself than anything else.

From Myth-America.com

July 25, 2015

Geek Freaks Across America, The Trip Continues

By Richard Harrigan

Several readers have asked me over the years if there is a Holy Grail, or more accurately, a Rosetta Stone, that paranormal researchers like Kevin and the rest of us on this blog, are actively questing after.

We all believed that if it was indeed impossible to unravel the mystery of this slippery phenomenon head-on, maybe we could chip away at it around the periphery. As Starkly would often say you had to search for "the telltale fingerprints" carelessly left behind. Maybe there was a forgotten clue that most others would deem insignificant.

Anyway, it seems clear now, that Starkly believed that this forgotten clue, this key to unlocking the mystery of everything strange, is buried in a cemetery in Aurora, Texas. This was his Rosetta Stone, the careless clue left behind at the scene of the crime. At last, here would be the physical evidence that everyone was searching for...the bones, the DNA of some alien race, or maybe ectoplasm, or maybe...something else entirely.

I have to admit, I never gave this nonsense much credit. Yet, unbelievably, The Nerd Legion can now verify that something decidedly bizarre occurred in Aurora in 1897. Unfortunately, I can't reveal any details yet. But one thing seems clear now as never before—the real end point for our summer journey was always Aurora, Texas. And that is precisely where we are headed right now, first driving through Nashville, Tennessee. Perhaps we will uncover the answer to the greatest mysteries of the unknown. Will we reveal the key clue unlocking the UFO puzzle, or alien abductions, or poltergeist hauntings? I don't know. But I hope we will find Kevin Starkly waiting for us patiently at the cemetery gate asking, "What took you so long?"

Posted by drrich

Post Comments

Kunstkammer Kids writes:

Don't it just beat all that you boys are finally coming to our neck of the woods? We've been following you on your blog since about last year. Why don't you boys come down I 40 out of Nashville and set a spell here at our Arcanium dime museum. We can sit up and shoot the breeze all night if you like, but you probably want to get all rested and refreshed before your big day in Texas. Can't say it's as classy as a Motel 6, but the price is right. The couch-surfing is free, but we may charge you some to get a sneak peek behind the door of the Arcanium! Contact us online and let's get together for some southern hospitality.

PEABODY'S LAST PATIENT

Doctor Howard Peabody stared at the rows and rows of identical steel sheds stretching into the distance like little Levittowns of deferred dreams and quickly concluded that this house call would be difficult, if not hopeless. He had driven more than two hours in the sweltering heat along dusty Oklahoma back roads to arrive at this godforsaken self-storage facility smack in the middle of nowhere. Over the years, Peabody had grown accustomed to meeting his special patients at discreet locations, usually far from their offices or homes. In fact, Peabody had done some of his best work in decrepit motel rooms, in the VIP lounges of exclusive clubs, and in the kitchens of four-star restaurants after closing time. But nobody before had ever asked to rendezvous at one of those narrow storage containers that barely had enough light to see, let alone the necessary space to operate.

Villages of self-storage units had started springing up all over the Sooner State, an outgrowth of sudden foreclosures and the mortgage meltdown of the last few years. Peabody wondered what secrets were locked inside, what family treasures sat neglected awaiting better days that would never come. The place was desolate. Nobody, not even a security guard, was in sight. Then, right along a row in the middle of the complex, he spotted his last special patient of the day waiting outside storage shed H699.

"Dr. Peabody, I presume?" They shook hands and all seemed normal enough and not at all like two strangers meeting along a dusty road in the middle of the night for a round of clandestine surgery.

Peabody's first reaction upon meeting the mysterious man he only knew as "Mr. B" was, "Oh shit, I hope I brought enough anesthesia."

The roly-poly gentleman had a body mass index that would probably wreak havoc with any drug titration estimates. That was one of the many reasons Peabody despised fat patients—he could never guess the proper dosage for medications. It was always trial and error, and too many errors at that. Mr. B had requested the removal of "an inconvenient growth" and Peabody prayed that the operation could be accomplished under a local.

Peabody couldn't help smiling as he tried to imagine what his proper father would make of all this. Peabody had kept his eccentric late-night activities relatively hidden from family and colleagues, although rumors had been whispered over the years. Peabody was particularly amused that even his regular 9-5 activities filled his family with unbearable disgust. His father threw a fit when his youngest son announced he would take up private practice in one of the poorest neighborhoods in the city. He had planned all along that his two sons—Howard and his older brother—would join him in lifting and sculpting some of the wealthiest sagging faces in Tulsa.

And mother was sorely dismayed when he rejected her choice for a proper wife. "Howard, I do hope you can join us for dinner at the club this Saturday," she said. "That lovely young lady, Mary Anne, will be joining us. You know her, don't you? Her Daddy, Dr. West, teaches at OU." Of course, Peabody declined the invitation.

His wealthy friends were appalled that Howard was a GP and not even a damn dermatologist for God's sake. Where was the money in that? Where was the prestige? Lesser men, maybe even cowardly men as Peabody imagined them, would only choose the safer path that was expected of them. Peabody smiled because more than anything else in his life, he was pleased with the small amount of freedom he had carved out for himself against all odds. It was a freedom that entailed making hard choices. But he entertained neither false modesty nor foolish regrets. Somebody had to help these poor creatures, so why not him? His practice in southeast Tulsa brought him into daily contact with the most hapless and helpless speci- mens of society. Here the barely pubescent girl pleaded for free birth con- trol without her mother's permission. Here the illegal day laborer sought opioids to take the edge off his aching back. Peabody made sure he kept all his proper forms in order so as not to trigger any inconvenient investiga- tions from the state watchdogs. Peabody thought of these "morality police" as little more than yapping dogs—border collies keeping the sheep in line.

Howard Peabody had always considered himself a good doctor. Perhaps not in the sense of a superlative or even accomplished professional—indeed, his surgical skills were only modest at best—but certainly in the all-important moral sense. He had seen and experienced more in his last ten years than perhaps any other doctor his age. It was a breathtakingly varied moral landscape where the choices were never easy or simple, but Howard believed he had always chosen wisely.

"I hope you don't mind that I asked you out here, so far from the city. I merely wished to finish some business before you, that is…before my operation."

Mr. B. had a slight accent that Peabody found difficult to place: Italian? Greek? At any rate, judging by the obese man's clothing and demeanor, he must certainly be one of his wealthier clients. In fact, Mr. B. seemed overdressed for the occasion. Perhaps he made his excuses and exited from a formal dinner in order to make his secret tryst for the evening. Peabody had given up years ago trying to second guess his patients' bizarre behavior and requests. He wasn't apathetic exactly, just judiciously incurious. It was not his business after all to judge these poor souls—it was just to relieve them of their suffering, whether real or imagined.

Peabody hated making polite conversation with his patients. It seemed so unnecessary, a waste of his time. He made a good show of simulating an interested response. "What kind of business are you conducting out here?"

Mr. B. fiddled with a ring of jangling keys he produced from his neatly embroidered vest. "I suppose you could say I'm in the export business. I have a number of these storage units that I keep in various cities around the western states."

With a quick motion that startled Peabody, Mr. B. rolled up the entry gate like a rickety garage door. "The items I've stored here are from my own personal collection gathered during my travels. Believe me, none of this is for sale. I like to check on it from time to time when I'm in town just to ensure that everything is in order. Now where is that light?"

It wasn't the darkness inside the container that made Peabody uneasy, but the slightly phosphorescent glow of some of the objects. What exactly did he collect? It wasn't much better when the fluorescent lights were switched on. The dim lamps didn't so much illuminate the room as chase a few more shadows into the corners. It took a few seconds for Peabody's eyes to grow accustomed to the light, but he still couldn't believe what he saw.

The narrow space was packed with metal laboratory shelves stocked with jumbled collections of dusty specimen jars. He felt like he was a child again at the Oklahoma State Fair sneaking behind the curtain of that forbidden freak show tent. One jar held the remains of a deformed human fetus. At least he thought it was human. On closer inspection, the head was far too large, and the fetus seemed more like a wrinkled old man that had shrunk to the size of a newborn. Peabody wondered if it was a horrific case of advanced Progeria Syndrome. On another shelf was a collection of ancient glass jars whose contents were obscured from view by cloudy water. Peabody could swear he heard a distinct humming or buzzing coming from the jars. Out of the corner of his eye he caught fleeting, tantalizing glimpses of creatures too bizarre to be real. One looked similar to pictures he'd seen of those dark deep-sea monstrosities, but it had seven eel-like heads attached to a reptilian body. He tried to convince himself that these were collections of dime museum gaffs—parts of different animals stitched together to create abominations that never existed in nature. But he noticed that some of the specimens appeared to twitch in the jars, moving ever so slightly. Peabody stepped back and decided that maybe it was best not to look at these things too closely.

The sudden wave of unexpected dread reminded Peabody of his first special patient almost ten years ago. Answering a desperate plea for help on a DIY medical online forum ("I think I've fucked myself up real bad"), Peabody found himself in the middle of a down-at-the-heels trailer park just outside Dallas attending to a Mexican male prostitute no older than 23. The young man shivered uncontrollably in the dry June air and wrapped himself deeper inside an oversized trench coat. Peabody could feel waves of fever heat radiating from the patient's sweat-drenched body.

As they agreed during their last email exchange, the young man had cleared some space on the small table in his efficiency kitchen effectively beginning its transformation into an efficiency OR. The problem was painfully obvious once he dropped his pants. He had hacked away at the bothersome remainder of his manhood with a serrated steak knife but was only partially successful with his do-it-yourself sex change operation. That is to say—it was a disaster. The mutilated penis was now a grotesque ground zero of raging infection threatening to poison his entire body.

Peabody required less anesthesia than he originally guessed—the thin hooker passed out within seconds on the kitchen table. The telenovela playing on the TV in the next room provided an incongruous but not unpleasant background soundtrack for the operation. The emaciated Mexican would need to recover for a few days and stick to a strict regimen of full-spectrum antibiotics to fight the wide-ranging infection, but he felt certain that his special patient could soon start a new life. In gratitude the young man insisted that Peabody take all of the jewelry he "inherited" from his grandmother. It was all stored in a Ziplock baggie hidden under the bed. The patient decided to keep only a pair of cheap jingle-jangle earrings that sounded for all the world like Christmas bells. The cache of jewelry turned out to be a bigger bounty than Peabody had any right to expect. Emerald brooches, a diamond engagement ring, and real ivory cameos, were indiscriminately mixed in with cheap costume jewelry and kitschy turquoise baubles.

Of course, the money was always secondary. He was proud to have saved a life that society had all but forgotten. Was it reckless and dangerous behavior? Perhaps to those lesser men Peabody despised, who measured their small, cowardly lives in triplicate forms and Blackberries.

The world changed profoundly for Peabody after that night, and in ways he never could have predicted. His daily routine now seemed worse than mundane. It was stifling. It would take all his stamina to simply refrain from screaming of boredom in the middle of the afternoon after hearing a dozen old ladies complaining of arthritis and high blood pressure. He had uncovered an underground economy for doctors willing to perform certain operations with no questions asked, and it frankly thrilled him. Peabody was proud that over the years he had attained a kind of notoriety for his services. He became quite an expert at removing unwanted limbs and performing unorthodox cosmetic surgery. Finally, he thought he was providing a valuable service to those patients who needed the most help because they had lost faith in the healthcare system.

As his special patients took up more and more of his time, Peabody started catering to wealthier patrons as well. Their demands were stranger, but no less necessary in their eyes. As the years blurred together, his memories of these late-night encounters resembled the hallucinations of an ICU patient. He could no longer readily distinguish whether some of his memories were of real events or only nightmares. And only he could possibly know because he shared these private stories with no other living soul. So he couldn't very well call his brother to verify the case of that car dealer who needed several holes drilled into his skull to release the personal demons trapped inside. Then there was the MIT engineer who had successfully attached a robotic claw where he had chopped off his own hand, but now needed help removing his perfectly healthy larynx so it could be replaced by an electronic voice box. And then there was the grand society matron who wanted another pair of breasts stitched to her back to help excite the fantasies of her younger lover.

No, it had been years since Peabody complained of boredom.

Most patients sought his help outright or were referred by other satisfied customers. Sometimes he searched for likely prospects by reading the various medical chat rooms online that most people don't even know exist. Peabody even turned to Craigslist, placing simple offers on the Services board: "Need medical help? Have you been turned away by other doctors? This MD understands your problems. No questions asked. House calls are my specialty."

It was a response to one such online listing that brought him out to this obscure stretch of road in the Oklahoma Panhandle on this stifling evening.

Attempting to distract himself from the things gathered on the shelves, Peabody made the mistake of looking up at the ceiling of the shed. At first glance, he thought it was an exotic life-size mermaid figurehead pulled from the prow of a ship. But he realized that this was no carved wooden figure suspended from wires but real flesh and bone—as real a mermaid as he could ever imagine, with a scaly tapering fish tail and shockingly human features from the waist up. As he stepped under it, he noticed to his horror that the creature was sliced down the middle with a Y-incision as one would fillet a corpse during an autopsy. Her arms were outstretched so he could clearly see that the flesh had been pulled aside and pinned in place, so the organs were clearly visible. The incision ran from her scaly stomach to her breastbone. But it was her face that disturbed him the most—the shriveled leathery flesh of her face and the eyeless sockets, and her mouth opened wide in a silent scream.

"I see you've noticed one of the true prizes of my collection." Peabody jumped nearly a foot as he had quite forgotten that Mr. B was still in the room. "This is the original Fiji Mermaid, the one talked about in sailors' legend that inspired a legion of fakes, including the one P.T. Barnum put on display in his American Museum in New York in 1842. This one was caught swimming among the Fiji Islands by a whaling ship around the turn of the 19th century, and it has remained hidden in private collections to the present day. They did a remarkable job preserving the specimen, don't you think Doctor? You can still see the webbed fingers."

"You mean all of this is supposed to be real?"

"Supposed to be real?" Mr. B. chuckled slightly. "I can assure you that everything here is the genuine article. I detest forgeries. In fact, I had to pass up several competent fakes before I finally came across this stunning artifact here."

His sausage fingers pointed to what looked like a human skull made of glass. With a sickening shudder, Peabody realized that this was one of the things glowing in the darkness. Even as he gazed at it now under the dull florescent light, he was certain the skull emitted an unearthly aura. Mr. B lifted it gingerly, lovingly, and he could see that the jawbone and skull were all carved from one solid piece.

"Of course, there are many crystal skulls including the famous ones at the British Museum and the Musèe de l'homme in Paris, all of them pretending to be the real thing. But this my good doctor, is the genuine prize that any student of antiquities would sell his soul to possess. Would you like to hold it?"

Peabody shook his head and perhaps protested too much. Mr. B. seemed offended.

"The other skulls were all carved using modern lapidary tools. But they were honest attempts to recreate this ancient original object. This was the revered holy item used in the most sacred of ceremonies by the high priests of the Mayan people in the great city of Chichén Itzá. It was roughly shaped from a block of quartz and then polished to perfection using coarse sand mixed with the blood of human sacrifices over a period of decades. It was a reminder to the Mayans of their own mortality, and of the insatiable appetites of their dark gods."

Peabody seemed drawn into the discussion against his better judgment. "Exactly what kind of collection is this?"

Mr. B. grinned with an air of self-satisfaction. Obviously, he didn't have many chances to discuss his work with others and he seemed to relish this opportunity. "I have spent most of my life cataloging and collecting the greatest hidden treasures of occult knowledge. Artifacts and specimens dismissed by mainstream science and described only in obscure journals. Lost things hidden for so long that they have been forgotten by mankind. I've gathered them here and in other places like this around the country."

Oddly, Peabody seemed relieved. He had seen this type of self-deluded loon before—the punk rocker who believed he was the reincarnation of the god Bacchus came to mind. They were tiresome, but not dangerous. Ever since he first stepped into this storage container, he felt an unshakeable chill of impending disaster, but now he was reassured. Maybe he would even enjoy a good laugh as this jolly fellow would inevitably pull out the lost Philosopher's Stone, or perhaps a fragment of the True Cross.

"Is there a good consumer demand for these kinds of...of hidden treasures?"

"Oh, most of these treasures are not for sale. My main business inventory is located elsewhere. I mostly hunt these items for my own personal satisfaction. You of all people, Dr. Peabody, must understand the satisfaction of a job well done."

Peabody shifted uneasily. The weight of his medical instruments was growing heavier by the minute. "It's getting late Mr. B., perhaps you can show me the operating table now."

Mr. B. seemed disappointed, as if he hoped this guided tour could continue a little longer. "Of course, I suppose I've prattled on for too long already. There's a table back here that should be suitable."

He moved deeper into the half light of the room and Peabody was struck anew by the oppressive heat and the confined space. Although, he had to admit that the interior seemed more spacious than he would have guessed by looking at the outside.

Mr. B. started clearing objects from a small table. Some he just pushed to the floor with a clatter, others he gingerly replaced on one of the many shelves. He held up a glass container that held the most beautiful feather Peabody had ever seen. It shimmered with a rose-tinted iridescence that seemed quite out of place with the other unnatural objects surrounding it. "This is a feather from the wings of the Archangel Gabriel. It was originally in a reliquary in El Escorial, near Madrid for centuries. Now it's mine. I only regret that I wasn't there myself to witness how it was plucked from his hide." It was then that Peabody noticed the buzzing and humming he heard earlier had altered imperceptibly into the sound of voices—distant muted voices—and perhaps also the sound of footsteps. Peabody abruptly turned half-expecting to see several shadowy shapes sneaking up behind him. But no one was there.

"Did you hear something just now?"

His last patient of the day didn't even bother looking up as he finished clearing the table. "It's probably coming from next door. I actually have more of my collection in the containers surrounding this one."

The voices stopped as did the footsteps. Peabody decided then and there that he would perform his surgery and exit this place as quickly as possible.

"Doctor Peabody, I almost forgot to show this to you. I thought you, as a man of science, would be particularly interested in this item." Before he could protest, Mr. B. had pulled a drop cloth from a nearby child-sized coffin.

"Here is the final resting place for the greatest achievement of John Murray Spears. He started out as a Universalist minister but soon came to believe that a group of spirit guides calling themselves the 'Band of Electricizes,' dedicated to elevating the human race through advanced technology, wanted him to create a new link to God, a man-made Messiah promising communion between the sacred and the mundane. Along with some devoted followers including his secret mistress, they gave 'birth,' in a manner of speaking, to a divine machine in 1853—a wonderful living hybrid that never existed before in nature. Unfortunately, some of the more traditionally religious did not see things exactly the same way. They accused him of blasphemy and one night they destroyed his wonderful invention, pulling it apart limb from limb."

Mr. B. pried open the coffin lid to reveal a messy jumble of wires and metal pipes and copper plates scattered with materials Peabody couldn't identify. But he was certain he saw human bones bolted to metal pieces; bone fragments enmeshed in electrical wire. There was a small femur and thigh bone and scapula. And sleek porcelain limbs like the parts of a doll. Among the bones and metal and doll limbs, Peabody also saw several glass eyes, the kind taxidermists use to create life-like specimens. His brain throbbed trying to mentally piece together the hideous jigsaw puzzle before him, as if refusing to see the total picture.

"It didn't turn out to be a very successful New Messiah. It barely had a chance to speak its first words before it was torn apart."

Peabody could barely hide his disgust. "Why are you telling me this insane story?"

"I'm truly sorry if I somehow offended you, Doctor Peabody. I meant no disrespect. I simply thought that as a man of medicine who has devoted most of his life to pushing the boundaries of conventional surgery, I thought you might enjoy this memento from a fellow pioneer."

Peabody wiped the sweat from his face. He was again uncomfortably aware of the stifling heat. "I don't know who you think I am, but I'm no pioneer like…like this." He pointed in the general direction of the small coffin.

Mr. B. laughed a truly unsettling laugh. "You are simply too modest, Dr. Peabody. I have kept an eye on you over the past several years, admiring your work from a distance. You are a special surgeon who doesn't kowtow to the ridiculous ethical guidelines of your fellow practitioners. Doctor… May I call you Howard?"

He nodded, although Peabody had no idea how this strange man knew his name. He made a point of never sharing his accomplishments with any of his special patients. Many times he never even shared his last name. And he was suspicious of anyone who claimed to admire his work over the years. "How do you know…?"

"I make it a habit to know a good many secrets about a great number of people," said Mr. B. as he removed the last specimen jar from the makeshift operating table. "I have to say I admire your particular brand of courage in advancing medical knowledge.

Convention be damned, I say. Yes, I'm reminded of great leaders such as Dr. Henry Cotton; Dr. Walter Freeman, who perfected the art of the lobotomy back in the 1950s; and of course, those pioneering physicians who participated in the syphilis studies at Tuskegee. There was important research conducted there to be sure, as long as it didn't involve curing them of syphilis, of course."

Peabody had heard enough. "Dozens of poor black sharecroppers died during those Tuskegee experiments because they were withheld proper medical treatment. When they couldn't keep it secret any longer…"

"But the experiments were never kept secret, Howard. Certainly you must remember that it was written up in all the proper journals over a period of 40 years. It was quite respectable until the—what do you call them—the 'morality police' came along and spoiled everything for those courageous physicians. The bleating sheep even demanded apologies. Apologies? I'm proud to say that not a single Tuskegee doctor ever apologized for anything."

Peabody was practically suffocating in the hot humid air. He felt as though he had this conversation before. Was it in a dream? "I never withheld treatment from any of my patients. I saved lives."

"Yes, you were quite free with your scalpel and surgical tools. Tell me Howard, have you kept up with your 'special patients' over the years? Have you checked in with them now and then to see how they're getting along in the wide world?"

"It's difficult to keep track of them. I don't even know their real names for the most part. Listen, it's not the type of work where you recommend a follow-up visit," said Peabody, who wondered why he was so defensive with Mr. B. It wasn't as though he needed to explain himself to this fat elf who collected Fiji mermaids and crystal skulls.

"You might be surprised to find out how some of them are doing, Howard. But then again, the whole point is just to relieve the poor souls of their suffering, whether real or imagined. Better not to bother with second-guessing your decisions. Isn't that right, Howard?"

The voices were back even louder than before. The volume must have been building imperceptibly in the twilight haze of the metal box. Although they were muffled, Peabody could sense these were angry voices, accusing voices. Try as he might, he couldn't decipher what they were saying. Did he hear his own name?

"Howard, did you hear me? I say, if one was given to second-guessing, then you would have thrown in the towel after that little operation on your darling niece. You have to admit that you always had your doubts about that affair from the beginning."

Of course, Peabody had never told another living soul about his niece. Not the whole story anyway. Not even his brother—especially not his brother. Earlier in the day he remembered looking at the photo of his 16-year-old niece on his cluttered desk. She was wearing that pretty little red bikini he remembered from that last family vacation in Galveston. His older brother finally found some use for the black sheep of the family after all, requesting some "services" to relieve his daughter of her "troubles." He thought he had locked away those memories forever, stashed away with his brother's obsequious thank-you letter in a hidden drawer in the armoire—a letter too quick to flatter, filled with innuendos and unanswered questions that Peabody regretted in later years never asking. He promised he would do anything if it all could just disappear. Peabody was feeling quite queasy now and grabbed the side of the table.

"Howard, you're looking a little unsteady there. Please don't misunderstand me. I admire how you just push aside any misgivings and still manage to convince yourself that you're the real hero of the story. It's a trait I look for in any true professional."

"How did you know about Alice, about my niece? Exactly who are you anyway?"

"I'm just like you, just another hard-working public servant." Mr. B. smiled broadly, and his teeth glowed with an odd phosphorescence. "Didn't you find it odd, Howard, that after all this time you were never caught or even investigated for a single secret surgery you performed? Did you really believe you accomplished this by yourself?"

Peabody was no longer certain of the passage of time. He couldn't even recall how long it had been since he first set foot inside the storage unit. Was it a few minutes? Was it an hour perhaps? And the sound of those damn voices was now so loud he could barely hear himself think. "Where are those voices coming from? It sounds like there's a meeting going on in the container right next to us. You can hear it, can't you?"

"I was hoping we could finally get down to business Howard. I've been looking for a new personal physician for the longest time and I dare say, I think I've finally found the man for the job."

For a moment Peabody had completely forgotten why he was here. Of course, there was still a bizarre operation to perform. There were always bizarre operations and unfortunate truths crowding his nights. Now he was sure this was a dream he had a long time ago. Yes, this was a familiar nightmare that he woke up from screaming, but now he knew he would never wake up from this.

Mr. B. pulled down his pants and there sprouting from his ass was a dark leathery tail that twisted and wriggled as though it had a life of its own. He flopped it down on the metal operating table with a dull thud and it slithered about like an eel fresh from a deep-sea fishing net. Peabody noticed as his eyesight started fading that the end of the tail was forked like a serpent's tongue.

"I've had it removed before, but the damned thing keeps growing back. Once that's finished I have so much more for you to fix. But first, you simply must see some familiar faces, and teeth, and claws, and other assorted body parts that are all just dying to get a hold of you."

Just before Peabody lost consciousness, he was acutely aware of the voices and noises in the next box over and for the first time he heard something familiar, a jingle-jangling that sounded for all the world like Christmas bells.

* * *

Published July 25 in Fanfiction.net

From *"A Guide to Roadside Attractions in Tennessee, Revised 2015 Edition"*

Most tourists speed down I-40 W like a bat out of hell heading to Fort Worth. Don't make that same mistake or you will miss out on one of the all-time creepiest roadside attractions this side of the Mississippi. Brothers Hank and Frank Weir of Kunstkammer Kids.com fame have recently opened a brick-and-mortar version of their online cabinet of curiosities and are daring the public to step through the front door.

Both Weir Brothers make appropriately bizarre hosts for this little freak show of horrors. They cut tall and formidable figures and Hank (or is it Frank?) affects a patch over his right eye which barely covers a truly hideous scar. If you want some additional entertainment value for your $1.00 admission fee just ask Hank how he got that little scratch—the story changes with every telling. The Weir Brothers don't like talking about their age ("We take after our Daddy who always looked younger than his years," says Hank), but they don't mind spinning the stories behind all the artifacts in their impressive collections. Some of the stuff is your standard two-headed turtles and fake South American shrunken heads that are the staples of most dime store museums, but the majority of goods here are things guaranteed never before seen anywhere else on Earth. And the brothers tell their mind-boggling tales with a down-home earnestness that's downright convincing. Many of the specimens in their shop are for sale, but the things in the next-door Arcanium are strictly for display only. I won't give away any of the contents here since experiencing the shocks and surprises around every corner is part of the fun. But I will say that stepping into the Arcanium is like opening the door to an unnatural history museum in the Twilight Zone.

And the boys are planning an expansion later this year that includes a Bone Maze imported from a small Czech village. They've worked out a deal with a tourist attraction in Prague and the Weir Brothers are shipping it over to Tennessee bone by bone. And here's the best part—they insist with a straight face that all the bones that make up this elaborate labyrinth are real human skeletons, all victims of the Black Plague.

Arcanium: A Roadside Collection of the Weird, Macabre, and the Occult is open Monday through Sunday, 10:00 AM to 6:00 PM. Suggested fee is $1.00 for adults (not recommended for children under 12). Located at 600 Addington Road, right off I-40 W. Call ahead to check for hours of operation.

Graffiti found in Old Town Square, Fort Collins, CO

THE PILOT AWAKENS

From collected text exchanges on July 26, 2015

Rich: Have u found the back door?

Tony: This place is BIG

Johnny: Where r u?

Tony: Passed 2 outbuildings

Johnny: 2 bathrooms?

Tony: No, they look like storage sheds—still no sign of life

Rich: *Nothing here in the shop either*

Johnny: Just a bunch of dusty potion jars, skeletons, and crap

Tony: Why do I have to sneak alone round back?

Johnny: Don't be a baby

Rich: I don't trust these guys—only know them by reputation and rumor

Tony: So Kevin has strange fans—what else is new?

Johnny: Some stranger than others

Rich: Just wanted to guarantee there r no surprises

Johnny: I hate surprises

Tony: Found the back door…locked shut

Johnny: So Tony, how's Kevin's girl doing?

Tony: Terrified. And Angel is NOT Kevin's girl

Johnny: Ha! Jealous much?

Tony: Are we 13?

Johnny: Dude, you had a crush on her since HS

Tony: OK so I love Angel. Happy?

Rich: Boys, were not passing notes in homeroom anymore.

Johnny: Going into the Arcanium next door

Tony: Wait 4 me I'm coming round

Johnny: Omg…the Weird Brothers are here!

Tony: Can't go this way, blocked by wall of bones

Johnny: Shit…it's Lurch with an eye patch!

Tony: I have a bad feeling about this

Johnny: I swear it's the Peacock brothers from X-Files

Rich: Expect they're hiding Mom under the bed

Tony: Wait 4 me

Johnny: Wtf! Wait til u see the Arcanium!

Tony: What?

Rich: It's the storage container from Peabody's Last Patient…
           exactly

Tony: So I guess were not sleeping over tonight?

From Myth-America.com

July 26, 2015

Meet the Kunstkammer Kids

By Richard Harrigan

We've never stepped foot in Nashville, nor do we know anyone who's ever visited Tennessee, but we endured the most unsettling species of déjà vu when we entered the roadside attraction run by the Kunstkammer Kids. We knew from their online reputation that the Weird Brothers (or Weir Brothers if you adhere to a dreary accuracy) were simply run-of-the-mill con men pawning off bizarre crap collected from dime museum closeouts and freak show sales around the country. But upon entering their prized Arcanium, I confess I might have seriously misjudged them. Walters got all weak in the knees and whispered that we were in the presence of truly dangerous men. You see, the place looked exactly as Starkly had described in his Peabody's Last Patient, a story he posted to Fanfiction.net just a day before we arrived in Nashville.

Everything was packed in there, from the dirty humming jars, to the crystal skull and deformed fetuses, to that horrifying mermaid hanging from the ceiling. How could Starkly have possibly known about it? He's never traveled to Tennessee in his life and he's never met Hank or Frank Weir. I've researched this thoroughly and there's no detailed description of the Arcanium anywhere, not online or in print. I don't know how Starkly saw it all, but it is probable that he intended it as a warning.

I could tell that Walters and Fermia were ready to get the hell out of there as soon as possible. Upon careful consideration, I judged the best course of action to simply behave as civilized as possible in the short time we had together. Admittedly, it was difficult ignoring the freak-show appearance of our hosts. One of them (Hank, I think) is over six-feet tall with a disfiguring scar and eye patch. Frank was the shorter, talkative one jabbering on about how much he admired Myth-America.com and the research Starkly was doing.

"I'm glad you could set a spell and visit about your trip to Aurora," said Frank.

Our discomfort must have seemed painfully obvious since Frank attempted humor to settle our nerves. But the bizarre chatter only reminded me that we must have slipped into some alternate dimension where standard rules of etiquette didn't apply.

"We've been told straight out—'you boys are ugly as sin'—so we best do our work far from any cameras, and that's the way we like it," said Frank.

And they asked us what we all did and where we lived. Hank was amused when Walters told him he was born in Brooklyn.

"I remember our Momma would always say, 'Brooklyn, Brooklyn, city of sin, no one comes out the way they came in.'"

And my mother always instructed me to behave as a gentlemen even when surrounded by hooligans. Her advice served me well countless times in the classroom and in awkward situations like this one. In an attempt at normal conversation I offered my condolences on Hank's eye problem, and he said something like "I had a little something growing next to my eye for a while. It turned out it was another little eye growing there except it didn't look right—maybe more like a goat or squid eye or something. Had to get a local doc around here to carve out that little bastard. You want to see how deep the scar is?"

I realized that this was probably the tenth different tall tale of what's wrong with Hank Weir's eye. Each one more outlandish than the next. Were they trying to scare us? Or was it just a clumsy attempt to gauge how gullible we were? In the calmest tone I made our excuses that we really couldn't stay much longer. The Weird Brothers were clearly disappointed and continued to suggest sleeping arrangements for the three of us out back in their shanty cabins. I insisted that we didn't want to inconvenience them further for the night. Then Hank (the taciturn one) showed his hand.

"So what are you boys planning to do in that Aurora cemetery? You plotting to dig up something that don't belong to you?"

They saw us all as competing collectors of the strange! Was all this rigmarole a ham-handed attempt to broker a deal? Perhaps they were no more dangerous than your standard ruthless businessman.

"Now don't be that way with our esteemed guests," said Frank. "They wouldn't try nothing illegal or underhanded, would you now?"

"Of course, that would be none of your business, but you can listen in on our podcast and find out," I said with a smile on my face. Saying "No" firmly, but with a polite smile was something else I learned from my mother.

"Sorry you fine gentlemen can't take us up on our offer of Southern hospitality, but maybe you could just humor us by taking a walk through our new Bone Maze before you leave. We just set it up not more than a month ago now," said Frank.

I think I shocked everyone by taking them up on their insane offer. Walters nearly fell off his chair. Of course, the brothers were inordinately delighted by this turn of events and escorted us around the corner to the entrance of the maze.

"We usually charge a separate admission fee for the Bone Maze, but for you fellas we'll just look the other way and let you wander in for free," said Hank.

"It was built for a little Czech church back in the 1700s, if you can believe it. I hear them Catlickers love their labyrinths," said Frank.

Walters pulled me over to the side and out of earshot of our hosts. He asked why we were wasting our time getting lost in this damn maze.

I assured both my compatriots that this was indeed the path of least resistance. Instead of facing God-knows-what threat from the Weir Brothers if we simply turned tail and ran out the door, this way we would backtrack out of the maze in five minutes and sneak away before they knew it.

Clearly, the maze was designed to frighten and conjure up thoughts of the transience of life, but it was still a physical maze occupying no more than 2,000 square feet. As I look at it now, I see that every surface is covered with layer upon layer of human skeletons. No matter where you turned there are legions of skulls staring you straight in the face. I'm sure the rest is some artfully arranged ossuary you might find in Paris or Rome. The jumbled matrix stretches at least nine feet high. I promise you now that this collection of bones might confuse the local yokels with some superstitious nonsense, but a maze is a maze, and we will simply use Tremaux's algorithm to find our way back out. Also, once I post this online we're provided an excellent insurance policy against any looney hanky-panky from Hank and Frank.

SORRY, UNABLE TO CONNECT TO SERVER

NO SERVICE

TRY AGAIN?

Personal correspondence from Anthony Fermia to Angela McQueen, July 26

Dearest Angel,

I hate to admit it, but you were right.

Visiting the Kunstkammer Kids place in Tennessee turned out to be the biggest mistake we could make.

When Rich said that we would love to walk through their maze, I think my jaw dropped to the ground. Poor Johnny was fuming. He wanted to get the hell out of that place as soon as possible and didn't take kindly to any suggestions that would delay our exit.

Rich sounded reassuring, but I had my doubts as soon as we stepped through the entrance. After some initial geeky discussion, I convinced everyone we should use the simpler wall follower wayfinding method instead of Tremaux's algorithm.

Night fell faster than any of us thought possible. We couldn't have wandered for more than 10 minutes and already the sky was darkening into deep twilight. Rich had his right hand in constant contact with the wall of the maze since we entered and never even lifted one finger. Now he reversed direction following the same path back to the entrance. It should have been a simple matter to retrace our steps back to our starting point. But we soon discovered that nothing was simple or predictable inside this damn Bone Maze.

"I don't remember passing that dead end before," said Johnny.

"I'm sure we passed it, you just don't remember it." Rich was attempting reassurance but failing miserably.

It's difficult to believe this labyrinth was ever sanctioned by the Church. Nothing holy here but more like a sacrilegious stacking of body parts. I suppose there's some primitive skill involved in connecting all the femurs, clavicles, and jawbones like a ghastly jigsaw puzzle. But any semblance of sanctity this labyrinth originally contained after it was built on the outskirts of Prague was lost in translation when the Weird Brothers reassembled it here for their own purposes.

I wondered out loud how many individual bodies were used to build this thing.

"Probably about 30,000, maybe as many as 50,000," said Rich.

Johnny thought they were all probably fakes, nothing more than movie props, but Rich quickly dissuaded us of that comforting notion. "No, this place smells like real human remains. You can't fake that aroma. However, I seriously doubt that these are all plague victims from the 14th century."

Rich pointed out a nearby skull and jawbone. "Look at all these alloy fillings. Nobody was getting that level of dental care in the 1340s."

"So you're saying some of these skeletons are…recent acquisitions?" asked Johnny.

"I'm saying that our hosts are probably not telling us the whole truth," said Rich.

After another 15 minutes scrabbling around in the ever-darkening twilight and bumping into cul-de-sacs that seemed to appear out of nowhere, it became painfully obvious to everyone that we were not where we thought we were.

"I don't understand," said Rich. "We should be right next to the entrance."

As you might imagine there was a lot of arguing and tons of blame to go around. I accused Rich of taking his hand off the wall at a critical junction right at the start. Rich insisted that we should have followed the foolproof Tremaux's algorithm instead. Johnny said the only fool around here was Rich for getting us into this damned predicament in the first place.

Just as I was *this* close to kicking Rich in his pompous ass, the nighttime lighting for the installation clicked on. Every skull, fibula, femur, and toe bone—everything white for that matter—glowed with a sickly bluish phosphorescence. We were all bathed in the glow of hidden UV lamps. It reminded me of Dante's room, except these were real human skeletons gleaming under the black-light rays and not Grateful Dead posters.

"That's perfect," said Johnny. "It figures these assholes would take a contemplative space exploring our mortality and tart it up with fun-house lights."

I'm ashamed to admit that I was contemplating my own mortality at that point. It seemed we were wandering aimlessly through the glowing skull and bone corridors for about a half hour, and we were no closer to finding the entrance. I want to say that we all lost track of time because of growing fear and panic, but the truth is even stranger. All of our watches had slowed to a crawl or stopped dead. Nobody wanted to say the obvious: that we were hopelessly lost inside a maze that seemed much larger on the inside than we first thought. So nobody said anything at all. It reminded me of some of my worst dreams where the dead are leading me into terrible places, and I have a cold dread in the pit of my stomach. I can't explain it, but I felt we were no longer alone in the maze. The hairs on the back of my neck pricked up as if someone was watching me. And I swear I felt that even before we heard the growling coming from behind us. Johnny heard it first.

"Is that a dog?"

It sounded more ferocious than any dog I've ever heard. And what-ever it was, it was large.

"What if our hosts collect living specimens as well," I said because I couldn't stop myself from speaking out loud what we were all secretly dreading. "What if they captured some horrible creatures, like a sasquatch, or werewolf, or maybe a black hound?"

"That's not a hell hound, they've let loose some junkyard guard dog," said Rich. "And I'm having no more of their little fun and games." He opened his cell phone and pressed 911 before he realized that he had no reception at all. Again no service, no posting anything online, nothing, even though we had talked to the Weird Brothers on the phone just on the front porch of their store.

"Let me guess, they built the Bone Maze over a dead zone?" said Johnny.

We picked up our pace trying to put as much distance between ourselves and whatever was following us through the bone maze. There was no entrance or exit in sight, just unending walls of skulls and skeletons everywhere you looked. And the growling and snuffling from that thing was getting closer. I think Rich actually convinced himself that it was nothing but a large dog, not even a wolf. But as it stalked us, literally just around the corner, not more than a corridor away in the labyrinth, I could hear its massive footsteps pounding the ground. Whatever it was, it was walking upright on two legs.

Johnny suggested that he climb up on my shoulders and look over the top of the maze. Maybe he could see a clear path out, or at least find out approximately where we were in this nightmare tangle of intersecting walls. We did the exact same thing to escape from that old cemetery after they locked the gates on us after closing time. Johnny quickly hopped up on my right shoulder first with a helpful lift from Rich, then steadied himself against the wall before planting his other foot on my left side. The wall was higher here than at the entrance but that seemed impossible. Then again, everything about this cursed maze seemed impossible. Without stopping for a second, Johnny tried to secure a handhold on the bony wall, anything to grab onto and pull himself up. But every time he found purchase in an eye socket or jawbone, he pulled away fingers that were cut and bleeding. Johnny's blood stained the bones and glowed brightly under the UV light. I swear all the skulls shifted in place to look down at us with row upon row of death grimaces.

"Damn, that felt like something bit me."

Not wanting to waste any more time, especially with the sound of the creature getting nearer, Johnny dropped back to the ground.

That's when all the lights went out in the maze.

After the first wave of animal panic passed over me, I felt an odd sense of relief. Everything around me was glowing with a painful electric vibrancy that hurt my eyes. The absolute darkness—except for the starry night sky above us—was almost soothing. Johnny, always prepared, pulled out a flashlight from one of his cargo pants pockets and led the way. There was a slight but noticeable mist rising from the ground, like the tendrils of steam that come off the pavement after a summer storm. We were now racing headlong through the twisting corridors guessing at which path to choose next. The creature behind us was matching our speed, moving faster as it smelled how tantalizingly close we were. And we could all hear the wild sniffing and insane scratching of claws on bone. Sometimes the low growling would break into an alarming howl that sent a cold shiver down my spine. The last time I felt this level of fear was in that dream I told you about, the one in Tesla's mountain laboratory.

So in the middle of all the madness, I stopped and closed my eyes. You may not believe me, but I thought of you and our last week together back in NYC. I remembered in my dream you appeared in the middle of Tesla's lab and you told me, "Don't worry, you'll know what to do." And for the first time I believed that maybe my curse had some larger purpose. That maybe my random conversations with the dead had some meaning beyond waking up in cold terror. In the middle of the bone maze, I closed my eyes and thought of you and prayed you were right.

Rich and Johnny came up behind me and in their flailing panic pushed me to the ground. I stumbled around the next corner and there she was staring me right in the face as if she had been patiently waiting for me for all eternity—the little girl with the ash-covered face and matted black hair.

"Hello, Mr. Fermi," she said in a familiar sing-song voice that seemed to come straight into my head.

She looked exactly the same as when I first met her inside the Shunned House. The years had not changed her even a little bit. But then I suppose the dead never age. Her plain smock looked like it dated back to the 1950s, or maybe it was a generation earlier. She looked like a six-year-old girl that had come through a horrific firestorm and was heartbreakingly unaware of what had happened to her. Judging from the puzzled expressions of Rich and Johnny, I realized very quickly that, just like last time, I was the only one who could see the little ghost girl. Her appearance seemed more solid than spectral until I realized that I could see her perfectly clear in the absolute darkness of the maze.

"Hi Abigail, what are you doing here?" I asked.

"This is a bad place. You have to leave here right away."

I couldn't agree with her more. But what she said next terrified me as much as anything I'd experienced that night.

"You have to go back now. You have to turn around. There's a crack in the wall where the ground shifted. Even the bad men don't know about it."

I would rather have chopped off my right hand than face whatever was chasing after us. But my protests to Abigail changed nothing.

"The nasty noises you hear are just a pretend monster. The real monster isn't in this maze. Those tricky bad men want you to be trapped in here forever. The crack is very, very small. You have to crawl on your belly to get out."

"Are you sure about this, Abigail? After all, you are a long way from home."

She nodded her head and I realized that there was nothing else to be done about it. We had to march headlong into whatever was slavering after us.

"Will you come with us," I asked.

"I can't stay long. This is such a bad place, but some parts are still a little tiny bit holy." Then her smile cracked the gray ash that was forever caked on her face. "But I'll stay long enough to show you the way."

I didn't know how to tell the guys about the change in plans, since they had no idea what was going on. It helped enormously that I was confident about what we had to do—scared as hell and wishing I was anywhere else in the world—but still confident. The dead love to screw around with the living as I've discovered to my chagrin. But Abigail has never lied to me, not even in my dreams. Before I could say anything, the little ghost girl skipped back down the corridor towards the beastly sounds as though she was heading off to a game of hide-and-seek.

"Abigail is here. She's going to lead us out of the maze, but we have to follow her wherever she goes," I said, and to my everlasting gratitude that seemed to be enough for Rich and Johnny.

We turned the corner and ran right into the thing following us.

God help me, it looked like a monstrous wolf standing at least eight-feet tall with claws the size of scythes. Rotting flesh fell away in chunks from its skull. Hollow eye sockets glowed blood red. I tried not to look at it too closely, but I shivered even at the glimpse of its bony muzzle filled with impossibly long teeth. The horror howled at us and we stopped in our tracks, but only for a second. The stench of matted decaying flesh and fur nearly made me gag.

Abigail ran right through it.

So we charged ahead as fast as we could go, eyes closed and screaming into the night like banshees. Passing through the nightmare creature felt like running through the thick black smoke of diesel exhaust. Choking and coughing, we slid on our bellies out through the crack in the skull wall—just as Abigail said.

I've never loved the sweet humid smell of summer air more than that night. And I've never missed you as much as I do now. Please keep safe. Love, Tony

* * *

From *Frank Leslie's Weekly Illustrated News*

March 21, 1868

The Destruction by Fire of Barnum's American Museum, New York

After twelve o'clock on the morning of March 3rd flames were discovered issuing from the windows on the third floor of P. T. Barnum's Museum Building, Nos. 539 and 541 Broadway. An alarm was promptly sounded, and in a very brief space of time several hundred people were at the scene, and the utmost excitement prevailed.

The Fire Department was rather tardy in its appearance on the premises, owing to the depth of the snow and an alarm of fire raised a short time previously, and when the steamers took up their position the discovery was made that a majority of the hydrants in the neighborhood were frozen to such an extent that they were practically useless. By the time, therefore, that the engines got in working order, the flames, aided by a high wind, and fed by the large amount of inflammable materials about the Museum, had gained such headway that it became apparent that neither the building, nor the animals and curiosities contained therein, could be saved from the ravages of the destroying element.

Above the snorts of the steam-engines, the orders of the engineers and the shouts of the spectators, rose clear and painfully, expressions of the intense agony to which the animals comprising the Menagerie were subjected. Monkeys, bears, hogs, lions, tigers, seals, and birds, united in a manner peculiar to their natures in swelling the volume of a death-song which occasioned responses of pity from those without the burning mass.

A very small proportion of the Curiosities were saved, and many of the most interesting and expensive animals, together with the entire collection of birds, perished in the flames. Through the incessant exertions of the policemen and citizens, a passageway was effected through the Mercer street entrance to the Menagerie building, when a series of ludicrous scenes, tinged not a little with the exciting element, were presented. When the fire had burned for more than an hour, and the entire interior of the Museum was a mass of flames, a sudden cry of wonder was raised at the appearance at one of the windows on Broadway of some animal too severely burned to be recognized.

Several of the Human Oddities of the Museum occupied apartments on an upper floor of the building, and a posse of policemen forced open the doors and rushed into the rooms to save the inmates from destruction. The Circassian Beauty, whose lustrous eyes and beautiful moss hair have made her one of the Museum favorites, was carried from the room by a stalwart gentleman, and was immediately followed by a procession of four bearing upon their shoulders the Fat Boy. Miss Swann, the Giantess, Mrs. Powers, the Fat Woman, the hairy little Esau, and the Albino children, were likewise rescued by a sympathetic company, and the entire party were conducted to the parlors of the Ansen House.

Police report that several witnesses swore two odd hooligans, all dressed in black, had disturbed the night watchman just before the conflagration, repeatedly asking for the "real Feejee Mermaid." One of the Albino boys rescued from the scene, said "They looked like they belonged with us, with the rest of the human monstrosities. One was tall and gaunt, the other short and squat. Never saw the likes of them before."

The origin of the suspicious fire is still under investigation.

* * *

From Angela McQueen's blog, *Where Angel Fears to Tread*

July 27, 2015

I don't usually go into a lot of gossipy crap here on my blog. Well, OK, I don't *totally* go into gossipy crap mode. But I thought this was as good a time as any to go all fangirl on you and chat about the Secrets of the Nerd Legion. And I thought I would start with (if you'll pardon the expression) their Origin Story.

Now Johnny and Rich had been best buds since nursery school or something when they were growing up in Brooklyn, but the rest of the Scooby Gang didn't get together until sophomore year at Prep. We sort of knew each other from hanging out in class and such, but it didn't get real social until Johnny (bless his heart) invited most of Ms. Hawthorne's Gothic Lit class to his parent's basement for an H.P. Lovecraft birthday party the summer of sophomore year. We were all there in the depths of the Walters' residence—me (wearing so much Goth makeup I must have looked like a crazed raccoon), Rich, Tony, Johnny, and about a half dozen other kids. I don't remember much about the party except that the Cthulhu cupcakes were de-lisssh! Oh, yeah…and there was this epic hair-raising séance where we all sat in the dark around a humongous round table. Everyone was doing it like it was some goof (or a chance to cop a feel in the dark) but I swear to God, this heavy table started vibrating and some THING spoke to us out of nowhere! Dominic and Patsy both swore on their grandmother's grave that they saw some spooky vapor cloud swirling over the table. I couldn't see a thing, but I sure as hell heard it. It was like this totally inhuman voice bellowing "Get out!" So, the table flips over and everyone goes tear-assing out of the house screaming and crying.

It was awesome!

I look around and the four of us are the only kids left standing in the basement. I remember saying something like, "What the hell was that?" And Tony said, "This kind of stuff happens to me a lot."

That's when I figured it might be cool to hang with these guys.

Kevin didn't enter the picture until senior year. But he wasn't the type of geek who was satisfied with sitting around playing D&D on a Saturday night. Kevin was always into serious weirdness and he hit it off with the others right from the start. He was (as my grandma would say) a total instigator and troublemaker. We would be out hanging from the rafters at some abandoned factory in Long Island City or sneaking around Green-Wood Cemetery after dark chasing ghost lights or some other shenanigans. I only stopped going out with the boys on their night-time adventures after they got back together after college. I began to feel like they didn't want me playing any Nerd Legion games, but Kevin explained it was really some uber-geek chivalry or something where he thought they were all protecting me.

Then we graduated and found our own lives apart from each other. College years were a blur, dude. I vaguely remember bad art, bad professors, better music, and too many loser boyfriends. What happened to the Nerd Legion? You know the drill—you promise to stay in touch, get together once in a while for a séance...blah, blah, blah...and nothing ever happens. I got into publicizing some local indie rock bands, traveling around the place. Tony was working the stacks in the New York Public Library, Rich was teaching other kids how to blow things up in physics class, and Johnny inherited a dive bar from his uncle and turned it into the Last Call art gallery. Kevin never did forgive him for that, Lol! And Kevin started Myth-America.com maybe three or four years after college. Then the Earthquake shook up NYC and Kevin's podcast & blog really took off. He got mucho media coverage for his...umm...how should I put this? For his personal dedication to investigating the weirdest shit out there. He was all over any UFO sightings, vampire cults, poltergeist activity, or strange animal reports (and I mean like "werewolf" strange, not "spotted owl" strange), and Meteor Girl. Did I mention Meteor Girl?

I do worry about those boys sometimes. I wonder how they ever survive from one day to the next without killing each other. Or forgetting to eat, or taking a shower, or changing clothes. I swear, the one event that totally rocked their world and made them like macho blood brothers—that time in the Shunned House—they needed the help of a six-year-old girl to save their hides and she was already dead something like what…a good fifty years? They get all quiet when you ask them what exactly happened in Providence. But I once did get Tony to tell me something I never heard before. He said that Abigail the friendly ghost told him that one of the next times they meet, she will take him into heaven. I tell you, these little girl ghosts are way too j-horror-creepy for my taste.

Don't get me wrong, the Nerd Legion are no pussy pushovers. When it hits the fan they can man up and take care of business. I've always said that if you scratch the surface of a nerd or brainiac or geek, or whatever you want to call a socially awkward obsessive, you'll find a scared, angry little kid who's totally fed up with the next bully lurking around the corner. One time at the Prep (was it junior year?) this goon from the rugby team starts pushing around Johnny. And Johnny's the shy, stick-figure type, so he's eminently push-able. Well, into the brawl flies Rich like some mad sumo-wrestler! I couldn't believe it because Rich is no way a street-fighting man, but he's grabbing whatever he can get his hands on and throwing it at Goonie. He starts with a cafeteria tray, then a backpack, and before long he's hurling shoes, stray dogs, lighting fixtures—whatever. And before Goonie knows what hit him, along comes Tony and he jams the goon's sorry ass into a locker and slams the door in his face. Needless to say that was one rugby player that wasn't going to play that scrum again! And then they got together and sewed their own costumes and little masks and promised to use their powers for good. Nah…just kidding. But all that other stuff really happened, I swear.

* * *

Handwritten note on top of page: *A rare moment of self-doubt? Mostly, Starkly believed in nothing…or nobody…except himself.*

From the Myth-America.com archives (posted June 9, 2015)

The One Where Kevin Starkly Explains it All

By Kevin Starkly

If I was going to tattoo something pithy and significant on my forehead or another prominent body part like that forgetful dude in *Memento*, it would be this: "Question everything." Now don't get me wrong. Mom and Pop Starkly brought up their baby boy the right way, sending me to St. Stan's school, and going to church every Sunday. I even signed up for altar boy duty. Let me tell you, learning Latin phrases sure came in handy when I tried deciphering some of that bizarro Alistair Crowley shit.

But I've discovered that reality is too fragile to trust one single paradigm over another one. It becomes particularly mind-boggling when investigating the high-strangeness I see every day. It's a great temptation in life to search for a belief system that answers all your questions, confirms all your doubts. We're drawn to the pitchman hawking "here's all the dogma your family will ever need." But when you're hunting Damned Things skittering near the edge of the abyss, it's a luxury I can't afford.

I've personally seen too many lives derailed by trusting in one theory or another. The history of ufology and parapsychology are literally littered with the corpses of well-meaning researchers who believed too strongly in the common wisdom of their time. There was poor Morris Ketchum Jessup, one of the most famous flying saucer researchers of the 1950s, he even coined the term "ufology," for God's sake. He went down the rabbit hole of government conspiracies with his uncovering of the infamous Philadelphia Experiment and then killed himself in 1959. And then there was Johann Schröpfer, the famous "phantasmagorical" spirit conjurer of 18th Century Germany who put on such a good show projecting spooks on smoke screens that he started to believe his own hype and killed himself in 1774.

And then there was Kevin Starkly, freelance paranormal investigator who believed that supposed "hauntings" could be explained as mass telekinesis unconsciously controlled by the human imagination. A pretty nifty theory really. Hell, I studied all the cases including the famous "Philip Experiments" performed by parapsychologists in 1970. A diverse group of researchers came together and consciously created an entity named "Philip" that soon developed a life of its own, and which they then proceeded to communicate with during a series of séances.

And I believed it right up until we were almost killed inside The Shunned House in Providence, Rhode Island. I think we all altered our theories after that little incident.

That being said, I'm almost afraid to mention my newest favorite theory—that the key to unlocking the mystery to alien abductions is hidden in lucid dreaming. I believe that alien intelligences are somehow altering our dreams and implanting these abduction scenarios. Everything about the abduction phenomenon just screams out that this is some bizarre species of vivid dreaming. By mastering the power of lucid dreaming, I think we have a better than average chance of confronting these alien intelligences by taking back our own dreams. But why are they doing it? I have no idea. But here's some bone-chilling speculation: What if this alien intelligence is secretly building another reality that we can't even begin to fathom? Every once in a while, the façade slips and we get a glimpse of this hallucinatory other world. Maybe there are small rips in this reality where you can cross over and see the Damned Things at play. And then, one night when the plan is in place, the aliens will replace our reality with the flick of a switch and humanity will wake up to its greatest nightmare.

But then again, what the hell do I know?

So "Question everything," indeed. I'm still good with that. And remember what your Mom always warned you, "Be careful what ideas you pick up because you don't know where they've been."

Posted by strangekevin

Comments

Oddball2001 writes:

Score! First comment, dude! Seriously, if you all want to know the truth behind our government's long-term plans for messing with our minds, or the details behind the secret U.S. conspiracy with the Greys read my latest posting at oddworld/alienconspiracy.

Wake up sheeple! Your government is run by criminals intent on selling you for body parts.

Rich Harrigan writes:

Spoken like a true scientist burned by one too many failed hypotheses. I mean that as a compliment by the way. I agree that dogma is no suitable replacement for rational thought, but before you use your own disappointments as an excuse to give up the search for truth altogether, allow me to quote one of your favorite authors:

"Belief has always been the enemy of truth; yet ironically, if our minds are supple enough, belief can sometimes open the door." – John Keel, *The Mothman Prophecies*

You see Starkly, sometimes I actually read the crap you give me.

Angela McQueen writes:

Don't get me wrong, Kevin. I know what you're saying. It's hard figuring out what to believe. How to separate the BS from the real deal, blah, blah, blah. But I don't think the answer is to throw up your hands and give up. I know I'm paraphrasing really badly here because I don't have time to look it up, but I think G. K. Chesterton said something like,

"When a Man starts questioning all belief, he doesn't then believe in nothing, he believes anything."

Questioning is cool and all, but I'm saying don't give up the search. Maybe you need to find an idea to hold on to. You know, like something strong to steady yourself against all the storms ahead.

* * *

Aurora Cemetery Gate, Aurora Texas

From the sign posted by the Texas Historical Society outside the Aurora Cemetery:

The oldest known graves, here, dating from as early as the 1860s, are those of the Randall and Rowlett families. Finis Dudley Beauchamp (1825-1893), a Confederate veteran from Mississippi, donated the 3-acre site to the newly-formed Aurora Lodge No. 479, A.F. & A.M., in 1877. For many years, this community burial ground was known as Masonic Cemetery. Beauchamp, his wife Caroline (1829-1915), and others in their family are buried here. An epidemic which struck the village in 1891 added hundreds of graves to the plot. Called "Spotted Fever" by the settlers, the disease is now thought to be a form of meningitis. Located in Aurora Cemetery is the gravestone of the infant Nellie Burris (1891-1893) with its often-quoted epitaph: "As I was so soon done, I don't know why I was begun."

This site is also well-known because of the legend that a spaceship crashed nearby in 1897 and the pilot, killed in the crash, was buried here. Struck by epidemic and crop failure and bypassed by the railroad, the original town of Aurora almost disappeared, but the cemetery remains in use with over 800 graves. Veterans of the Civil War, World Wars I and II, and the Korean and Vietnam conflicts are interred here.

From the Facebook page of bikerdude17

July 25, 2015

This town sucks.

Really, I mean what kind of loser place calls itself "the town which almost wasn't?" I'm not joking dude. You can read the town history in a little booklet they sell at the main gift shop right on the highway on 114.

My cousin thinks this town sucks too, and he has to live here which makes it even suckier. Cal—that's my cousin—he's sort of cool. He's been showing me around the place checking out the "hot spots" – HA! Most of his crew are gone for the summer off to more exciting places than this— which would be like anywhere else.

Cal has some sweet BMX bikes that we've been shooting around town when my Aunt Mary thinks were in bed. I used to think Aunt Mary was cool when I was younger, but she's just like my Mom now. Dude, it's my summer vacation, I'm supposed to have SOME fun. I think it's required by law.

Cal showed me this bitching cemetery last night which was kind of cool. He said there's this legend about a flying saucer that crashed in the town like a 100 years ago and they buried this little alien right under this old oak tree in the cemetery. And he says the ghost of the alien appears floating by the tree once a year to try to finish its secret mission.

Dude, I was like totally believing him until he starts laughing like crazy. He said that the whole story was some wild hoax made up by tele-graph operators who were bored out of their minds. I guess boredom is like a tradition here. Cal says nobody in town believes the story, except for Miss Evans who swore she saw it happen when she was just a little girl. But she's dead now.

He did show me the spot where everyone says they buried the alien. There's no headstone or nothing—just a depression in the ground. But here's the freaky part—everywhere else in this damn cemetery the grass is growing bright green like a freaking golf course, but on the alien grave the grass is withering and dying and it's all red, like rust or dried blood.

The big excitement for tonight is that we're going out for dinner to the Bar-B-Q for baby back ribs! Dude, I can't wait to get back to Denver!

From the transcript of the Myth-America.com podcast

July 28, 2015

JOHN: Welcome to the much-delayed and
much-maligned Geek Freaks Across
America Tour brought to you by Myth-
America.com. I'm John Walters filling in for Kevin Starkly. Kevin plays
a better master-of-ceremonies than
I do, but unfortunately he can't be
with us tonight since he disappeared
off the face of the Earth right at the
end of our first installment over two
weeks ago.

TONY: Keep your voice down. Do you want someone to spot us out here?

(sound of shoveling)

JOHN: (Lowering his voice) But I sense the
spirit of Kevin hovering above us
tonight as we boldly move to the last
location of our trip. At least I hope
this is the last location. I'm here
with Tony Fermia who, I'm overjoyed to
report, rejoined our little group a few
days ago.

TONY: I think we're missing a shovel and some
rope. Where did Rich disappear to?

JOHN: He went back to the car to get those head-mounted flashlights. Anyway, Kevin promised you all back on July 10 that we would travel across America to explore haunted places, track strange creatures, and dig up every lurid secret buried in the ground. Well, tonight we've gathered here in the cemetery in Aurora, Texas, to hopefully unearth one of the greatest secrets of all time. Back on April 17, 1897, a strange airship crashed into this sleepy north Texas town and the pilot of that craft—identified as an inhabitant not of this world—was buried right here under our feet. Now there's been a lot of controversy over the years about the veracity of this story, but Kevin always believed that the outrageous tale was absolutely true. And God help me, I believe it's true as well.

(more digging and grunting)

TONY: The tour hasn't exactly gone the way Kevin planned it.

JOHN: That's an understatement.

TONY: Actually, nobody knows what Kevin had
           in mind since he didn't write any itin-
           erary before he disappeared before
           our eyes in the forgotten ruins of
           Harrisville back in the Pine Barrens
           of New Jersey. But that didn't stop
           the Nerd Legion from traveling to a
           Starship Invasion convention that ended
           tragically at the famous Serpent Mound
           in Ohio.

JOHN: I nearly had my head cracked open. It
           still hurts right back here. And then
           we got side-tracked into that God awful
           Arcanium place outside Nashville.

TONY: The less said about that damned place
           the better, but here's my consumer tip
           for the day—I don't recommend getting
           lost in their Bone Maze. And for anyone
           just joining us, that brings us to our
           activity this evening.

           (more shoveling)

           We are clandestinely engaged in ille-
           gally digging up the corpse of an
           alleged extraterrestrial pilot.

JOHN: Kids, do not try this at home.

           (more digging and grunting)

Kevin would probably give you some history of the Aurora crash controversy offering some witty personal insights and snarky bon mots. But I'm already getting exhausted so I'm just going to shut up and keep digging.

ANGEL: Hey! Anybody need an extra flashlight?

TONY: What? Angel babe, what...what are you doing here?

JOHN: Wait, I thought you were...

ANGEL: Well, here's the thing. I remembered as soon as I got to Montauk that I can't stand, and I mean like I really, really, really can't stand my cousin Joyce. So, bye-bye Montauk, hello Aurora! Besides, as an honorary member of the Nerd Legion we got to stick together, amiright?

TONY: I thought you...I thought we agreed that you would stay safe.

ANGEL: I know. But then I realized that the best place I wanted to be...the only place I wanted to be...was next to you. No matter what happens.

JOHN: Well I'm glad you're here to help out. Did I happen to mention how pissed I am that Kevin is not with us right now? I was so hoping that he would be here waiting for us and that this was all some elaborate scheme to…to…I don't know.

TONY: (Startled) What was that flash? Did someone take our picture?

(Rumbling thunder)

ANGEL: Scaredy cat! It's just lightning. Evening thunderstorms are like the weather du jour in Texas this time of year.

(More thunder)

JOHN: Perfect! We're digging in a graveyard during a thunderstorm. I expect Boris Karloff and Béla Lugosi will join us any minute now.

(A sharp crack of thunder very close)

TONY: I read that the whole crashed airship story lay buried in obscurity under the Texas soil until a UFO researcher named Hayden Hewes single-handedly resurrected the forgotten tale back in 1973.

ANGEL: Why are you talking like some narrator
            from the Travel Channel? Shit, are you
            recording this for the podcast? And who
            is Howard Huge?

JOHN: Hayden Hewes was the director of the
            International UFO Bureau and yes,
            we're recording everything. Hewes said
            he uncovered several metal fragments
            of what he claimed were pieces of the
            original crashed craft.

TONY: And then other folks claimed there was
            some metal buried right here in the
            supposed grave of the alien astronaut.

            (More rolling thunder, shoveling, and a
            light rain starts to fall)

JOHN: The forgotten story started generating
            tons of media coverage. Local Dallas
            papers picked it up, then it ran on
            the national newswires. Even the local
            TV stations started talking about the
            famous crashed saucer in Aurora, Texas.
            Hewes insisted that the body should be
            exhumed and studied by medical experts.
            But the local sheriff refused to comply.

TONY: Didn't he say that it was…that digging
            up a body was a possible public health
            hazard? I think he said that the "spot-
            ted fever" bug that claimed hundreds of
            lives decades ago could still be deadly
            if it came back up to the surface.

(sound of digging)

ANGEL: That sounds like a load of bullshit.
           Probably the townies just didn't want a
           bunch of strangers digging up grandma
           and grandpa by accident. But what hap-
           pened after that?

TONY: The metal fragments came back and lab
           results were inconclusive. And the
           metal pieces detected in the alien's
           grave mysteriously disappeared without
           a trace, along with the tombstone. So
           the story of the crashed airship and
           its strange pilot once again disap-
           peared off the front pages and dropped
           over the edge into limbo.

JOHN: And now here we are digging through
           obscurity to find the truth. I hon-
           estly have no idea what we're going to
           unearth here tonight. What do you think
           an extraterrestrial skeleton would
           look like?

           (still shoveling)

TONY: Probably a big skull with big eye sock-
           ets. Or maybe it changes form after
           death. Maybe it's nothing now but a
           throbbing blob of alien protoplasm.

ANGEL: Gross! Maybe it's not dead at all.
           Maybe it's just…hibernating.

JOHN: Hey, what if it's not a phys-
             ical entity, but more like an
             energy projection?

             (some grunting and shoveling)

ANGEL: I just hope we don't score some jail
             time for all of us.

JOHN: You know what Kevin would say? 'Better
             to beg forgiveness, than ask permis-
             sion.' God help me, I've now stooped to
             quoting Kevin.

             (deafening crack of thunder)

ANGEL: Damn, that was close.

JOHN: By the way, did I happen to mention how
             pissed I am that Kevin isn't here to
             finish the job that he started?

             (sound of more digging and more fre-
             quent thunderclaps)

TONY: Yeah, several times.

             If it's any consolation I thought he
             would meet us here too. I imagined that
             he would jump up from behind a tomb-
             stone and give us all a good scare.
             Remember the time he did that when we
             were all in Green-Wood?

JOHN: I remember. That was back in…

(the clunk of a metal shovel strik-
ing wood)

I think I've hit something.

TONY: What? But we're only down about
four feet.

JOHN: They must have buried the poor bastard
in a hurry. Damn, I think we can dig
the rest of this up in a few minutes.

(Frantic shoveling and agitation. The
rain is still falling)

Look, it's a child's coffin. We're going
to need more light than just this lamp
and the lightning to see what we're
doing. Where the hell is Rich?

TONY: Keep your voice down. Someone is going
to hear us.

VOICE: How about this? We've brought along our
own flashlights to the party.

2nd VOICE: Momma always said you should
come prepared.

(Another thunderclap)

JOHN: Oh shit!

FRANK: Now boys, there's no reason to get
yourselves riled up. We're here to help
you finish your work tonight.

HANK: And once you dig up whatever is in that grave, we'll be carting it off back home to add to our private collection in Tennessee.

FRANK: A real ET under glass, yes sir, now that's going to be a regular four-star addition.

JOHN: And what makes you both think we're going to stand back and let you do that?

ANGEL: Maybe we should just, you know, shut up.

FRANK: You're going to listen to us…

JOHN: What are you going to do? Flash us another look at your yellowing teeth and scare us away?

HANK: (yelling) You are going to listen to us or I'm taking this here toad sticker and slicing your throats faster than you can cry "Mommy."

TONY: What the hell is that thing?

FRANK: A ceremonial dagger from Tibet—a phur-pa —sharp as hell too. I still can't believe we couldn't even get a bid of $300 for it.

HANK: There just ain't no appreciation for genuine artifacts anymore.

ANGEL: Why do you want to hurt us? What did we
            ever do to you?

FRANK: It ain't nothing personal Missy. You've
            just put yourselves in an inconve-
            nient spot between us and our prize. My
            brother Hank and I don't take kindly to
            obstacles or unpleasant surprises.

JOHN: Wait a minute. Which one of you jerks
            nearly cracked my skull?

FRANK: Now that was just a misunderstanding,
            plain and simple. We wanted to see what
            information your friend Kevin had about
            the alien buried in Aurora. He seemed
            damned sure it was above board and
            all, but in our business you can't be
            too sure. Just wanted to see if it was
            authentic, you know. I guess I got a
            tad angry when I discovered you didn't
            have the object I needed.

HANK: I still say you should have hit
            him harder.

TONY: Why didn't you come here and dig up the
            remains for yourselves?

HANK: Our time is too valuable to go running
            around the country for nothing.

FRANK: We didn't want to look foolish and go
            pell-mell on a wild goose chase. But
            then you boys went racing off to Aurora,
            so we knew it was the real deal. We've
            been collecting for a long time now.
            How long has it been Hank?

HANK: One hundred years? Maybe two hundred?

FRANK: And you would be surprised how many
            conniving folks try to pass off fakes
            as the genuine articles. We just get
            aggravated by the sheer mendacity of
            some folks. Someone once tried to sell
            us a fake Feejee mermaid, for example.

HANK: We taught that collector a lesson,
            didn't we?

FRANK: Yes sir!

JOHN: I used to think you guys were just col-
            orful eccentrics, but now I know you're
            a couple of murdering psychopaths.

FRANK: Now there's no need for name-calling.
            You go digging up secrets your own way,
            and we'll dig up secrets our way. Live
            and let live is what I always say.

HANK: You wouldn't believe the hidden knowl-
          edge we've uncovered over the years.
          Sometimes they were out in plain sight
          if you had the eyes to see it—in estate
          sales, museum displays and cemeter-
          ies. Sometimes the secrets were more
          closely guarded.

FRANK: Just keep digging boys. You're close to
          done right now.

          (more shoveling, rumbling thunder in
          the distance)

TONY: It's just a cheap pine coffin.

JOHN: Only the best for our Martians. We'll
          haul this up to you guys, but we'll
          need a hand to get ourselves out
          of here.

HANK: That's right, just lift it up here.

          (sound of movement)

FRANK: You know, I think you two look fine just
          where you are. And how about if I just
          hold on to this little Missy here just
          in case you get any fancy notions.

ANGEL: Let go of me you psycho!

TONY: Hey! Don't you touch her!

JOHN: She hasn't done anything…

HANK: Well now, we wouldn't have to worry
          about any of this, if you all just
          stayed lost in our labyrinth like
          we planned.

JOHN: Sorry, but we didn't want to hang out
          in your maze.

HANK: That was a fine trick you boys pulled
          off. We still don't know how you man-
          aged to find your way out of the lab-
          yrinth, but now you've made this all
          so inconvenient.

ANGEL: Let me just kick your inconvenient ass!

FRANK: This little Missy is a feisty one,
          ain't she?

HANK: Reminds me of that librarian lady in
          that book town up north in New York.

FRANK: Promised not to kill her if she just
          handed over those special manuscripts.
          Then I plucked her eyes out of her
          head. Surrounded by books and no eyes
          to read them (chuckles).

HANK: Of course, she begged us to kill
          her then.

          (another sharp thunderclap, rain is
          pouring down)

FRANK: Tell you what. While you boys are down
          there why don't you hand up your sup-
          plies first.

HANK: Just give me your shovels and lamp. And
          don't forget your cell phones.

JOHN: Hey pretty boy, why don't you hop down
          here and get them for yourself? I prom-
          ise I'll smack you with my iPad.

HANK: (Yelling): That's it. That is no way to
          speak to your elders.

          (Another thunderclap and then screams
          are heard. There are sounds of a strug-
          gle and shouting. The recorder drops
          to the ground. There are ten seconds
          of muffled voices before the recording
          ends.)

From the Facebook page of bikerdude17

July 28, 2015

OK, I have to write down what I just saw at the cemetery even if no one believes me and even if Aunt Mary catches me. I'm afraid if I don't write this down fast it'll like disappear from my brain or else I'll convince myself it was all just a dream, or maybe a nightmare.

It was all Cal's idea. He wakes me out of a dead sleep and says we're hooking up with Tina and her little sister at the ball field. Dude, it's like 1 AM or something. But I figure Tina's sister is hot so I'll go along for the ride. I mean she's only 16, but she's still hot.

Anyway, we get to the ball field right off the main 114 highway and guess who's a no-show? No Tina or little sis in sight. Cal is really pissed and says he's going back home.

At this point, I'm wide awake and looking for something to do so I tell Cal I'll follow him home in a few minutes. He's cool with that. At first I figure I'll do some wheelies down Main Street, but I only get as far as the end of Cemetery Road which is directly across the road from the ball field before it starts raining and the sky is full of thunder and lightning and shit. And at the end of Cemetery Road is the town cemetery. Duh!

I'm going around the south end of the cemetery and I figure I'll sneak in and check out the spaceman's grave that Cal showed me before. Which would be a good idea except there's like a party going on at the grave already right in the middle of the thunderstorm. There's like four dudes that I've never seen in my life digging up the grave! Actually, only two are doing all the digging. The other two dudes who look like zombie rejects from *The Walking Dead* are just standing there and watching. And the big ugly one with an eye patch is waving around some freaky dagger. Dude, that baby has three sharp blade edges running down the side! And the smaller guy is holding on to this hot chick who's wearing shorts and Doc Marten's. I mean she's old, like 25 or something, but she's still hot.

While I'm trying to figure out if anyone can see me from where I'm hiding in the weeds, the two digging dudes lift this coffin out of the ground. The damn thing looks too small to be real until I remember what Cal said about the alien being short like a ten-year-old.

Then everybody starts yelling at each other. I can't make out what they all are shouting about because the thunder is so loud and I'm not that close. But I hear a lot of threats coming from the big ugly dudes especially the tall one with the dagger.

I'm thinking I should be calling 911 on their asses, when I see this shadow racing toward the bunch. He's moving so fast that no one sees him coming before it's too late. It's some short fat dude carrying a shovel and he hauls off and whacks the tall bastard right upside his ugly head. CHONK! I could hear it all the way over where I was hiding. I thought his eye patch would go flying right off, but instead he drops the knife and looks real unsteady. Before the big dude can even think about standing straight again, the fat one throws the shovel at his head a second time. BOOM! The tall bastard falls over like a demolition chimney right into the grave. And the two dudes stuck down there clamber up the sonovabitch like a ladder.

My dad always said that if you're breaking up a bar fight—and as an MP in Manila he broke up brawls like every Saturday night—you take down the biggest, meanest muthafuka first and everyone else usually falls in line. I'm not saying these grave-robbing dudes are street smart—like I don't know if I would have brought a shovel to a knife fight—but the first moves were sweet. I figure the shorter ugly bastard is going to call it quits after his partner goes down for the count. The chick is trying to pull away from him and plants one of those Doc Marten's right in his balls! He doubles over in pain and I'm thinking game over. But he comes right back and punches that girl and just flattens her. Then two dudes that crawled out of the pit start double-teaming the last ugly bastard standing letting loose some pure whoop ass. The skinny dude plants a roundhouse punch square in his face. But that ugly sonovabitch is giving as good as he's getting. He's throwing punches and body blocks like a wild man. I figure this dude has seen like a brawl or two in his day. The skinny dude gets clocked with a flashlight across his skull and joins the girl flopping in the mud like a choking guppy.

And the last ugly dude is wicked fast. Before I know it he's holding the damn knife in his hand! Now I'm thinking I better call 911 pronto before someone gets real dead real fast.

But here's when things got really strange. I've got to think real hard to remember what weird shit happened first. First, I heard this humming or buzzing like a swarm of bees out for a night drive. Then the freaky dagger starts bleeding! I don't mean like the guy accidentally pricked his finger bleeding. I mean like someone turned on the bloody faucet bleeding. Mr. Pug Ugly looks down at the knife and even from where I'm hiding I see that he's scared silly like he's seen a ghost. He drops the knife and it's still bleeding on the ground like a wounded animal. Without missing a beat, one of the other dudes cold cocks him in the face with the shovel's wooden shaft. I can hear his nose crack. Then the fat dude decks him with a ham-fisted uppercut and the sonovabitch trips over the coffin and goes flailing into the grave to join his best bud.

I realize that the thunder and rain have stopped now but the air seems charged with electricity. I can feel my skin tingling and I don't like it. The buzzing is getting louder like the static on an old TV. Now I see it. I'm not sure what I see and even now I don't want to remember it because I'm damn sure I'm not supposed to be seeing it. There are little lights floating everywhere like fucking neon blue fireflies. I'm sitting here still shaking like a baby thinking about it. The air over the grave is filled with them—hundreds of them—and they all dive into the grave like killer bees or something. The three dudes and the chick are standing there paralyzed like statues. I don't know what the damn lights are doing to the ugly bastards in the grave and I don't want to know. I hop on my bike and I speed out of there like a bat out of hell. I don't care if I have to stay here another week, I'm never setting foot in that cemetery again.

From the Myth-America.com blog

July 28, 2015

Aurora—Reconsidered

By Richard Harrigan

When I think about our recent excursion to Aurora, I'm reminded of that old joke about the drunk searching for his missing car keys. You know how it goes: Late one night a guy comes across a drunk on his hands and knees looking for something under a streetlight.

"What are you looking for?" asks the guy.

"I dropped my car keys about two blocks from here and I'm trying to find them."

So the guy asks, "Why don't you look for them back where you dropped them?"

And the drunk answers, "Because the light's better over here."

I'm afraid we've all been like the drunk scrambling about looking for something where we damn well knew it didn't exist. It wasn't a misguided quest necessarily. It was just the wrong quest. You can hear the whole podcast of our misadventure in the Aurora cemetery by clicking **here**.

I suppose some greater good did result inadvertently from our road trip. It turns out that the infamous Kunstkammer Kids—noted collectors and apparently self-confessed killers of collectors—have disappeared off the face of the Earth, joining our friend Starkly in that electric blue oblivion.

At the very least, I'm sure it will wreak havoc on their feedback reviews on eBay.

After the Weird Brothers dissolved into the ether, we pried open the casket that my friends had so laboriously dug up from the ground.

Unfortunately, the casket was empty. Whoever or whatever was in there had been removed years ago. It took only a short while to replace the coffin and refill the shallow grave.

I offered my profuse apologies to my comrades for returning to the Prius and then staying there to spy on the Weird Brothers as I caught them sneaking into the cemetery.

I believed the best I could offer at that point was the well-timed element of surprise. In the end I think they valued my propitious entrance more than they would have appreciated an extra hand digging up sod. I forgot how exhausting it was to run across a graveyard carrying a hefty shovel. Luckily for me—and unluckily for Brother Hank—my two initial blows were well-placed.

Of course, that's when Brother Frank knocked the wind out of me with a stunning blow to my solar plexus.

I'm ashamed that I committed a cardinal sin: I made the mistake of underestimating our enemies. Despite evidence to the contrary, I believed the Kuntzkammer Kids were harmless collectors of the macabre, no more a threat than that fellow who runs the sideshow revue at Coney Island. I didn't imagine they were killing collectors of the arcane across the country. Thankfully, the Weird Brothers misunderstood us as well. They thought us a bunch of poseurs, a team of tyros that would run in fear from the unknown and let the big boys have their way. I shall never forget that uncomprehending stare from Big Hank when I materialized from the shadows and smacked him in the head. It was quite gratifying.

Presently, Walters is filling up the tank and checking the oil and performing other obscure car ablution rituals that are a mystery to me. We would all appreciate a well-deserved rest first, but we decided unanimously to "get the hell out of Dodge" as Walters said. Fermia and Angel are purchasing a good three-day supply of the much-prized bags of Twinkies and cheese puffs for the trip home. I can see them holding each other for dear life at the grocery store across the highway. Me? I'm now enjoying a cup of "cowboy coffee" at the Tater Junction, the Wi-Fi hotspot in town. Who knew? There's a young girl who's up past her bedtime undulating before an appreciative crowd to the strains of "Rattlesnake Shake" —the classic one by Fleetwood Mac—playing on the jukebox.

The night's events have focused our resolve to find our missing friend. These last weeks we deluded ourselves into believing that the most important mission was to uncover this grave in the Aurora cemetery. But all this time we were really hoping we would reconnect with Starkly. And in truth, that was really our mission all along.

Now Fermia believes he has correctly interpreted a Nikola Tesla dream he had the other day. Initially, he thought Tesla was leading him here to the cemetery in Texas. But now we are heading back home to New York to the place where I sincerely hope we will be reunited with our absent comrade.

Posted by drrich

From the dream journal of Anthony Fermia

July 27

Last night I dreamed about Tesla again. I was relieved that instead of a mad scientist laboratory in Colorado Springs he was sitting at a dining table on the second floor of the Old Town Bar in lower Manhattan. The place looked remarkably unchanged from the last time I visited, and then I realized it was probably one of the few places left in NYC that has looked about the same for the last century.

"Please Antonio, come and join me," said Tesla.

There were a number of well-dressed people sitting around us. If I wanted, I could have studied every detail of their dress down to the mother-of-pearl petticoat buttons. I satisfied myself with just studying the old-fashioned menu that highlighted such turn-of-the-last-century fare as Oysters Rockefeller and sauerbraten.

"I hope you don't mind that I've taken the liberty of ordering some clam chowder for the both of us." Tesla seemed pleasant but slightly anxious.

Within a minute the soup was served and oddly enough, I remember it tasting very salty.

"Do you know that these fine bowls hold 6.3 cubic inches of chowder? I find that I need to confirm the volume of all the foods I eat and then I must consume it whole in a number of bites divisible by three. This bowl of chowder, for example, can be consumed in exactly 12 portions. Do you often find yourself obsessed with measuring all your repeated acts so that they are divisible by three, Antonio?"

"No, Niko, I can't say I have."

"No? Well, no matter. If I missed counting for a certain activity I felt impelled to do it all over again, even if it took hours. Would you like something to drink?"

I remember asking for a beer, but I was preoccupied with other concerns.

"Niko, where are you trying to lead me? I get the sense from you that there is something urgent you need me to do."

Tesla fussed with rearranging the silverware before he answered. "I have believed for many years that my will has been pushed and prodded by outside forces to accomplish some greater good. I have no knowledge of how these forces work, I simply know they have guided me through some of my major accomplishments."

"Are you guiding me now? Are these same forces guiding me?"

"Did you know that when I was very young, I could imagine distant people and places with a clarity and detail that was truly frightening? I soon discovered that I could simply go on in my vision further and further, getting new impressions all the time. So I began to travel—in my mind, of course. Every night when alone, I would start on my journeys to see new places, cities, and countries."

Tesla looked around nervously as though someone or something was eavesdropping on our conversation.

"I think I always suspected that this was some gift bestowed on me, though I never knew my benefactor. These were scenes from my future, from places and acquaintances I would meet later in life."

I noticed that while he was talking, Tesla had neatly sliced his filet mignon into 15 bite-size chunks. "While I was only a boy, I once pictured in my imagination a big wheel run by the roaring waters of Niagara Falls. I told my uncle that I would go to America and carry out this scheme. My poor uncle had no use for this kind of nonsense. Yet, thirty years later I was able to see my ideas carried out at Niagara and marveled at the unfathomable mystery of the mind."

He continued talking but my attention drifted as I noticed that the bustling atmosphere around us in the restaurant had subtly changed. Nearby tables were now empty where before patrons were happily tucking into their pork chops and steaks.

"After I recovered from a life-threatening illness, my strange mental powers metamorphosed into another unique gift. I observed to my delight that I could visualize the most complex mechanisms with the greatest facility. I needed no models, drawings, or experiments. I could picture them all as real in my mind, as though I was observing someone else's handiwork.

"One afternoon in Budapest I was enjoying a walk with my friend in the City Park and reciting poetry. I recall it was something from Goethe's *Faust*. Yes, now I remember it. The sun was just setting and it reminded me of the glorious passage.. "

He started to say something in German, *Sie rückt und weicht...* something I didn't understand. He stopped abruptly and looked away as if suddenly remembering something more pertinent, or perhaps simply realizing he needed to translate. He began again, this time looking past me into the distance.

"Oh, came a magic cloak into my hands

To carry me to distant lands,

I should not trade it for the choicest gown,

Nor for the cloak and garments of the crown."

Tesla turned and stared directly into my eyes.

"Then an idea came like a flash of lightning into my mind and in an instant the truth was revealed. The images I saw were wonderfully sharp and clear and had the solidity of metal and stone. I drew with a stick on the sand, the diagram shown six years later in my address before the American Institute of Electrical Engineers. There was my Alternating Current motor fully realized before my eyes! Pygmalion seeing his statue come to life could not have been more deeply moved."

I noticed that it had grown darker outside when I could have sworn it was bright daylight not a moment ago. Tesla leaned in closer and looked directly into my eyes, "I am convinced that I am but an automaton devoid of free will in thought and action and merely responsible to the forces of the environment."

"I don't understand. Are you saying someone is controlling you?"

"There are mysteries and secrets I may not share with you now, Antonio. But you will uncover them in time yourself. There came a time in my research where I needed to make a drastic decision. Would I follow my visions blindly to whatever dark path they were leading me? Or would I seek another direction?"

"Niko, please tell me if I'm on the right path. Will we find Kevin?"

He stared straight ahead and ignored my question entirely. The dead are often stubborn in telling their stories.

"At that time, as at many other times in the past, my thoughts turned towards my mother's teaching. Did I ever tell you about my mother, Antonio?"

He had never mentioned either of his parents before, and he now seemed filled with a deep melancholy. It was the first sign of genuine emotion I could recall from Tesla. Outside it was the darkest night.

"My mother was a truly great woman, of rare skill, courage, and fortitude. She worked indefatigably, from break of day till late at night, and most of our apparel and furnishings were the product of her hands. Did you know that even when she was past sixty, her fingers were still nimble enough to tie three knots in an eyelash?"

"What did your mother tell you, Niko?"

"My mother had taught me to seek all truth in the Bible. The gift of mental power comes from God, Divine Being, and if we concentrate our minds on that truth, we become in tune with this great power. At this time I made a further careful study of the Bible and discovered the key in Revelations."

And then the ground opened up underneath and the Earth swallowed me whole. I dropped down into the darkness clawing at empty space. After a few seconds of pure terror that seemed like an eternity I hit bottom. I could see no light and the blackness engulfed me completely. And I was completely afraid. I reached out my arms and I could feel the walls of earth surrounding me, closing in on me. I could hear Tesla's disembodied voice floating above me:

"I saw a star fall from heaven unto the earth: and to him was given the key of the bottomless pit. And he opened the bottomless pit; and there arose a smoke out of the pit, as the smoke of a great furnace; and the sun and the air were darkened by reason of the smoke of the pit. And there came out of the smoke locusts upon the earth.

And unto them was given power..."

I shouted, "Where are you? Where am I?"

The earth moved closer still all around me, squeezing the breath from my lungs. Was this what it was like to be buried alive? Then I heard Tesla's voice one last time:

"A thousand secrets of nature which I might have stumbled upon accidentally, I would have gladly given up for that one secret which I had wrested from her against all odds and at the peril of my own existence. Go here Antonio and you will find everything you seek."

A sudden, soundless explosion of light filled the space and blinded me.

I screamed myself awake.

Graffiti spotted on the corner of 8th and Market Street, San Francisco:

THE PILOT AWAKENS FOR ALL OF US

From After the Quake Twitter feed:

@Afterthequake

Yesterday, I cut my wrists on my way back home from the office.

But the bleeding was not enough.

From Dr. Jeanette Stryker's personal email

July 21, 2015

Dear Angela, I understand perfectly dear child your impatience with mastering lucid dreaming. Just remember we are, all of us, possessed of the most powerful alternative reality generator ever devised—our own brains. And we interface with this reality every single night in our own dreams. Imagine the events of consequence we can create; imagine the untapped lives we can bring to fruition when we learn to hone our control of that interface.

Sometimes the greatest service performed by our lucid dreams is the ability to confront our greatest fears. The situations, peoples, and things that paralyze us into blithering idiots in the waking world become subservient to our will at night. The phobias to creepy, crawly things that go bump in the night are transformed into our loving pets, no more formidable than a cuddly kitten in our eyes. And why is this possible? Because dear Angela, it is our own dream world manufactured by our magnificent brains. We become the directors of our own inner dramas and farces. Do these lucid dreams help us master our fears once we get out of bed? Our research has shown that this manner of directed dreaming is far more effective than many other anti-phobia techniques including exposure therapy.

There has been much speculation on whether lucid dreamers become addicted to their dreamtime as one becomes addicted to Minecraft or Worlds of Warcraft, or whatever is the latest video game fad of the week. I believe these concerns are entirely overblown. Remember we are dealing with a natural expression of human experience. To deny our dreams is a death sentence as surely as if we were deprived of sleep or food or water. It is not an artificial reality found inside a computer grid manufactured in Korea or Japan. It is a world of dreamtime created in our own minds that is probably as old as the human species.

I've spent years researching dreams and using my knowledge to tutor others on how to unlock the power of lucid dreaming here at the

Dreamtime Research Institute, but there are still many puzzles and mysteries to vex us.

The greatest unknown, of course, is why do we dream at all? Biologists and psychiatrists are utterly stumped as to why our brains remain engaged in this seemingly pointless activity once the body has called it a day. Some theorize it is simply a way for us to randomly sort through the accumulated detritus of our waking time. But to what purpose?

Perhaps dreamtime evolved as a survival skill for our little species. Maybe this notion that we could conceive of another reality, of a different time and place, maybe this is what gave us the advantage over all those other hominids competing against us. If I were a gambling woman I would assuredly have placed my bets on those strapping Neanderthals with the larger brain capacity. Yet, somehow, little *Homo sapiens* soldiered on through to the present day, the last of their kind still standing.

Maybe, and this is surely speculation of the basest kind, the dreams of our ancestors prepared them for the epic hunt they needed to face the next day. And maybe having dreamed of a successful kill they were more prepared than our Neanderthal brothers who had no such mental skills.

I often think that the secret to our survival may have been as simple as dreaming of tomorrow and seeing ourselves living in that new day. Wouldn't it be absolutely brilliant if our future was assured simply because we dreamed one night of a better day ahead surrounded by our children and grandchildren?

Cheers! – "Doc" Stryker

* * *

INVASION DAY

It's not difficult to remain invisible in New York City if you just put your mind to it. Of course, it's easier if nobody in particular is hunting for you. Most people accomplish this task every day without even thinking about it. You simply must live as mundane, obscure, and boring an existence as humanly possible without slipping into a coma. Seriously, just ask the non-descript *schlub* sitting next to you on the C train. Admittedly, boring and mundane aren't in my usual repertoire of social skills, but even this old dog can learn a few new tricks if I want to live to see another day.

I've taken to avoiding well-traveled areas most of the time, places where public and private security cameras are monitoring the flock 24-7. I never set foot inside a bank and I never, ever, use a single credit card. It's too easy for them to trace my transactions. I took enough of a risk slipping into libraries to post my stories online. But how else could I communicate the secrets revealed to me? I had to unite the guys with Dr. Stryker and I had to warn them about the Kunstkammer Kooks.

I was so far off the radar; nobody knew if I was dead or alive.

It was wonderfully exhilarating in a freaky, freeing way. I walked like a ghost through the city at night, hiding my face even from strangers. Of course, I couldn't contact any of my friends or acquaintances. They were under surveillance even if they didn't know it. All of my phones were bugged, all my computers hacked. All of my old haunts were compromised.

I was drawn inevitably to the multitude of forgotten ruins of New York City that exist in a splendid limbo. Just like me they are caught between life and death. They stand as crumbling wrecks awaiting judgment: either a sentence of rebirth or destruction.

I found myself one day on Roosevelt Island staring at the old Smallpox Hospital on the southern tip. I thought I caught a glimpse of somebody who shouldn't be there. I couldn't be certain though because during the last few days I found myself floating in and out of consciousness unexpectedly. Perhaps it was a post-hypnotic suggestion implanted in my brain. Or perhaps I really did see Jeanette Stryker walking towards the Coler Goldwater Hospital on the northern end of Roosevelt Island.

I certainly couldn't mistake her for anyone else. You know how you imagine people looking in your mind's eye after chatting with them on the phone, and the reality is never as exciting when you finally meet them in person? For the longest time, I only knew Dr. Stryker as a delightfully Brit babe voice on my iPhone. And wouldn't you know once we met, I found she was more Dame Judi Dench rather than Billie Piper. Another fantasy bites the dust.

But why would she be working here in a rehabilitation facility? I've watched many of the patients stream out of here in the morning convoy of wheelchairs and motorized gurneys, some accompanied by nurses riding shotgun, others running solo. But then I realized that her lucid dreaming techniques would be ideal for some of these patients. Wouldn't it be wonderful for a paraplegic to dream into existence another reality where he is an Olympic superstar?

To make sure this wasn't just wishful thinking on my part, I hung around the island for the rest of the day. I was dying to investigate some of the haunting reports I heard about The Octagon—one of the recently renovated old buildings located on the North end of the island—but under my circumstances that was next to impossible. Seriously, don't you think you would be tempting fate and pissing off some angry spirits if you built a luxury condo right in the middle of a former insane asylum? The solar panels are cool, though.

I realized that throughout its checkered history, whether it was called Blackwell's Island and you were locking away prisoners in the penitentiary, or it was called Welfare Island and you were quarantining patients in Ryker's Smallpox Hospital, this was always a place where you could hide all the secrets you wanted.

At around 6 pm, I saw her leaving the hospital. This time there was no mistake. I recognized her stocky frame and curly red hair as easily as I would recognize Angel or Richie in a crowded bar. But what could I do? I desperately wanted to say something, but I knew that could endanger her. I followed her along Main Street until she came to the island's large parking lot and I knew it would be difficult to remain undetected ducking around cars and SUVs.

"Whoever you are, you're not terribly adept at stalking, are you?"

Damn, the old bird still has a good eye! It was hopeless to keep pretending that I was any good at tailing people and if I kept hiding behind the cars, she would probably end up calling the police. I stepped out from the shadows for the first time in two weeks. It had been so long since I spoke aloud to anyone, even I didn't recognize my own voice.

"Sorry Jeanette, I didn't mean to scare you."

She stepped away from her Mini Cooper and eyed me suspiciously. Then she gasped reflexively as though she had seen a ghost. Or maybe she was just gagging at the smell. Not having many opportunities for a shower, I was particularly fragrant at this point.

"Good Lord, is that you Kevin? Thank God, you're still alive. Your friends are looking all over for you."

I didn't know what to say. I had been incommunicado so long that I momentarily lost the ability to communicate entirely. Finally, I managed to say, "I shouldn't be talking to you at all."

"Nonsense! What happened to you, dear boy?"

"I was abducted," I said, because it was the simplest answer I could think of and I knew that Jeanette, of all people, would know everything that meant. "I was abducted just like the rest. Afterwards, I was transported somehow and found myself floating in Minetta Lake."

The next thing I remembered I was waking up in the most luxurious bed I had ever known. I was so confused, I honestly believed for a few seconds that I had just awakened from a nightmare. Did I really see Dr. Stryker the night before? Have I really been hiding in plain sight in New

York City for the past two weeks, or was that all some elaborate recurring dream? I vaguely remembered Jeanette offering me the keys to her apartment on Roosevelt Island.

"It's my little pied-a-terre I keep when I work late at the hospital, and I can't bring myself to hiking all the way back home."

I remembered something else too. She said that after I rested, she wanted me to visit her at Goldwater to see her work. She said that there was important research going on that I absolutely must witness firsthand.

I must have slept all night and through most of the day because by the time I showered and ate a jar of yogurt from Jeanette's fridge, folks were wrapping up their lunch breaks and getting back to work. Through force of habit, I snuck around the side streets avoiding the Main Street security cameras and I entered the hospital using a little-used service door.

"Thank God, you're finally here Kevin. I was about to begin a new experiment." Jeanette showed me into a large circular room located on the top floor of the southernmost tower of Goldwater. There were at least a dozen beds wrapped around the perimeter of the room. Each one had its own compact alcove equipped with EEG monitoring equipment and other devices I didn't recognize. Every bed was occupied by one of the poor patients undergoing rehab treatment at the hospital. Most of the sleepers were missing a limb or two and wheelchairs were scattered about like folding card tables.

"They really are a jolly good crew of volunteers. They've quite taken to helping me in my dream research, though I suspect they have no idea how serious this project has become."

"What kind of dream research are you conducting here?"

She leaned in closer to me with a hint of conspiratorial intimacy, "You'll be pleased to hear Kevin that I think we've sorted out, finally, a testable hypothesis concerning the nature of the alien abduction phenomenon."

The theory she related to me was chilling. Jeanette always believed that the abduction experience was intimately related to our dream state. We agreed on this practically from the first moment we met online and compared notes during a Budd Hopkins abductee conference. But we also agreed that these abductions were not simply random hallucinations generated by the human brain.

"I believe that these abductions are a violation of our dreamtime from an outside force. They are an outright invasion of our dreams if you will. You led us in the right direction Kevin with your musings on the possible manipulation of reality through dreams."

For years, I believed that lucid dreaming held the key to understanding these bizarre violations of our unconscious mind. If we could control our dreams we had a chance of fighting them on their own turf.

"We think they are attempting to change us, to mold us, through our dreams. To what end, I can't possibly know. But they've recently attempted to hide their presence, so I fear something is afoot. The incidences of reported alien abductions keep growing every year and yet you have to search the farthest corners of the internet to read anything about it."

It was more of a sweeping conspiracy theory than even I ever imagined, but it certainly made sense. If some alien race was covertly rewiring the human brain they wouldn't want us actively chatting about that possibility now, would they? God forbid, we might stumble on a plan to stop them dead in their tracks. And here's the killer part: Jeanette Stryker believes she may have stumbled on to that plan.

"Our dreams are ephemeral, but the architecture of the human brain is real. The cortices and lobes communicate with each other through electric signals jumping from synapse to synapse and you can monitor and measure all of it. These creatures may be attempting to breach our defenses, but I believe we can give them a sound thrashing using the very electrical signals they are using to alter our perceptions."

Jeanette told me about the transcranial magnetic stimulation research she's been involved with over the years. There was a portable TMS device that translates electric signals into a magnetic field that passes through the skull and into the brain. By adjusting the signal, they found they could fine tune brain activity the same way you could dial up radio stations.

"At first, the notion was to control migraines or treat drug-resistant depression. But I realized that this device might be more successful than lucid dreaming in overriding the abduction scenario. Even under the best circumstances, a lucid dreamer is locked in a battle of wills against an alien threat fighting for control of their own dreams. But the TMS device gives us a new weapon to add to our arsenal, and a distinct advantage."

The plan was simple but brilliant. At a prearranged signal, once it was clear that alien activity was taking place in the sleeper's brain, Jeanette would activate the TMS device and literally overload the alien's circuits. She hoped scrambling their once-familiar terrain would force them into a strategic retreat, or possibly even injure them big time.

"I have to hand it to you Jeanette, you've come up with a way to zap alien invaders that isn't part of a video game."

But the sleepers around us were not actively engaged in any zapping whatsoever and it concerned the good doctor. Previously, at least one lucid dreamer had experienced an alien encounter during each session, but this time no one was taking the bait.

"They are all in deep REM sleep at the moment, but perhaps I'm a bit hasty, expecting to hit a grand slam the first time out of the gate, so to speak."

"You're mixing your sports metaphors, but I think I know what you mean. If nothing happens tonight, you can keep trying tomorrow."

Jeanette looked at me with an off-kilter glance—the one where she arches her left eyebrow as she affects a bemused smile—that told me she was hatching another wild ill-advised plan. "You know, Kevin, you would make a perfect subject for this experiment. Now wait, just hear me out before you say another word. You're already an accomplished lucid dreamer and unlike most of my patients here at Goldwater, you've experienced a bona fide abduction scenario, which by the way, I again must offer my condolences."

I began to protest, but even as I opened my mouth I knew she was right. During my initial meetings with Jeanette I discovered that I had a natural talent for waking up within my dreams—to gain awareness of my dreaming while still asleep. Admittedly, it's one of those wacky quirks, like curling the tip of your tongue or finding out you're super-susceptible to hypnosis, that has limited real value in life. And to think my parents never believed I would develop any marketable skills!

And that's how it came to pass that I found myself transformed from a twilight dweller lurking about the ragged edge of society to a doctor-approved guinea pig helping to save the world—all in the course of a single day.

At 5 pm, I was ready to play my part. A band of electrodes were wrapped around my head and the TMS device was positioned at the top of my head.

"I think you'll find our dream protocols particularly familiar, Kevin. I've taken to using your song suggestion as the triggering event for all my patients now. When you hear it you'll know you're in deep REM sleep. Try to be aware of your dream activity and if you sense any alien intruders press the button in your hand to activate the TMS surge. I would recommend creating a reality for the device within your dream so you'll find it easier to use. Maybe an electric torch perhaps, or a handgun?"

I smiled and closed my eyes. The subdued lighting in the room and the rhythmic beeps lulled me to sleep in a wink. I passed through the usual number of half-remembered dreamscapes before settling on terrain dredged up from the deepest, darkest places of REM sleep. I can always identify these dreams because they are the most like the waking world. Everything vibrates with an almost hyper-reality.

I found myself back among the ruins of Harrisville in the Jersey Pine Barrens. It was a sultry summer midnight with mosquitoes droning around my ears. It was so eerily similar to the actual night of my abduction I half expected to see Rich and Johnny and Tony trooping behind me complaining about small flashlights and the shortage of good snacks. But this time was different. I looked down at my right hand—which in the real world was holding the TMS buzzer—and found I had subconsciously created a five-fingered hand blaster just like Captain Ramses and his gang in *Starship Invasions*. I decided it was a far cooler and more elegant choice than the behemoth Space Marine rifles from *Aliens* or the prissy little ray guns from *Men In Black*, so I kept it.

Now I was the hunter and not the hunted. They could throw anything at me, even those damn buzzing blue lights. This time I was ready to fight back.

Just in case, I kept repeating to myself, "If this isn't nice, I must be dreaming." The clarity of the landscape was so startling, it would be easy to fool myself into thinking that I really was walking around the crumbling factory walls of Harrisville, instead of sleeping on a hospital bed on Roosevelt Island.

I had the uneasy feeling that I was being watched and expected something unpleasant to jump out at me at any second from behind a tree or bush. I kept walking in a circle around the ruins waiting for a sign, anything at all, from the intruders, but nothing manifested itself. There was not a single sound or sight out of the ordinary. Were they deliberately hiding from me?

That's when I saw Rich coming at me through the underbrush holding a large hypodermic needle. Oddly enough, he was wearing the same inappropriate outfit he wore when I last saw him in the Pine Barrens—a long-sleeved plaid shirt and corduroy pants.

Was this an alien manifestation? It might be a clever ruse to use the memories of my own friends to lull me into a false sense of security. Or maybe this was an image I had created myself for some reason. Not taking any chances, I raised my hand blaster and pointed my shooting finger at Rich.

"Don't shoot jackass, it's me, Richard. I'm part of the post-hypnotic suggestion you received from Dr. Stryker."

Something about a post-hypnotic message sounded familiar, so I lowered my arm.

"What the hell are you doing here?"

At this point, Rich was at my side sweating profusely. "Something has gone… terribly wrong outside your dream." He stopped to catch his breath. "Dr. Stryker created this escape image as an emergency exit if you will. As I inject you in your dream, she is administering an epinephrine push to wake you up."

I didn't want to think about what was happening in the real world that would force Jeannette to take these drastic measures, so I did what I do best and changed the subject entirely.

"If Jeannette needed to implant an escape image into my subconscious, why didn't she make it some hot nurse wearing black fishnet stockings and high heels?"

"Just shut up and hold still. I think this might hurt a little bit."

As Rich plunged the needle into my chest, a hot electric stabbing pain raged through my entire body.

The next thing I knew, I was sitting straight up in my hospital bed on Roosevelt Island with electrodes still dangling from my forehead. I was abruptly back in the real world with nothing to show for my hunting expedition. All questions I had about the abrupt change in plans disappeared the moment I looked around. There, surrounding my bed as though clumsily reenacting the last scene in the *Wizard of Oz*, were my closest friends— Rich, Johnny, Tony, and even Angel—the same friends I had successfully avoided for the last two weeks.

I think I managed to stammer out "What?" or something equally erudite.

"You really didn't think you were going to just saunter into Dr. Stryker's lab from out of nowhere and she wasn't going to tell us all about it?" said Johnny.

"Welcome back," said Tony. "I'm sorry we have to meet under these circumstances."

Angel bent over and seriously locked lips. "I didn't know if I would kiss you or punch you out," she said. "So I decided on the more embarrassing choice."

It's funny. I owed a whole world of people an apology—friends, relatives, parents, colleagues—and the only person I tried to offer any explanation to at all was Angel. "I desperately wanted to tell you what happened, but I was afraid I would endanger the lives of everybody close to me."

Angel nodded her head and looked down at the floor. "I kind of figured it was stuff like that. You don't have to worry about the part about endangering lives because we woke you just in time to see your nightmare come true. Take a look."

I staggered to the closest window—I think my right foot had fallen asleep—and bumped into Richie who helped steady me.

"At first, I thought it was some mass hallucination, but then once the attacks started..."

You know how it is when you look at something unbelievable and at first you're not quite sure what you're seeing? Like passing the scene of a car accident and you're initially confused for a second if you're looking at scraps of metal or pieces of a human body scattered on the road. It's as if the brain has to process the full horror of it piece by piece because it can't comprehend it all at once. That's how I felt when I first gazed at the Manhattan skyline in the early evening twilight. I was first struck by the eerie stillness of it all—no cars moving on the highway, no choppers taking off from the heliports, nothing moving at all in the summer breeze. Then slowly I noticed the burning wreckage scattered about the landscape. Was that a crashed fighter jet next to the United Nations with black smoke billowing from it? There seemed to be flames everywhere but not a single fire engine responding. I looked even closer, and I could finally see crowds of people moving unsteadily through the empty streets like legions of zombies. Some were pointing every which way, gesticulating madly. Most of them just trudged silently through the streets, wiping their eyes absentmindedly. I guess they couldn't believe what was happening either.

Then I looked up and saw them all floating there. They sat in the sky like flat black manhole covers pushing against the clouds—each one was massive, easily a quarter mile in diameter. They looked like giant holes in the heavens.

And then I realized with a nauseating sickness in the pit of my stomach that it was too late now. While I was asleep the world had changed forever. In fact, everything I knew to be true no longer had any meaning and everyone was waiting with bated breath to discover what this new world would bring.

"Thank God, you're awake, Kevin," said Jeanette as she rushed into the laboratory cradling a cell phone to her ear. "I'm afraid some of the other sleepers were not as fortunate."

I looked over at the other beds surrounding us. One or two of the cots were empty, but most of the patients were still lying there unconscious.

"Why aren't they awake?"

"I'm afraid we have terribly misjudged the aliens' plans for our world. They never intended to simply satisfy themselves with the occupation of our dreamtime. The ultimate goal was to manifest themselves in physical form and invade our reality. Somehow—I don't understand completely how—they have breached the divide between our world and dreamtime. What you see happening here is taking place all over the Earth. These black mandalas started appearing in the skies soon after you went to sleep.

Nobody seems to know if they are ships or apertures in space or something entirely different. We can't get close enough to them to find out." She threw down the phone in disgust and looked out the row of windows facing the battleground that once was Manhattan. She was a general still coming to terms with the fact that her latest strategy was a miserable failure.

"The damned thing doesn't work. Nothing bloody works."

Then I remembered the wreckage of the F-16 and wondered how many other sacrifices were made within the first moments of contact.

Rich was still at my side also staring at the horrific landscape outside. "I think it was some electromagnetic pulse unleashed just at the moment they materialized in the skies. We always speculated that the phenomenon had an electrical component with subsequent physical effects. Most electrical connections were fried instantly. Computers, GPS units, cell phones—practically everything else—is a useless heap of metal. Some landlines are still functional, but the information is sporadic."

"And the patients sleeping here?"

Jeanette straightened her back and regained her composure. She seemed more weary rather than frightened. "I can't seem to wake them. They appear to be perfectly healthy, yet they can't be roused into consciousness. I haven't heard of anything like it in the literature since the bizarre encephalitis lethargica that swept through America and Europe during the 1920s. I suspect it all has something to do with the invasion, but I can't fathom how or why."

I had to get away from the damned windows. I couldn't stand there another second, so I sat down at a desk in the middle of the room. Johnny sat next to me. "You know, if we managed to get ourselves over to the Old Town Bar, I bet all the drinks would be on the house, even the top shelf stuff."

I smiled and said, "Hell, maybe I can even persuade you to finally uncork that bottle of Krug 1996 Champagne you have hidden away, you stingy bastard."

"It's not exactly the occasion I was planning for, but…" He trailed off and looked out the window. "I'm glad you're back with us Kevin. I can't imagine a better person to share a ringside seat at the Apocalypse than you."

It's an odd species of camaraderie to share with anyone—a fine appreciation for the End Times—but it was perfectly in keeping with all our years together. At times death seemed one step behind us. I just never imagined that the rest of the world would be in lockstep with us contemplating the end of all things all at the same time.

Of course, there was one essential element missing from the battleground outside.

"Has anyone seen the aliens?"

"There are scattered reports of strange creatures," said Johnny, "but nothing confirmed. It's this damn silence that's so unnerving. There's this hum of ordinary life that we take so much for granted. Cars, television, radio, all the mundane machines that surround us, and when they disappear all at once, the effect is creepy."

A minute later I would pray for the return of that comforting silence. At first, I thought I heard a distant murmuring, like a crowd of people talking in the next room. Then it became clearer that the sound was close at hand but terribly low.

"Is it just me or do you all hear voices?" said Tony.

"This time it's not just you," I said. "But where is it coming from?"

Angel figured it out first. "Holy shit, the patients are all talking in their sleep!"

But not just talking. They were all saying the exact same sentence, and eventually they all started saying it at the same time and they said it louder and louder, until it was at a level that one might term conversational, if you could engage in conversation with a comatose patient.

"We have awakened," they said.

The truly frightening part wasn't that all 10 of them were chanting this same bizarre sentence repeatedly for over a minute. What was frightening and creepy was the knowledge that some alien influence was directing their speech. They were helplessly in thrall to some inhuman manipulation, for what purpose nobody could dare guess.

"We have awakened."

Of course, it made some maddening sense that if the invading creatures had effectively knocked out all our electronic systems worldwide, the things still needed some means to communicate with us. I never imagined that their loudspeakers would be human.

"We have been made flesh and now travel freely across the land," said a sleeper whose right leg was amputated at the hip.

"We travel freely," echoed another sleeper nearby whose both arms were replaced by prosthetic claws.

Angel delicately placed her hand over her mouth as though she were about to gag. "The aliens are using these people as their mouthpieces?"

"I fear the situation is far worse than that," said Jeanette who was busily searching for something through several cluttered drawers. "I think that the aliens are feeding off the consciousness of these patients and God knows how many other sleepers around the world. They require human thought to manifest themselves in our reality. And they are causing this incapacitating 'sleeping sickness' in order to perpetuate their plans."

"If they wake, will the alien ships just disappear?" Angel suspected the real answer to her question but hoped that she was dead wrong.

Jeanette had gathered a collection of hypodermic needles in sterile packages but was still hunting for something else. "Dear, I think these poor souls have no hope of waking from their nightmare."

The thought projections created by the greatest mystics of all time, the tulpas conjured up by lamas in Tibet, demons brought to life by heretics during the Inquisition, all these creations from the ether required active thought and genuine belief to perpetuate and sustain them. But how do you break the spell that summoned them?

"We have to kill them, don't we?" said a terrified Angel. "We have to kill the sleepers before they can bring more aliens into existence."

"No, dear child, we must attack the creatures they have conjured up, not the helpless sleepers."

I'd lost track of Rich for a few minutes, but obviously he was busy at work along with Jeanette. But his expertise was in physics, and I don't believe he took a single day of premed training, yet there was Rich running about carrying a tray of drugs.

That's what the invasion of dreamtime was all about. It was never the end strategy. It was just the first beachhead in the grand battle plan. I guess it was foolish to believe that the aliens would settle for possession of our thoughts when they could have our entire planet for themselves.

We started to hear distant screams coming from the streets below.

"We have awakened," said all the sleepers in one voice. For all I know, maybe every single sleeper around the world was saying the same sentence in every language known to mankind.

"We have awakened, and we are already all around you."

That's when we heard the first screams from inside the hospital. There was a tumbling of bodies in the hallway and a shattering of glass. Whatever was moving through the hospital hallway was getting closer to the laboratory.

"Block the door and prepare to make a stand," said Rich.

We all rolled anything we could get our hands on towards the main door and the one emergency exit. Carts, beds, metal cabinets, even bed-pans, were piled in a jumble blocking the doors. There was no talk of escape plans because we all knew without saying a word that there was no escape from the inevitable. All across the city, maybe even all across the civilized world, humanity was making its last stand in offices and conference rooms, in laundries and supermarkets, and even in family basements. The time for running was over.

I looked around me and marveled at the brave oddball collection of people I call my friends. Angel was holding a fire extinguisher at the ready. Tony had armed himself with a fire ax pulled from the wall. Rich, bless his heart, carried a tray of hypodermic needles filled with God-knows-what as though he was prepping for a game of darts at the pub. And Johnny cocked a Smith and Wesson revolver in his right hand. When the hell did Johnny get a gun? Are you now allowed to carry a gun in NYC to defend your art gallery? Myself, I made do with an aluminum chair I held over my head prepared to crash down on the first alien skull in sight. I thought this was perhaps the most unlikely collection of warriors I had ever seen. At the same time, I could not imagine standing back-to-back with any more courageous bunch of jackasses at the end of all days.

The lights in the room started flickering. I hadn't noticed before that despite the blackout in the rest of the city, the hospital lights and power were still on. Now they flickered and sputtered for the last time and went out.

"Damn! There goes the emergency generator."

The last rays of the setting sun transformed the laboratory into a harsh realm of long stark shadows and bright light. Very soon the sunshine would dwindle to a sliver of light and the shadows would take over completely. "I have some torches at the ready in that top cabinet to your left, Tony," said Jeanette.

But we never needed the flashlights because our invaders were in too much of a hurry to wait for nightfall.

"We are already all around you," said the sleepers in one voice. And God help us, they weren't lying.

The shadows by the main doorway rippled as though they were underwater. Something large and terrible had shifted into existence in the darkness. In the blink of an eye, a monstrous millipede uncoiled, its shiny, black exoskeleton glistening in the shadows. The thing shot upwards segment by segment, until it rose to nearly eight feet tall, brushing the ceiling. It was as thick around as a man's torso and covered with rows of pincer-like legs rippling in waves up and down its body. The bulbous beetle head, hideously out of proportion to the rest of it, was a misshapen mash-up of insect parts I couldn't bear to look at for more than a second. I remember catching a glimpse of frantically waving antennae covered with bristles, and several compound eyes staring unblinking at us, and slavering, constantly moving mouthparts that looked like nothing else alive on Earth. I choked back a scream, as I stood in absolute terror wondering where I could run. But the spell was broken by Johnny firing his revolver and unloading several bullets into the damn thing. As if on cue, we all attacked.

I don't know if the bullets found any vital organs, but the stream of foam from the fire extinguisher wielded by Angel certainly slowed it down. Momentarily confused, almost uncertain as to where it was. But the creature quickly reoriented itself and surged towards us knocking over carts and chairs and whatever else was in its path. The millipede thing was frighteningly muscular, overturning a large wooden desk with just the slightest touch, and its carapace deflected anything we threw at it. Most of Rich's needles bounced off harmlessly. Tony correctly judged that the bug's head was a relatively soft target and swung hard with his axe as it closed in on him. It landed with a satisfying squelch right in the squishy middle of a compound eye the size of a dinner plate. A hideous shrieking filled the room. But the sound didn't originate from the drooling mouthparts of the alien, but from the lips of every comatose patient in the room.

The screaming stopped and the alien—with axe still firmly embedded in its head—rolled up to its full height. The quivering flappers, labia, or whatever made up its mouth, opened wide and it regurgitated a stream of wet sausage-like things that splashed to the floor. At first, I thought the thing was mortally wounded. But to my horror, I quickly saw that this was its ultimate line of attack.

Whatever came out of its mouth laid there like a steaming pile of disgorged intestines. Then it started to move, squirming into life. The pile metamorphosed into a nest of smaller millipede monsters all skittering across the floor on hundreds of needle-like legs. Dozens of them—all no more than one or two feet in length—swarmed all over us with incredible speed. I reflexively squashed several with the chair legs before I could fully grasp what was happening. Johnny wasn't as lucky as several crawled up his body like crazed cockroaches. After standing uncomprehendingly still for a second or two he started swatting at them. One or two fell to the floor with a clatter, but most of them, easily a half dozen more, scampered towards his head. One encircled his eyes like a shiny black blindfold, another wrapped its body across his mouth. He tried frantically to pull them off his face, but the damn pincher legs had lodged themselves firmly under the skin. Within seconds Johnny's head was completely covered by the millipedes.

And then something stranger and infinitely more horrifying happened. Johnny abruptly stopped struggling as though some sedating drug had taken effect, and he sat himself calmly down on the floor as though having a head wrapped by alien millipedes was the most natural thing in the world. And I understood how they would conquer us: one brain at a time claimed for our arthropod overlords. Johnny now joined the other sleepers dreaming into existence more holes in the sky and more nightmare invaders.

Angel reached out to Johnny, still unaware that there was no way to pull him to safety.

"Don't touch him," screamed Jeanette. "We need to pull back to the emergency exit."

We gathered in a tight group near the back of the room, huddled in the last pool of daylight. The smaller millipedes scampered up the walls and on to the ceiling, no doubt preparing to drop on our heads.

"Is that what's going to happen to all of us?" said Angel fighting back her tears. "Are we going to be covered by...by those things like Johnny?"

"No, that need not be our fate dear child," said Jeanette as she gathered the last of the hypodermic needles. "I have enough here to inject the rest of us. We may not be able to stop them, but we can still deny them our consciousness."

"You go first, Kevin," said Tony. "I'll try holding them back."

"We've been observing your earth," said one of the sleepers, an older man whose one remaining arm was covered in tattoos. "And now we'll make contact with you."

And then I heard the familiar music. Faintly at first, but then imperceptibly building in volume, the sound filled the air in the darkened room.

"Do you hear that music?" I asked stupidly, not even comprehending what I was saying.

The patients were not saying "Surrender!" or "Exterminate!" or even "Resistance is futile!" They were all repeating the lyrics from *Calling Occupants of Interplanetary Craft*.

The music was everywhere now. I would never claim to be the sharpest guy in the room, but even I finally understood what was happening.

"If this isn't nice, I must be dreaming," I said. I looked at the chaos all around me with new eyes. For the first time, I looked at the titles of several scholarly journals and found they were indecipherable gibberish. The clock on the wall clearly showed 5 pm, which was utterly impossible.

"If this isn't nice, I must be dreaming." And I raised my right hand and pointed my five-fingered hand blaster at the towering hundred-legged alien in front of me. Ruby laser rays shot out from my fingertips and struck the thing squarely in its monstrous head. It shrieked in genuine ass-kicking pain this time and reality flickered for a few seconds like an old television signal. The dream doppelgangers of my friends faded from view. T h e jolt of transcranial magnetic stimulation originating from the real-world Goldwater Hospital was frying their alien circuits.

The room around me shifted abruptly like a shaky jump cut in a bad foreign flick. For a few seconds I was back in the ruins of Harrisville from the first part of my dream. Then I was back in the battle-scarred dream-time version of Goldwater. The only constant was the hideous monster bug twisting in agony. I kept pressing the damn buzzer button until the muscles in my fingers started to cramp. The alien deception was almost flawless, but they couldn't control what was happening outside of the dreaming and that was its downfall. The thing finally exploded in a spectacular shower of shredded exoskeleton and insect guts.

After what seemed like an eternity, I opened my eyes and awakened in my hospital bed.

Published on www.fanfiction.net on July 30, 2015

* * *

Smallpox Hospital Ruins, Roosevelt Island, NYC

Dear Friends and Family,

I hope you enjoyed the Invasion Day piece I posted today. It will be the last story I'll ever write. It was exactly how I wanted my own story to end—with guns blazing, screaming victory in the face of the most hopeless defeat. So I desperately manufactured that reality by putting pen to paper. We all carry secret stories within us. Some stories we reveal only to our closest friends and family. Other stories we only tell ourselves in the darkest night when we know nobody is listening. Sometimes we fool ourselves into thinking we have no story at all.

Here's my story: I'm a brave hero who will rescue the people he loves from the unknown. Just like the doctor in Night Terror, I'll figure out a way to protect others from the approaching evil. I don't think I fully appreciated how powerful that story was in making sense of my own life until the last several days.

I had a strange thought this morning that it should be autumn already. There was something about the chill in the air, the fragile poignancy that attaches itself to every activity. Even with another blanket on the bed, you're stopped cold by an unwelcome shiver in the morning. I'm easily tempted into thinking that I could just stay here under the covers forever and never get up ever again. The light of day is extinguished too fast. You blink and night has crept in and conquered everything. The leaves start dying and only then show their true colors.

So Tony, you're absolutely right. You too Mom and Dad. I'm really a jackass. But even I'm smart enough to figure out what happens next. I can't remember everything that happened once those crazy blue lights surrounded me in Harrisville. It's all fuzzy, like those fleeting dreams you have napping on the subway between stations. But I'm damn certain of one thing: I've got to keep myself and my fucking secrets hidden away forever. Nobody must ever find out what really happened in Aurora, Texas in 1897. Never in my wildest nightmares did I think it would cause such devastation to me and all my friends, to the whole world. I'm the trigger for this whole shit show. Somehow—I don't know exactly how—but somehow I've caused all this. All the suicides, the missing people, the army of homeless and helpless victims. I know that sounds crazy, but I also know it's true. So a real super fail in my career as a hero, right?

At least I wrote the stories to keep you all safe from the Kunstkammer Kooks. It was the only way to warn you without revealing myself. I pray that worked. Listen, I'm not asking for forgiveness. I don't deserve it. Just forget all about me. Burn everything I own and salt the ground. Maybe, just maybe this will stop it all from happening.

That's why I'm hiding all this time. That's me desperately avoiding the inevitable. There's this icicle razor feeling in my gut—cutting me to the bone—that's pushing me, forcing me inexorably towards my monumental fuck-up. I couldn't tell you all to stop looking for me because you damn geniuses wouldn't listen. Thankfully, I've hidden my important evidence where nobody will ever find it. So the only answer I keep coming up with is this: I have to remove myself from the playing field permanently. Maybe if I'm no longer in the game, I can't lose it. Can't commit any unforced errors, right? Yeah, that answer sucks, but I can't come up with anything better.

Believe me, this is the only way to keep the world safe. Ladies and gentlemen, you're welcome to come up with better endings to your own stories, but mine is finished.

Handwritten note at bottom of page: *Manuscript found on the body of Kevin Starkly on July 30, 2015. Police concluded he committed suicide by jumping from the top of Ryker's Smallpox Hospital and breaking his neck.*

RIP Old Friend: **Non hodie Quod heri**—*I am not today what I was yesterday.*

Handwritten note on top of page: *Unpublished piece from Night Tours zine files*

Written by Starkly?

An Aboriginal Dreamtime Lesson

The Oracle picked up the Book of Law and began reading.

"In the beginning there was the Dreamtime and all Earth lay sleeping in the darkness and nothingness. One day the Rainbow Serpent awoke from her sleep and burst out from under the ground. She snaked all over the barren surface leaving the marks of her winding tracks across the landscape. Then she returned to where she burst through the ground, and called to all the Ancestor Beings, 'Come out!'

First, the frogs came out and started to laugh with delight. When the frogs laughed, water rained down because their bellies were heavy with water. The water filled the tracks left behind by the Rainbow Serpent and made all the lakes and rivers we see today.

Next all the other animals awoke and followed the Rainbow Serpent— Ant, Grasshopper, Emu, Eagle, Crow, Kangaroo, Lizard, and more. Soon, grass and trees sprang up.

The Rainbow Serpent made laws that they all were to obey, but some refused to listen. She said, 'Those who keep my laws will be rewarded and I will give them human form. But those who break my laws will be punished and turned to stone.'

The lawbreakers were turned to all the mountains and hills we see today."

The Oracle then asked, "And what was the first and greatest of the laws?"

One hand went up. "You shall not be proud and steal the secrets of the Rainbow Serpent from the Dreamtime," said the small creature who was once human. But she could not lower her arm because it had quickly frozen in place and turned to stone.

* * *

From *The Last Days of Nikola Tesla: Secrets Behind the World's Greatest Mad Scientist* **by E.G. Hardwicke (Penguin Books, 2013)**

No one would be more delighted with all the crazy kudzu growth of tangled conspiracy theories and genuine puzzles surrounding the last days of Nikola Tesla than Tesla himself. He was a secretive man who paradoxically craved attention from fans and foes alike, expertly massaging the mass media of his time. He would tease the world with outrageous pronouncements timed especially for his famous birthday parties or leak partial details of his work to major newspapers and magazines. Of course, his secrecy was a double-edged sword. That which is well hidden is often too soon forgotten.

Most already know about the wild speculations about supposed "death-ray" blueprints confiscated by the U.S. military, the rumors of a secret will hidden away in an underground vault in the Tesla Museum in Belgrade, and the great riddle concerning the final resting place of hundreds of his unpatented research papers, but few know about this obscure but puzzling incident from January 7, 1943.

Tesla was gravely ill at the time and bedridden by doctor's orders. The great man lapsed in and out of consciousness. Earlier that day he requested a Postal Telegraph messenger boy named Bill Kerrigan to feed his favorite flock of pigeons in Bryant Park. Tesla then instructed Kerrigan to deliver a plain manila envelope to Robert Underwood Johnson at 35 South Fifth Avenue and made it clear that this should be done with the utmost urgency. Johnson was the former editor of *Century* magazine and a close friend of Tesla for many years.

Light rain from earlier in the evening turned to a freezing downpour as Kerrigan sought out the address with no luck. He eventually realized that 35 South Fifth was the location of Tesla's old laboratory from the 1880s and was long since gone, erased from the new street grid once South Fifth was renamed West Broadway. Undeterred, he raced through the storm and found the correct address at 327 Lexington Avenue but learned from the current owner that Robert Underwood Johnson had unfortunately passed away.

When Kerrigan returned soaking wet back to the Hotel New Yorker, Tesla refused to believe his old friend was gone. "Don't be foolish boy, I just spoke with Robert the other night," he said. "Now give him this letter immediately."

Not sure of what to do, Kerrigan went to his supervisor.

Both thought the circumstances warranted that the letter should be opened. After all, there might be important information that *someone* should know about.

What they found inside was more bizarre than anyone could have guessed.

Written in block letters on a plain white paper were the words ABRUFEN SIE DAS NACHT-PAKET—translated literally from German as "Retrieve the Night Package."

Did Tesla have some secret arrangement with his old confidante? Was he referring to one of the many boxes of arcane equipment stored away in the basement of the hotel? Oddly, there is no mention of a "night package" to be found in any of the voluminous correspondence between Tesla and the Johnsons, either Robert or his wife Katherine. Or maybe it was just a simple delusion.

Obviously both Kerrigan and his supervisor thought so since they didn't bother to disturb Tesla again that night. Surely it could wait until morning.

A hotel maid named Alice Monaghan, ignoring the "Do Not Disturb" sign on the door, discovered that Tesla had died in his sleep sometime during the night of January 7. The official cause of death was simply listed as "coronary thrombosis" –a heart attack.

From the plaque placed near the entrance to Tesla's Wardenclyffe laboratory

In this building designed by Stanford White, architect,

Nikola Tesla, born Smiljan, Yugoslavia 1856, Died New York, USA 1943,

Constructed in 1901-1905 Wardenclyffe,

Huge radio station with antenna tower 187 feet high (Destroyed 1917),

Which was to serve as his first World Communications System.

In memory of 120th anniversary of Tesla's birth and 200th anniversary of USA independence. July 10, 1976

* * *

From the dream journal of Anthony Fermia

July 30, 2015

Last night I dreamed we once again descended into the abyss at Wardenclyffe.

We were all there—me, Rich, Johnny, Angel, and even Kevin, although he wasn't really with us that day. We would discover later that even as we drove out to Shoreham he was already dead, but of course we had no way of knowing that at the time. Angel insisted on coming along because she had possession of all of Kevin's "spelunking shit" that we needed to rappel down into the pit.

It all felt exactly as it did that night in late July when we arrived at Wardenclyffe. A small breeze provided some relief from the oppressive heat, and I could smell ozone in the air from an approaching storm. We cut through the fence and snuck past the lone security guard. It didn't take long to find the shaft that was uncovered more than a month earlier by the big earthquake. It was surrounded by a few sawhorses and French barricades that would hopefully prevent the curious from accidentally dropping to their death while the bureaucrats decided what to do next. The hole was a good 12 feet in diameter and deeper than anything I could have imagined. Our flashlight beams searched in vain for the bottom of the thing but found only more darkness in the depths. We knew it was probably deeper than a ten-story building and none of us had ever attempted anything like this before, but that didn't slow us down one bit.

Even though Rich had a paralyzing fear of heights, he volunteered to go first. "It only makes sense that if this gear can support me, it can support all of us."

Within minutes, Rich was in harness and slowly lowered into the pit. It wasn't long before he disappeared from view completely—he was just a small dot of light and a disembodied voice on the radio. He wasn't terribly good at rappelling, and he kept slipping down too fast and too erratically.

Johnny yelled into the radio, "Rich, you're bouncing around like a damn jackrabbit. Slow down!"

"I'm fine. I think I can finally see the bottom of this…"

And that was the last we heard from Rich on the radio. I think we all panicked a little at that point. Johnny wanted to pull him out of there immediately and get the hell back home, but I cautioned that moving him before we knew the extent of his injuries would be dangerous. I remember teaming up with Angel and the two of us plunging into the abyss together. Time was working against us, so we knew we had to act as quickly as possible.

Rich was unconscious, but otherwise unharmed. He apparently hit his head against an outcropping along the side of the shaft while he was carelessly swinging about.

In the dream Kevin says, "Let's just leave Rich here while we explore ahead. I'm sure that's what he would want us to do."

But of course in reality, I was the one who suggested we leave Rich lying on the ground, not Kevin. I'm still not sure which is worse: me for my insistence on continuing to explore the bottom of the shaft, or everyone else for following along without voicing a single objection.

We didn't have far to travel. Within a few feet of where we landed, we discovered what looked like a small storage room that had been sealed away since 1917. Layers of dust and dirt covered an assortment of wooden crates piled to the ceiling. But we all recognized our prize as soon as we laid eyes on it. In the middle of the room was a metal sphere covered with numerous spikes like an oversize sea urchin. It had a thick glass window, like the viewing port on a bathysphere but larger. There was only room inside for one small body the size of a child. None of us dared look through the window.

"Is that...is that what I think it is?" asked Angel. I nodded because we all sensed this was the final resting place for the Aurora pilot.

"Okay guys, let's get of here now and call the police." said Johnny, who could always be counted on to point out the most sensible thing.

It was the first time in this impulsive adventure that I actually thought about the end result of our little quest. Maybe I always believed that we would find Kevin before anything else, and we could call it quits. And in the back of my mind I think I secretly wished that the Aurora story really wasn't true, that maybe it was all a tall tale concocted by Lawless Starkly to scare his kid.

"There's no way we can haul that sphere up to the top," said Angel. "It must weigh like a ton. Maybe we can take some pictures, some cool video, and get the hell out of here."

Of course, I realize now in hindsight that was exactly what we should have done. We should have taken enough pictures as evidence to prove we were there and that this secret room existed at the bottom of the pit. But that didn't happen.

In the dream Kevin whispers to me, "You know Tesla has been guiding you here all along. He's been guiding all of us."

"But he worked on this damn project for years with no success," I protested. "He probably wired it up to his tower for some secret reason. It was all a failure. Maybe he wanted to use it like an alien battery, or maybe he wanted to awaken it like some Frankenstein's monster."

But Kevin insisted, "We know something that the genius Tesla never knew, that nobody in the whole damn world knows, except the people in this room."

"What are you talking about?"

"We know its name." Kevin smiled that smile he always gave when he wanted you to agree with whatever crackpot observation he was making.

But of course, in reality I said, "Max As Abraxas."

"What did you say, Tony?" asked Johnny.

Again I said, "Max As Abraxas."

Nothing happened.

"Say it one more time," said the dream Kevin. Lawless wrote that it didn't sound like much of a proper name to him. Sounds more like an incantation, doesn't it?

"Max As Abraxas!"

And after the last syllable sounded there was a blinding flash in the underground chamber, and the room filled with light for the first time in nearly a century. We all closed our eyes and turned away from the spike-covered sphere, barely able to breathe. But I could hear the sound of rusty bolts dropping to the ground and of a metal portal creaking open.

When I opened my eyes again the room was dark with only the dim glow of the hallway light to reassure me. I was back in my bedroom in Corona, Queens, and I was ten years old. Once again, I was paralyzed with fear looking at my bedroom door. I noticed now that someone or something was blocking the light from the hallway. I couldn't make out the figure very clearly in the darkness, but I could sense it turning to face me. The head seemed all wrong, as though it was way out of proportion to the rest of its body. Almost against my will, I remembered a little more than last time. Before the darkness engulfed me, I saw two glowing red eyes staring straight at me. And then it opened all its other eyes at once and they all blinked.

From the note found at the bottom of the pit at Wardenclyffe

Dear Luka,

For the sake of our friendship, I hope you will find it in your heart to forgive me now that you know the secret of my mysterious "night package." You'll agree that *nacht-paket* seemed apropos for something hidden in a nest of German spies (at least according to our overwrought tabloids). Please believe me when I tell you I brought this creature here with the best of intentions and the highest regard for scientific research. Sadly, I failed in my mission, and I failed this wretched thing even more.

Now it is up to you to continue my work.

It makes no more sense for me to insist that this poor creature locked in this metal sphere is my property than it is for any man to claim ownership of the clouds in the heavens, or perhaps the waves of the oceans. In truth, I lay claim only to being its rescuer.

I know not what manner of creature it is, nor from which planet it claims as home. I know only that when I first read the story of its arrival, I understood immediately that this was the same heaven-sent messenger I saw crash to the Earth in a vision years ago. I had just graduated from Polytechnic and was laid low with a dire illness from which my recovery was not at all assured. I understood also, in ways that I still cannot fully explain, that this creature, whether Martian or Survivor from the Stars, would be my greatest ally.

At the earliest opportunity, while construction on my laboratory in Colorado Springs was well underway, I traveled secretly to the Masonic Cemetery in Aurora, Texas. While unearthing the creature from its grave and then reburying its shoddy pine coffin in the middle of the night I had the most remarkable vision. I saw fully formed before my eyes, the design for its final container which stands before you as the centerpiece in this chamber, in much the same way I perceived the design for my alternating current motor.

The design apparently shares the same lineage as the wondrous diving helmet conceived by the Brothers Carmagnolle in Marseille in the early 1880s. Thinking this was some indication that it needed a different atmospheric pressure in order to revive itself, I quickly rigged a re-circulating air filter and connected it to the sphere. Alas, changes in air pressure produced no visible signs of life in the creature whatsoever. It neither stirred, but neither did it naturally decay. My idea is that the development of life might lead to forms of existence very different from the ones with which we are familiar. There may be creatures, and perhaps entire civilizations, that are unconcerned with nourishment as we understand it. Why should a living being not be able to obtain all the energy it needs from the environment, instead of through consumption of food, and transform the natural forces around it into life-sustaining energy?

Also under cover of night, I brought my "package" here and literally built Wardenclyffe around it. It was retrieved in darkness and found its new home in darkness as well. The truth is that this creature was always at the heart of all my experiments here on Long Island.

If this intelligent being could be revived in some way, through the free transmission of the Earth's energy, I would be the first man to relay the secrets of the universe to a waiting world hungry for answers. So like Dr. Frankenstein I sought every way imaginable to bring life back to its silent heart. I would stand as a Prometheus for a new century stealing fire from the gods. What a tremendous stir this would make in the world! No one, not even my prime benefactor, Mr. Morgan, understands completely the mission I have undertaken here in my Radio City.

Unfortunately, you stand amidst my greatest failure. The secrets from this silent ally have so far eluded me. If you are reading this then my unspoken fear has become reality and I am no longer able to carry on my research. I now depend on you my old friend to finally reveal this secret to the world. Please keep the secret passage to the underground chamber open (Scherff assures me this is so, though he knows not the reason) for if it is covered over all hope is lost. Let the greatest minds work together to wake this sleeping messenger from beyond and grant mankind's greatest wish. May it unlock free wireless transmission of power creating an industrial revolution as the world has never seen before? Maybe it will unlock even greater wonders than any human mind can imagine.

I don't know why these visions had been sent to taunt me and frustrate my desires. But I hope you will demonstrate soon that in my experiments under Wardenclyffe I was not merely beholding a fool's vision but had caught sight of a great and profound truth.

Your friend,

Nikola

From the hypnotic regression transcript of John Walters

August 2, 2015

Stryker: *You are now back to that night in Shoreham, Long Island. You are back at that place called Wardenclyffe. What do you remember?*

John: It's hot here. I thought there might be some relief from the heat because its dark, but the ground is just…it's just radiating more heat.

Stryker: *Are you alone?*

John: No, we're all here. The whole Nerd Legion assembled. But Kevin's not here. Damn, where is he?

Stryker: *Very well John, now listen to me carefully. You are now at the bottom of the pit at Wardenclyffe. Tell me what you see there.*

John: No, I don't want to go back there.

Stryker: *It's alright John. It's just a short visit. You'll soon be safe again.*

John: Okay.

Stryker: *What do you see?*

John: I'm telling everyone we have to get out of here and help Rich.

Stryker: *Is Richard hurt?*

John: He's knocked unconscious. I think the back of his head is bleeding a little. But Tony is saying, "Let's just find what we came for first, then we can go."

Stryker: *Then what happens?*

John: Angel agrees with Tony that we should look around first. I'm scared. We should leave now. Rich is just lying there bleeding and we're screwing around. It's not right.

Stryker: *Do you find anything down there?*

John: Yes, we find the...Do I have to stay here?

Stryker: *Just for a little longer John. Now what do you see?*

John: Tony breaks open this forgotten side door. There's like a small storage room back there.

Stryker: *Is there anything still in that room?*

John: There are a bunch of wooden packing crates. God only knows what's in those boxes. Everything is thick with dust. I can't stop coughing. It smells like gunpowder...no, like ozone. Like a coming storm. Angel finds an old envelope on a metal table and she slips it into her backpack. That letter must have been sitting unopened on that table for what, 90, almost 100 years?

Oh, what's that thing?

Stryker: *What else do you see?*

John: It looks like a bathysphere. It's a big metal ball covered with metal spikes. It's like a Louise Bourgeois sculpture, or maybe like an undersea mine.

Did they have bathyspheres back in the early 1900s?

Stryker: *Is it very big?*

John: No, it's smaller than the one I remember at the Coney Island Aquarium. In fact, it only looks big enough to hold… to hold a child.

Stryker: *What happens next?*

John: It's funny. Nobody says anything, but I just know we're all thinking the same thing. This thing, this metal ball, must be holding the Aurora alien.

Stryker: *Can you see what's inside, or can you open it?*

John: There's a window, like a small porthole, but I don't want to look inside. I'm really scared. Nobody wants to look inside first.

Stryker: *Then what happens?*

John: Tony starts chanting something.

Chanting?

No, he's…he's saying its name. He's
saying Max As Abraxas like he's calling to it after all these decades. Like
he's reciting a spell.

Does anyone else say anything?

It all happens so fast. I want him to
shut up. I told Tony to stop talking.

Oh no, it's too late.

Is something wrong?

Damn, it's all wrong. We're not supposed to be down here. Now there's
light pouring out of that metal ball.
Oww, my eyes are hurting! It's so
bright I have to look away. We all turn
away from it.

Can you see anything?

I don't want to see it again. Can I
please go back home now?

*Just for a little while longer John.
Now what do you see?*

I hear something first before I see
anything. I hear a metal door creaking open. I think it's coming from
the sphere, but I can't be sure
because I can't see it through the
blinding light.

Then the light is gone. Poof! Like someone threw the switch off. I turn around now and I'm really terrified now because I see someone else standing there in the middle of the room.

Who is it?

I think it's him…it…whatever. I think it's the alien pilot that crashed in Aurora. Oh my God. How can he be standing there?

How can you see him in the dark?

I don't know. It's like it's not totally dark like before. Maybe he's glowing.

Can you tell me what he looks like?

No, I don't want to look at it.

Please John, just take a quick look. He can't hurt you now.

Okay. He…I think it's a he because it looks like a small boy wrapped up in black bandages. Maybe like a ten-year-old boy, about three feet tall.

He has normal arms and legs?

Uh-huh. It looks like he has normal human-like fingers too. I can't see his feet.

What else do you notice?

Oh, his head is much too big. It looks
swollen. It's twice the size of a normal head. And the eyes…

What about the eyes?

His head is covered with little red
eyes. They're all looking around and
blinking at the same time. They cover
his head in all the places where
they're not supposed to be. There must
be 20, maybe 25 of them. Where the eyes
should be white, they're all red.

Are there any other facial features?

He doesn't seem to have a nose or ears
that I can make out. He has no hair at
all. Oh, but there is a mouth. He has
a normal, an otherwise normal-look-
ing mouth. I can't take my eyes off him.
I don't want to see this, but I can't
help myself.

Do you feel compelled to look?

Uh-huh, like I have no choice. It's funny, I get the impression he's wearing a helmet, but it doesn't look like any helmet I've ever seen. I'm just staring at him. Especially those red blinking eyes. I'm looking closely at him now and I see that what I first thought were bandages wrapped around him are actually markings on his skin… drawings like tattoos. Maybe like writing, but I can't make it out. Ohhh.

What happened?

They moved. I mean I saw the markings moving across his skin like they're alive. Black things coiling around his body like a nest of snakes…like maggots crawling through a corpse, and…I don't want to look at him anymore. Please make it stop. Make me…stop looking.

Please Johnny, you're safe now. What are the others doing?

The others? That's funny. I can't see them. They must be right next to me because the room isn't that large, but I can't see them.

Does anyone say anything?

Yes, he talks to us. I mean, I don't see his mouth move, but I can hear him talking inside my head.

What does he say?

He asks, "What time is it?" Just like
that. Just like some customer at the
gallery checking the time.

And do you say anything?

For some reason, I don't know why I
say this, but I tell him, "The time is
now." I don't know why I said that.
It's like I was instructed to say it
all along. And he smiles. He actually smiles and I can see normal teeth
in his mouth. And he says, "That's a
good answer."

How does his voice sound? Is it…

He sounds reassuring. I mean inside my
head his voice sounds like a normal
adult male. He sounds like he's talking
to an old friend. The tone is like
"Isn't this a funny spot we've found
ourselves in, but we're all going to be
fine," but he doesn't actually say that.

What does he say?

He says, "You know my name. You must
know Lawless Scott Starkly. What's
your name?"

So I introduce myself to him and I tell
him the year. I don't get the sense
that he seems alarmed that he's been
locked away for over 100 years. I think
he has a different sense of time than
we do.

Why do you say that?

I don't know. It's just a feeling I
have that time is more abstract to
him. It's like a game, not like a com-
modity that can be saved or wasted. I
don't know why I sense that. Oddly, I
don't feel terrified any longer. I just
feel a curious strangeness. Like this
should be happening to someone else and
not me.

Does he say anything else?

No. But I asked him a question. I ask,
"What are you? Where do you come from?"

Does he answer you?

He says, "I'm just like you." The
answer is so absurd I start to laugh.
He sees my amusement and he tries to
clarify, "We share the same ancestors,
a long time ago."

Is he claiming to be human?

Yes, but not *Homo sapiens*, like us.
He's another species of hominid that
broke away from a common ancestor many
years ago. Maybe a million, two million
years ago?

He says, "We walked the plains of
Africa with your ancestors many, many
years ago, but we choose a different
path of evolution."

What does he mean by "a different path?"

I'm not sure. He says something which
I don't understand. He says, "We went
to grow in the dreamtime away from the
world." Maybe it was some hidden place
or maybe another reality altogether. I
don't know.

Do you ask any other questions?

I think I told him that I'm confused.
I'm confused because I thought, we
all thought really, that he was some
alien creature from another planet in
outer space.

He seems confused when I tell him this. His eyes, all his eyes blink, and they all look at me and he says, "There is nothing in space. There is not another single intelligent creature anywhere in space. We are all alone on this world." I don't understand how he could possibly know something like that, but he says it with such utter conviction that I feel a chill down my spine.

Does he say anything else?

Uh-huh. He says that his people have given us…I guess he means *Homo sapiens*… they have given us many gifts over the years. Oh, he says they taught us agriculture, and writing, and laws. They even instructed some of us…I get the feeling he's referring to specific people here…they taught some of us how to make certain machines. But he says the greatest gift they gave our species was something that couldn't be built. Oh, I see.

What did he say?

He said, "We gave you the First Dream
about 40,000 years ago." I'm not sure
what he means, but obviously he thinks
this is something very important. Then
he says, "I have missed so much speaking with you in the dreamtime. Our
peoples communicated with each other
often, but now we hardly talk at all.
Why don't you speak with us anymore?"

And what do you say?

I don't know what to answer. So I offer
some lame apologies. And he tells me,
"No, I owe you a great deal because I
was dead to the world sleeping under
the earth and you have awakened me.
What can I do to repay you?"

Repay you?

Yes, that's what he says, but it makes
no sense to me. Again he says, "I know
what to do for you and your generation,
I have just the right gift for you."

What gift is he talking about?

I don't think I like this part coming
up now. Can I go back home now?

Don't worry. It's almost over now John.
What does he say?

He asks me, "Wouldn't you like to know what happens next?" And I wish I said please, please, please don't give me any gift. I don't want to know anything. But instead, God help me, I say, "Yes, can you tell me?"

What does he say?

He reaches out his right hand and he says, "I'll tell everyone. Just touch my hand." I don't really want to touch him because I'm afraid he'll feel as strange as he looks. But his hand seems normal enough, like the hand of a little boy. I find myself reaching out to him and grabbing hold of his right hand. And...and...

What's happening to you now?

This is strange. I'm lifted upwards
into some black vortex, like I'm caught
in a tornado funnel, and I'm spinning wildly around. I'm no longer in
the hidden room. I'm somewhere else in
another place and I can't control my
movements. The only way I can describe
it is if you're riding the Cyclone in
Coney Island and you're just coming
over the hill heading down into that
first drop and you get that crazy ass-
lifting-off-the-edge-of-your-seat feeling and you don't know if you're flying
into space or dropping into a bottomless pit. It's exhilarating and terrifying all at the same time.

What do you see?

I'm passing all these scenes, like
flashes of scenes anyway, from people's
lives. Like rooms passing in a vast
mansion. There are vignettes swirling around me like a whirlwind. But if
I look closely at these scenes, they
begin to seem familiar. Oh, now I know.
These are all scenes from my life and
I'm in all of them. And they're all
happening simultaneously. How is that
possible? I have to step out into the
whirlwind. It's the only way to experience my future, but I'm afraid. I close
my eyes and I jump out...

What happened? Where are you?

(pause)

Please leave me alone. Can't you see
I'm worried about my wife?

Your wife?

Barbara seemed fine earlier. She just
wanted to take a little rest in the
back room of the gallery. You know how
she hates these opening night shin-
digs. Then someone starts telling me
that they attacked another shopping
mall out on Long Island, but this time
they killed only about 100 or so people. But I don't want to hear about
it. I wanted to…what was I saying? Oh
yes. So Barbara is always bored out of
her mind. She just nurses a glass of
white wine for the evening and makes
faces at me from across the room. She's
always trying to crack me up just as
I'm talking to an artist or trying to
close a deal with a new buyer. The EMS
guys are with her now. She's going to
be fine, right?

*Johnny, how long has it been since you
visited Wardenclyffe?*

Wardenclyffe? That was years ago.
Anyway, I went to check on her and
she's shaking uncontrollably. She's
having these, what do you call them?
She's having convulsions on the couch
in the back room. She's talking gibberish and I don't think she even knows
that I'm there. I called 911 immediately and they're on their way right
now. I mean, they're here right now.
I'm so nervous, I don't even know what
I'm saying. How did this happen so
fast? I think she was sleeping in the
back for only a short time. What was
it? 30 minutes? 45 minutes?

I had to cancel the rest of the preview
opening. You know Barbara hates these
opening nights. Leslie is home watching
the girls for us. Guess I should call
them and tell them that mommy is feeling sick. What's this?

What happened?

Oh, now I remember. It's Barbara's
necklace. She wanted me to hold it for
her while she napped in the back. Guess
I've been rubbing them in my hands like
worry beads all this time. Forgot I had
them until just now. Tahitian pearls.
The necklace is made of Tahitians
pearls. It was my first anniversary
present for Barbara. EMS is taking her
out on a stretcher now. That must be
pretty serious. Why isn't she moving?
She's going to be fine, right? Yes, I'm
going in the ambulance with her. Have
to get my coat. Oh Jesus…

Johnny?

The necklace broke in my hands. Damn!
It just all…it all fell apart just now
as I was holding it. The pearls are
bouncing all over the floor. I have to
get them back together. She loved this
necklace. I'm crawling on my hands and
knees trying to catch them all. Please
hold the ambulance. Please. Can't you
see I'm trying to find all the pearls?
If they would only stop rolling, I
could string them together again and
everything would be back to normal.
Please just let me find them. Oh God,
please let me fix this. They've all
rolled under the chairs and tables.

(pause)

Oh, here it is. The roll of duct tape was in the closet all along. If you think it's too cold, I'll close the window for you. I just love to leave it open and smell that pine tree in the backyard.

Johnny? Where are you now?

I'm back home, of course. There's no place left to find materials anymore. All the stores are empty. Everyone has to fend for themselves. Thank God, I found this old cardboard box upstairs in the attic. No wood to be found anywhere you know.

What are you doing?

Isn't it obvious? It's what all good mommies and daddies are doing all over the city. Hell, I guess all over the world. It's funny. It's almost Christmastime but I've forgotten all about it. I don't much feel like celebrating anything you know. It's a season for condolences now. It's the year nobody celebrated Christmas.

Why are you sad, Johnny?

All the little ones are dying. Well, it's affecting the old and the very sick too, but it's the little ones dying that is so heartbreaking. I saw on one of the webs that some pundits are calling it the Great Culling. All the weakest are taken from us—the frail and the hopeless. But why take the babies? I'm glad Barbara isn't alive to see this day. She would be devastated. She would walk down Eastern Parkway and see all the bodies piled up in the streets like…like trash. Oh, some people make an attempt to wrap them in blankets or bags or whatever they can find. Sometimes they're too tired to make much of any attempt at all. Little bodies discarded like dead Christmas trees. And she would never stop crying. Just as I've never stopped crying. They say some people are just tossing them in the East River. Others are burning them like piles of autumn leaves in Central Park. Of course, you can't believe half of what you see on the webs these days.

Did you know this was the box where we kept Kimmy's favorite ornaments?

I thought that was…you know, appropriate. Kimmy would get so excited when we took the box downstairs. She always wanted to be the first to put her "special ones" on the tree. Barbara was always so good about stopping them from fighting when it was on the verge of getting out of control. She would say, "Okay, you can put yours on first, but then your big sister gets the honor of putting the star on the top." And that would settle it. Barbara was so good with the girls. Joan especially misses her so much. I miss her so much. Kimmy was too young to understand about Mommy…about Mommy going away. What was I saying? Oh yes, now I remember. Afterwards, after Joan placed her "sparkle star" on the tippy top of the tree, Kimmy would curl up in the box and fall asleep. She seemed so small in that big cardboard box just last year. Now, she's just grown enough that it's a perfect fit. Look for yourself.

Did I ever tell you that Barbara wasn't
supposed to have any children after
Joan? That's what the doctors warned.
But when Kimmy came along, we thought
that was a sign. We thought that it was
a sign that…that the world had something special planned for Kimmy. She
was our miracle baby…our poor little
miracle. Anyway, that's why I need the
duct tape. I need to close up the box
and wrap it up tightly. Wrap it up like
a Christmas present to God. I feel too
tired and drained to carry her tonight.
Maybe I'll keep her in the backyard
just for one last night…just one more
night under the pine tree.

(pauses)

It's too dark here. Why don't they turn
on the lights?

Are you still at home Johnny?

No, I don't want to come here.

Are you back at the gallery?

No. Nobody makes art anymore. I'm at the conversion station. The one on Fourth Avenue. They said something happened to Joan…something about the procedure not taking. That's exactly what I warned her about. I told her that these people don't know what they're doing.

A conversion station?

Yes, the one on Fourth. I told her it's mankind's last gasp of arrogance and stupidity. They think they can scare away disease and death by replacing flesh with metal. Oh, what have they done to my Joan? I don't want to go in the room and see her. Isn't that terrible? What kind of Daddy am I? I guess that's why they have the lights so low… so you can't see what they've done.

Joan, are you in there? Oh, here's a dimmer control on the wall. Maybe I can adjust the lights better. Oh my God…

What do you see Johnny?

They haven't even picked her up off the
floor. She's crumpled on the ground.
She's just a jumble of flesh fused with
hot metal. Oh Joan, what have they done
to you? She's pulling herself across
the tiled floor with her arms. Her arms
still look mostly human, but her legs…
her legs are splayed out behind her.
The pumps…what do they call them? The
motor pumps and flanges and bolts are
useless. It's just dragging behind her…
this twisted mass of wires and struts,
this simulacrum of human legs…she's
just pulling it behind her. Oh God,
there's so much metal and mesh wrapped
around her, I can't even see what she's
wearing. Oh no, they shaved off all her
beautiful hair for the cranium implant.
All her beautiful black hair is gone. I
can't look any more. I have to turn off
the lights again. What's that?

What's going on now?

Joan is saying something. At least
she's opening up her mouth. I think
if I get a little closer I can make
it out.

What is she saying?

She says, "You promised you would be here Daddy." Oh God, all I want to do is cradle her, hold my big girl in my arms and tell her that I love her so much. I want to tell her that my heart is so full of love for her and no matter where she goes in her life or where she travels, my love will follow her anywhere in the world and she will feel it and her heart…and her heart will grow stronger and she will be so strong she can face anything…we can face anything together. But God help me, the only thing I can say is "I'm sorry…I'm sorry…I'm sorry." And I run out of that damned room as fast as I can. I'm running down Fourth Avenue for about a block before I realize that I can't even see where I'm going, I can't see because of all the tears in my eyes. Oh, what am I going to do now?

Johnny?

Please tell me. What can I do?

Johnny, listen to me. You are going to take yourself above all this. You're going to watch the rest of your life as though you were watching…like you were watching a movie. You can feel yourself floating above it. Now you're going to fast forward through the scenes in the movie. We're fast forwarding to the end of the movie. Do you understand me?

Uh-huh.

Now you're coming to the last scene you remember seeing. This is the last scene and then we're all finished. Where are you now Johnny?

They finished the evacuation of the city
yesterday. They marched all the people
away in this long unending parade of
cars and carriages and trucks and ambu-
lances and bikes. It went on forever.
I watched some of it going by outside
the house. They couldn't force anyone
to leave, you know. The dead and dying
they just left them behind in the big
rush. They left all the dying behind
them. It was like the circus leaving
town, except with none of the color
and gaiety but only the…only the emptiness. The authorities…you know…the
authorities don't have the power to do
anything anymore. They can only issue
those insipid color-coded warnings.
What do they call them? Amber alerts?
Yellow for heightened caution. Green
for go. Stop on the red. Purple haze.

Anyway, I watched them all go away down the street. But I'm too old to go anywhere, so I'm staying right here at my house. Well, it's not my house anymore, is it? I mean the state confiscated all private property years ago. I'm here at the house with all the others left behind. Christ, every room is packed. That's why I like to stay out here in the backyard. Did I tell you that it was Barbara who inspired me to try gardening? Nothing really grows in the soil anymore, but I still enjoy puttering around back here pretending that it makes a difference.

You know sometimes whole days go past and I don't think about Barbara even once. Then out of the blue I'll see a little girl on the street that reminds me of Joan, or I'll pass a spot where Kimmy used to love to race. And it hits me hard like a sucker punch to my gut. And I have to stop in my tracks…I mean physically stop in my tracks because the wind is knocked out of me.

Why are you staying behind Johnny?

That's funny. Nobody has called me
Johnny for such a long time. They have
numbers and colors for everything, but
hardly any names anymore. More effi-
cient, don't you know. Except it's just
a pathetic attempt to hide the truth.
And the truth is that they can't gov-
ern anything. Shit, they can't even
pick up the bodies anymore. It used to
be they collected the metal and glass
on Tuesday morning, paper on Thursday,
and the dead on Saturday. Now they…I'm
sorry, what did you ask me?

Why aren't you leaving Johnny?

I don't know. Maybe I'm just too old
to care what happens to me. Or maybe…
maybe I think I deserve whatever I get.
I don't deserve to live. Everyone I
know has either left me…or I've abandoned them. Can't say I blame them. I'm
ashamed of some of the terrible things
I've done in the past to stay alive.
The people I've hurt. I'm particularly
ashamed of the time…do you promise to
keep a secret?

You don't have to tell me anything.

It doesn't matter anymore. I'll tell
you anyway. I exchanged my wedding
ring, my precious wedding ring, for a
night of pleasure with a woman I hardly
knew. I promised Barbara I would never
take that ring off my finger. Did I tell
you it was the only piece of jewelry I ever wore? But I was so lonely,
I couldn't think of anything else to
sell. It was designed by an artist
Barbara knew and she carved these gor-
geous Celtic patterns around the ring.
The lines intertwined around each
other and around the ring into infin-
ity. Now it belongs to some woman whose
name I can't remember. She loved the
lines twisting together and our bodies
wrapped around each other. Does it matter that I was thinking of Barbara as
we made love? No, I guess not.

So now I'm looking forward to my death.
All these aches and pains in my joints
keep me uncomfortable all day long.
But I won't have any of those damna-
ble implants or augments in my body. No
sir! I've aged so much in just the last
ten years. All the horrors I've committed, all the suffering I've caused,
all to satisfy my selfish needs, have
eaten me from the inside out. I can't
sleep anymore. I don't have any dreams
left. No one dreams anymore. Oh...I hear
the sirens now. Whatever poor souls
are left are scampering away desperate
to find shelter. I think I'll just stay
standing right here. Oh my, I've never
seen anything like that before.

What do you see?

There's a storm cloud of flames rush-
ing across the dead city. It consumes
everything in its path in a flash of
light. It must be hurtling towards me
at incredible speed, but it all seems
to move in slow motion. Oh, it has such
terrible beauty, like a herd of stam-
peding wild horses. The force of it
pulverizes everything into splinters
and bones and dust and then the splinters ignite and blaze into nothing.
The heat from the cloud of flames is so
intense even at this distance that it's
scorching my face, blinding...my eyes.

(Screams)

Johnny, you feel no pain anymore. Do you hear me? You are floating above the scene. You are not part of the action anymore. You are now back at Wardenclyffe with the others. Johnny, do you hear me?

(Screams again)

(Aside) *These envisioning scenarios are quite common in abduction cases, but I've never encountered anything quite like this before. Johnny, do you hear me?*

Uh-huh

Where are you now?

We're all back above ground. How did we climb out of the pit?

Is the creature…is Abraxas still with you?

Yes, he's standing a few feet away from me. Oh look, he's brought that bathy-sphere thing up with him as well. I didn't see him do this, so I'm presum-ing he did.

Does he say anything to you?

No, and I want to stop him. Wait! He's
moving to the back of the metal sphere
and I think he wants to go inside. But
I have so much I want to ask him first.

I want to know…I ask him if this life
I've seen… I ask if this life I experienced is just one possibility? Do I
have the opportunity to choose a different path? Now that I know what will
happen can I change the course of
my life?

Does he answer you?

He says, "This is the future of your
species. You can no more change your
future than you can alter the course
of a raging river. It has already happened." And I sense that it's all true
because I feel as though I've lived an
entire life in just…in just the amount
of time we were in the pit. It has
already happened in some insane fashion
I can't fathom because I've lived it. I
expect to look down and see the scars
of it on my body.

And as he's getting inside the sphere,
I ask one more time…I ask him if there
is anything we can do to change this
future? How can we save ourselves?" And
he says, "No. There is no changing.
There is no saving."

Does he go back inside the sphere?

Uh-huh. Once he's inside and the portal
closes the spiky metal ball lifts up
into the air in the most marvelous way.
It floats up effortlessly like the shower
of embers swirling above a bonfire. The
bathysphere must weigh a ton, but it
floats away into the night sky as though
it was weightless. It sways and dances
like a leaf in the wind. I keep looking. I keep looking until it's a speck
against the face of the full moon. Oh,
it's gone.

How do you feel now that he's gone?

I feel something like regret. Isn't
that strange? I mean I should feel
relieved that it's all over and…It's
not fair. If I can't change anything
why must I suffer through this horrible existence a second time? You know
when I felt truly relieved? I felt this
absolute elation when the firestorm consumed me. There was excruciating pain
in that searing heat, but I thought
"It's finally over. I'm finally released
from this curse." But it's a cheat.
It's not over, is it? In fact, the horrors are just about to start. Oh God, I
don't want to suffer through this again.
How can I stop this? How can…

*Listen to me carefully, Johnny. When
you wake up you will remember nothing of your time at Wardenclyffe. Do you
understand me? When you wake up you
will only remember the descent into
the pit. You will remember meeting the
creature named Max As Abraxas, but you
will forget everything he told you.
You will forget completely the life
he forced you to experience. You will
forget everything as though nothing
ever happened. The last thing you will
remember is the metal sphere floating
off into the sky and disappearing. And
you will live your life anew as though
for the first time. You understand
me, Johnny? When I count to three,
you will wake up feeling refreshed
and reinvigorated. You will remember
nothing unpleasant from your time at
Wardenclyffe. Just a puzzling encounter
that makes no sense at all. You will
forget everything else because there is
nothing to remember. You are starting
to come to full consciousness now. Are
you ready? One...two...three.*

* * *

From Angela McQueen's blog, *Where Angel Fears to Tread*
August 15, 2015

So the last time we all got cozy together I was totally into fan girl
mode and spilling the beans on the Origin Story of the Nerd Legion. So

today I'm following up with a posting about—wait for it—the End of the Nerd Legion. That's right, the End of the Nerd Legion—Not a Hoax, Not an Imaginary Story. Except this time I'm not real sure where to begin. I guess it ended for most of us at Wardenclyffe (you know, that last surviving Tesla shrine out on Long Island) but I don't remember most of what went down there so don't start asking me for details. All I know is that we met this weird dude named Abraxas or Max Ass or some such who had more eyes sprouting out of his head than my old college roommate had zits—I swear to God! But then I was back in my bedroom feeling myself floating up through the ceiling and into the freezing night air. I was totally replaying my abduction experience! But then I figured out that this meeting with Abraxas in July somehow—in some trippy, timey-whimey way—WAS my abduction experience from back in February and at the same time it was Tony's nightmare encounter when he was ten years old. I know, I don't understand it all either.

But that meeting in Wardenclyffe—believe me, I got the best of it. Tony too, because he doesn't remember much of what happened either. But then there's poor Johnny. He hasn't been the same since we rappelled down into that damn pit. And then there's Rich who has like disappeared off the face of the Earth. Nobody knows where he's gone off to—he hasn't been in touch with anyone. He just jumped into that rented Nerdmobile and hasn't been heard from since. School started this week, but Rich hasn't set foot into a single class. Now Rich was unconscious the whole time in Wardenclyffe which was a piss poor shame because he's the scary-smart one in this posse and he might have a real prayer of figuring out this shit. So that's it. No more Nerd Legion.

I mean, you can imagine I have more questions than answers. What did we ever do to deserve this experience? Why was our little group of geeks so special? And then it hit me like it was staring me right in the face the whole time. We're NOT so special. Duh! So I'm thinking—what if EVERYBODY meets Abraxas? No wait, hear me out about this first. I mean, we triggered the whole thing, we initiated the first contact by waking him (it?) up from its beauty sleep. But I think we all meet Abraxas. Maybe not all at the same time. Maybe some remember it when they were kids, and maybe for some it hasn't happened yet. I mean just because Abraxas did it once and for all, it doesn't mean WE all have to experience it at the same time. See, I don't think this weird dude experiences time in the same way we all experience it—you know the old boring linear "one-thing-happens-after-another" way. I think Abraxas experiences everything in this scrambled, non-linear, "everything-happening-simultaneously" thingie. Tony said that maybe that's how God experiences time too. And that's when my head started hurting really bad. All this time travel and time distortion shit always confuses the hell out of me. I mean, I'm still like Wtf over the ending to Donnie Darko!

When some of us meet Abraxas we remember it like a bona fide abduction encounter. But maybe others only remember it like a dream or a nightmare. You know, like when you wake up shivering and it's not even cold? Or like when you wake up crying and you feel this real profound loss and a breathtaking loneliness that makes you want to run out into the street just to make sure the world is still there? I'm thinking most don't even remember his message about what happens to us next. But there are others who meet Abraxas and they remember EVERYTHING. Poor Johnny, he remembered everything. I hope to God that he stays OK. And all those poor people who have been committing suicide left and right—they probably remembered more than they wanted to know too.

And Kevin Starkly is dead. Kevin's dead. I still can't wrap my head around that even as I'm typing this. I've cried so much for that poor boy over the last few days that I'm glad I didn't have to say anything at his funeral. What could I say? That I wished his last desperate plan really worked? That his obsession made him a hero and not just another victim?

Kevin Starkly was a genuine throwback, dude, an old-fashioned pitchman like you'd see on late night tv hawking non-stick frying pans and shit. Except Kevin was best at pitching himself. He sold himself as THE one and only guide into the unknown, charting our way past the monsters hiding in the dark. The only guide your family will ever need. His one big dream was to find a way to protect all of us from the boogeyman under the bed. You know some people spend most of their short lives squeezing out one dream. Then they're all used up. They've got nothing else to live for, or no one else to live for. I guess sometimes we have to sacrifice our old dreams to keep a new dream alive. And Kevin? I think Kevin understood dreams. He just never understood that some dreams will kill you.

And Tony has stayed with me a lot lately. He's not like the other boys I've known over the years. I mean, first off, he's not a jerk. That puts him at like a big advantage already hands down. We talk about our future together and I swear to God I think he's hanging in there for the long haul. Before I would be paralyzed with fear going to sleep at night because I thought I would fly up into space at any moment and be lost. But now Tony holds me tight and I hold him and you know we sort of anchor each other. And I'm not afraid anymore. I mean I never thought I'd say that ever again. Last night I finally threw away those crappy handcuffs. I was tempted to sell them on eBay, but I wound up tossing them in the metal recycling bin along with the wire coat hangers and Coke cans.

* * *

From personal correspondence from Dr. Stryker

August 20, 2015

Dear Richard,

I trust you won't take my informality as too presumptuous, but I am absolutely rubbish at observing proper etiquette. And addressing you as Dr. Harrigan seems hopelessly stilted, especially after what we have all been through together.

As you requested, I'm sending my correspondence with Angela McQueen under separate cover. She is such a very bright girl you know! I agree that these are important puzzle pieces that need to fall into place. Since you know they are confidential client correspondence, I won't insult you by insisting they be kept private.

But as to your questions regarding the nature of Abraxas and his kind, I'm afraid I've probably given it too, too much thought over the last several weeks. Forgive me if I lapse into the jargon of standard pedagogy, but at my age it's a difficult habit to break.

Foremost, I have no reason to disbelieve who he says he is. In fact, I have no idea why any self-respecting higher intelligence would claim any kinship with us lowly *Homo sapiens* unless it were true. Even if we are distant second cousins, once removed, I'll grant that Abraxas is truthful when he says that his kind are nothing more than another hominid species, a *Homo occultus* if you will—the Hidden Man. Sorry, I couldn't resist the urge for proper nomenclature.

As you probably know, it's only been during the last century that anthropologists have uncovered the fossil remains of about twenty-something human ancestors. As one of my former professors was fond of pointing out, you could place all the evidence unearthed to date—every foot bone and thigh bone and hip bone—and still not completely cover the surface of your average dining room table. No one seriously believes that we've completely mapped all the missing branches in our hominid family tree. Remember back in 2004 when anthropologists discovered the skull of a heretofore unknown ancestor hidden away on an Indonesian island? Of course, there was some debate that little *Homo floresiensis* was not a real new species at all but merely a mutation of someone we already safely cataloged, but that was bollocks. Here was a genuine unknown hominid species that lived contemporaneously with *Homo sapiens* at least as recently as 18,000 years ago and we had no idea who they were or where they came from. So it does not stretch my credulity to the breaking point at all to assume that some intelligent species, some *Homo occultus*, has coexisted with modern humanity, undetected, to the present day especially if that species doesn't wish to be discovered.

And your question about whether they are truly more advanced than we are? I don't have enough data to formulate a better answer, but for what it's worth, I think they simply have different talents.

My training wasn't in physical anthropology, but I believe, based on observations of these creatures over the centuries, that this is a good starting hypothesis: These hidden ancestors separated from some common lineage on the plains of Africa maybe a million years ago, maybe later. Recent research indicates that the major evolutionary trend of our species was not merely a growing braincase but also a growing skill set. While *Homo ergaster* struggled with tool-making, and later *Homo sapiens* struggled with taming the natural world through language and fire and agriculture, our hidden friends branched out in an altogether different direction. While we evolved the trappings of material civilization, they developed and mastered the immaterial world. *Homo occultus* harnessed spiritual and mental energies, using powers that only Zen masters, lamas, and aboriginal shamans have rediscovered as vestigial talents. Using some ability that I can't explain, they apparently can shift in and out of dreamtime. Their dreaming is more real to them than our waking world. If I didn't already suspect that nobody would publish it, I would be tempted to write a paper analyzing their whole evolutionary scheme. But clearly, all traces of their existence faded from our perception altogether.

Most times they wished to live in secret, but the desire to interact with their long-lost cousins proved to be irresistible, didn't it? These brief encounters scattered throughout history metamorphosed into the stuff of legends. They became sacred encounters with the Gods Who Came Down from the Sky or dreaded meetings with Trolls from the Center of the Earth or just a puzzling rendezvous with one of the Wee Folk. Over the centuries they changed their guises, since they apparently could change their own appearance as easily as they could shift through space, and they masqueraded as gods with the heads of jackals, or demons with dark skin, or incubus or succubus with pleasing shapes, or aliens with huge heads and disturbing eyes. But always, they looked like us—just a little different.

Sometimes they came to share their secrets, but most times they came simply for sport. For example, let's examine the given name chosen by our little friend. As you rightly suspected, the name Abraxas is so freighted with such mystical significance that it would be impossible to ignore its connotations. During my research I uncovered this brilliant quote from Jung, I believe it was in Stuart Holroyd's *The Elements of Gnosticism*:

"[Abraxas] is truly the terrible one... He is the monster of the underworld... He is the bright light of day and the deepest night of madness... He is the mightiest manifest being, and in him creation becomes frightened of itself..."

Makes one shiver contemplating that creature's original mission, doesn't it? What had it planned for humankind in 1897 at the very start of the 20th century? It's staggering to think we experience Abraxas now in a weakened state after a century hidden under the Earth. I hope this is somewhat helpful, if not a bit disturbing.

I look forward to hearing your own thoughts on this soon.

Cheers,

Jeanette Stryker

* * *

From the note attached to the manuscript

Before I continue, I want to make it clear that I don't blame Tesla for what happened. I've come to believe that he was duped into this course of action—even beyond death—just as Fermia and Walters and Starkly were duped. They were all useful fools manipulated by The Pilot. It was a course of action set into motion after Abraxas crashed into Aurora and then rose from his little coffin and introduced himself to Lawless Starkly. It continued even as Tesla counted off multiples of three as he dug up that same coffin in the Aurora Cemetery.

We were all useful fools, weren't we?

Starkly was so obsessed with finding the Aurora pilot that he neglected to consider the possibility that it was all a trap.

I couldn't save you Starkly, but I forgive you. That's just what friends do.

I feel somewhat like J. Robert Oppenheimer when he witnessed the fruits of his labor unleashing the terrible power of the atom.

"I am become Death, the Destroyer of Worlds." He spent the rest of his life unsuccessfully trying to push that blazing genie back into its bottle.

Once recovered from my concussion underground I was still too close to recent events to truly make any sense of it all. Then with Starkly's funeral following soon after I was still in no fit shape to intellectually explore the puzzle that presented itself. I've always told my students that you can't begin constructing a correct theorem if you don't adequately understand the basic axioms first. Mustering all these journal entries, retrieving personal emails and text messages, most of them surreptitiously—please accept my apologies dear friends if I dared uncover any truths you wish had remained hidden—has proven an exhausting enterprise, but I believe I've pieced together a basic chronology. Amassing the other odd resources and newspaper clippings involved more straightforward research. In this regard I am forever indebted to Starkly for providing me access over the years to a truly staggering collection of obscure and bizarre volumes, many of which are no longer in print.

Of all the evidence uncovered by our little group, the one significant experience that has eluded me has been my own face-to-face meeting with our dreaded Awakened Pilot. I hope to correct this oversight and eventually have the pleasure of making his acquaintance on my own terms and in my own time. But how to accomplish this?

Why, you may ask, is a physics teacher running around the country spouting off mystical nonsense about meeting some creature that apparently transcends time and space?

First, I should explain that since I am a member in good standing of the Church of Quantum Mechanics I no doubt believe more impossible things every day before breakfast than Aleister Crowley or Madame Blavatsky ever did.

And second, while I am a skeptic, I am not an idiot.

Initially, I briefly entertained the notion that this was all some innocent mistake. Perhaps Abraxas had no idea what the effect of his horrifying future visions would have on an unsuspecting humanity. That he had no inkling of all the suffering and anguish it would cause, all the suicides and lost souls unmoored from their present reality living in perpetual fear and hopelessness. Or maybe it was some variety of interspecies "tough love," a well-intentioned kick to our lazy asses to spur us all to action.

But now I believe that Abraxas never had our best interests at heart.

In my research I found that Abraxas was associated with many spells for removing illnesses. However, one in particular tickled me to no end. The dutiful worshipper would write down the spell in descending order, deconstructing it, if you will, until the word was gone—along with the illness. Like this:

A - B - R - A - C - A - D - A - B - R - A

A - B - R - A - C - A - D - A - B - R

A - B - R - A - C - A - D - A - B

A - B - R - A - C - A - D - A

A - B - R - A - C - A - D

A - B - R - A - C - A

A - B - R - A - C

A - B - R - A

A - B - R

A - B

A

Abracadabra! And "POOF," it disappears. I found it inordinately significant that the only popular cultural remnant we have of Abraxas and his influence in this world is the word most commonly associated with a cheap magician's trick. Suddenly, the true nature of our encounter with Abraxas became clear to me. He was not a grateful gift-giver, but a patient prankster. He was that most awful and elusive of classical archetypes—the Trickster.

Abraxas would have us believe that every shining light in the course of human history was an aberration. He would have us believe that in our twilight time humanity would choose destruction instead of life, helplessness instead of hope. That our best qualities are powerless over our worst. Here's my considered hypothesis: I'm betting he's lying.

The reason I doubt the veracity of Abraxas is because of one puzzle piece that caught my attention but was soon forgotten in the course of events. But on gathering together all these papers it struck me anew and I was still at a loss to explain it. How did Starkly know the details of the Weird Brothers' Arcanium? How was he able to describe it in exact detail in his story when no description existed of the place—and I researched this thoroughly, believe me—and he demonstrably never set foot in the place himself? The answer was so simple, yet it opened up a new avenue into my understanding of Abraxas and his gift. Starkly *did* visit the Arcanium but in another alternative timeline glimpsed during his encounter with Abraxas. In this *other* future he accompanied the rest of us to Tennessee and witnessed the lair of the Kunstkammer Kids and probably even awakened Abraxas himself at Wardenclyffe. And seeing this future he sought to warn us in advance. But if his future vision differed so dramatically from our own reality what other differences exist between the future presented by the Trickster and our world? The great lie perpetuated by this creature is that the horrific future vision he forces us to live is our only future, when in fact, it is only *one possible future among many*. This realization is also based in no small part on my readings of physicists Michio Kaku and Itzhak Bars and their theories of parallel dimensions and timelines.

I have no doubt that this ability to summon a future timeline is a real talent, but he has wielded that talent as a crude cudgel.

As I've traveled around the country these last few weeks, I've had a chance to test my theory. In my conversations with many of the lost souls wandering across the backroads, I've compared their visions and I've found their accounts contradict each other in both trivial and substantial ways. I've actually managed to convey the full meaning of these inconsistencies to a few people. And like even the slowest students in my classes, they eventually realize that they can change the future they've seen. They are not cursed to repeat this litany of horrors. But too many are beyond all reasoning.

I think Angela got it precisely correct. We all meet Abraxas eventually. But we all encounter him in one of several different ways. Of course, there is only one meeting as far as the Pilot is concerned. This one "cascade event" for lack of a better term, took place for him once and for all time. But the event is experienced differently by each observer, and in fact, is experienced differently than the initiator of the cascade itself. The repercussion of this one event is changing hundreds of thousands of lives as it ripples outward in all directions like a pebble dropped into a still pond, affecting both the past and the future. Most people, I hope the majority of them, feel the presence of the Pilot as an invasion of dreamtime. It is an unsettling vision of half-remembered apocalyptic images and garbled warnings. None are completely forgotten upon awakening. I believe this is how Angela and Fermia encountered Abraxas.

But the more potent meeting is one where the participant is transported physically—usually in a shower of glowing blue lights—to a face-to-face encounter. I believe this is what happened to Starkly, and the Weird Brothers, and Holly Evers and God knows how many other people. And they remember everything as though they lived an entire lifetime in a matter of hours. If any experienced a pleasant, comforting vision of the future, I have yet to meet them. These are the cursed victims who soon lose all hope and inevitably die by their own hands.

And little phantom Abigail was right again. The real monster wasn't the Jersey Devil, or the Beast in the Bone Maze, or even the Kunstkammer Kids. The monster was always Abraxas. For what it's worth, I believe this was always his mission, even back in 1897. It was to infect the dreams of mankind. To bring his "gift" of despair and hopelessness and sow chaos everywhere. Or maybe he always intended to sleep for over a century. Maybe his plan necessitated some rest—like recharging a battery—somehow siphoning power from the Earth itself.

I couldn't understand why some observers experienced their meeting differently. I wondered if this was a random phenomenon based on nothing but chance. But there was a common thread, which I initially missed: All of those who were transported physically to their rendezvous with The Pilot had trespassed upon an invisible gateway point. At those special points the cascade event was able to break through to our waking reality. Previous generations who sensed the strange differences in these places called them cursed, or haunted, or the domain of fairies and elves. Liminal places just outside the range of our common experience, where strange whispers are heard, where dark things go bump in the night. It makes perfect sense that the most dramatic physical encounters would occur in cemeteries, forgotten ghost towns, odd crossroads, and mystical spots associated with the spirit world. These were the ancient thresholds where *Homo occultus* had interacted with our kind since the beginning of recorded history. It is in these very places where our species first learned how to deal with these interlopers into our reality. And perhaps Homo occultus use these spaces as portals traveling from one to another.

So that is why I am traveling across the country to visit every one of these damned locations. I am seeking out ghosts and ghouls and aliens and cursed things of every stripe in the hope that eventually I will see myself surrounded by those buzzing blue neon lights just as thousands have seen them before me. And I will find myself inevitably face-to-face with The Pilot. But unlike all the others, I will come prepared.

When he asks me "What time is it?" I will patiently smile and reply that it's "Time to die you lying little bastard." And then I will plunge the triple-bladed phur-pa dagger that I borrowed from the Weird Brothers at the Aurora Cemetery into his hominid heart. It was a weapon designed to kill demons after all, and this one supposedly was used by a minor deity to hunt nagas—nasty snake creatures. According to the *Dictionnaire Infernal*, Abraxas is often pictured as "a demon with the head of a king and with serpents for his legs." Now that's a bit of synchronicity, don't you think?

I am become Demon Hunter, the Destroyer of Gods, the Assassin of Fools.

If I have a chance, I will explain that his greatest mistake was not in tricking the greatest minds of our species with disastrous schemes for transmitting unlimited power through the Earth, or spinning gold from lead, or uniting man and God through some insane metal prophet. No, his greatest mistake was coming up with a scheme that hurt my friends.

Of course, this is the ultimate experiment to prove my hypothesis. And like every good scientist I am not absolutely certain how it will work. I don't even know *if* it will work. Maybe my theory is incorrect or incomplete and my action will have no affect at all over the course of events. Maybe the great roaring stream of time can't be altered after all. Will the injury to The Pilot create a new alternate reality where his awakening never took place? Or will the stabbing of The Pilot create a second equal and opposite "cascade event" that cancels out absolutely the effects of the first? Like two equal and opposite pulses that completely destroy each other when they overlap.

Maybe all time starting with the discovery of Max As Abraxas in Tesla's infernal pit will reverse itself in some great cosmic "do-over." Maybe the memory of all of this will be forever erased from our minds because it never happened. I guess that's one way to prove my success. If there is no record of any of this ever happening in the media, no mention of any of these events on the blogosphere, in fact, no mention anywhere except the writings you're now holding in your hands, you should read that as a good sign.

However you find this document, please pray that I was more successful than poor Starkly.

FRIDAY, SEPTEMBER 11, 2015

Katy Olmos woke abruptly from a nightmare filled with monsters and men.

She saw a thing in her dreams covered with twisting eyestalks chasing her through an underground labyrinth. Tripping over corpses littering the tunnel, she finally escaped by clawing her way through a fiery *sipapu* like it was some gateway from Hell.

Katy looked over at the kitchen table and saw the manuscript. She still had no idea what to do with it. Being the only person in the world who knew of its existence—apart from the man who compiled it—thrilled her in a way she barely understood.

Pueblo Bonito was now the scene of an active police investigation closed to the public, so Katy spent most of the day chatting with some of the other park rangers at the Visitor Center. Everyone swarmed around her, asking questions about everything that happened the day before. One of the older rangers, Trevor, mentioned that the stranger was recovering nicely in a local hospital. Suffering from shock and dehydration, he had no memory of how he got there and certainly no idea of why he was covered in blood.

"*Madre Dios*! It's weird, right?" said Trevor. "No car in the parking lot, no tour bus. Did he fucking walk the 125 miles from Albuquerque?"

"Maybe he was dropped off in a UFO." Everyone laughed, except Katy.

Police were likewise baffled since they found no weapons, no body, no crime scene.

"I hear the guy's record is clean. Not even a parking ticket," said Trevor. "Unless they find something else around the kiva today, the cops will probably release him. I mean, what are they going to charge him with? Trespassing?"

What is the proper punishment for a Demon Killer? thought Katy. Would it be a felony, or only a misdemeanor, like hunting deer out of season?

Driving home, Katy tried to convince herself that the story wasn't real. Maybe some parts were true, but the rest was just fiction, just cosplaying among friends.

But she kept seeing Harrigan's face and hearing his desperate plea:

"Did it work? Just tell me if it worked!"

One man's decision to sacrifice his own soul, or even his own life, in order to cancel the poisoned fruits of another man's obsession.

Whatever she would finally do with the manuscript, handing it over to the police was definitely out of the question. Even if Harrigan remembered nothing, the narrative he documented in those pages would only make things…complicated.

Katy told Pablo she wasn't feeling well and instead spent most of Friday night listening for the first time to some of the podcasts archived on the Myth-America site. Hesitant at first, she finally put on her headphones and decided to hear the truth for herself.

Katy smiled as she listened to the Pine Barrens podcast of July 10. Tony Fermia sounded exactly as she imagined. Kevin Starkly was a surprise. His voice was tinny with an odd Brooklyn accent and didn't sound very much like a loudmouth asshole. The podcast chronicled an uneventful evening camping out in the forgotten town of Harrisville.

Except for a terrifying scream that may or may not have originated from the Jersey Devil, nothing much happened.

Nothing much at all…not even a mention of floating blue lights.

In fact, there was no mention of any cross-country trek by the Nerd Legion at all.

Much to her surprise, Katy found herself wiping away tears of relief as she listened.

After taking off her headphones, she realized there was really only one thing left to do. Katy grabbed a large Fed Ex envelope, stuffed the manila folder with all its papers and clippings inside. She found the New

York City address easily online and decided at the last moment to include a short note. It read:

Dear Kevin Starkly,

Please don't worry about your friend Richard Harrigan. He's recuperating at San Juan Regional Medical Center in Farmington, New Mexico. Who I am is not important. The only thing you need to know is that I found a manuscript written by Richard when I first met him at Chaco Canyon National Park.

I've enclosed the manuscript here. I think you may like to read it.

END

Thank you for reading my book! If you enjoyed it, I would greatly appreciate it if you could leave a review over on Amazon and/or Goodreads so others can discover it for themselves. You wouldn't believe how critical reviews are for the success of any book and for an author's career. So please (picture me on bended knee here), please leave a review before you forget.

Also, please visit www.michaelwalkerbooks.com and sign up for my free newsletter. Subscribers will receive an exclusive haunted house short story featuring some of your favorite Nerd Legion characters!

ABOUT THE AUTHOR

Michael F. Walker is a lover of all things strange and macabre. Before writing his debut novel, *The Aurora Revelations*, he promoted the curators and curiosities, relics and specimens at the American Museum of Natural History in New York City for 20 years, covering everything from new dinosaur discoveries and space shows to renovations of decades-old dioramas, and flashlight tours of the museum after dark. Prior to that, Walker was manager of public relations at the New York Hall of Science, worked in corporate communications for Metropolitan Life, and publicized nationally renowned writers at *Parade* magazine. A graduate of St. John's University in NYC, Walker started his career as a newscaster with KOKH-TV and as a senior editor for KAUT-TV, both in Oklahoma City. He lives with his wife and daughter in a ramshackle old house in Brooklyn, NY that looks haunted but (probably) isn't. You can contact Walker at www.michaelwalkerbooks.com and subscribe to his free newsletter.